Carol Edgarian and Tom Jenks

The Writer's Life

Carol Edgarian and Tom Jenks are married and live in San Francisco. Ms. Edgarian is the author of the novel *Rise the Euphrates* and is currently at work on her next novel. Mr. Jenks is the author of the novel *Our Happiness*. His short fiction has appeared in *Story* and *Ploughshares* and has been nominated for a National Magazine Award. A former editor of *Esquire*, he edited, with Raymond Carver, *American Short Story Masterpieces*.

The Writer's Life

The Writer's Life

Intimate Thoughts on Work, Love,

Inspiration, and Fame

from the Diaries of

the World's Great Writers

Edited by

Carol Edgarian and Tom Jenks

Vintage Books
A Division of Random House, Inc.
New York

A VINTAGE ORIGINAL, NOVEMBER 1997
FIRST EDITION

Copyright © 1997 by Carol Edgarian and Tom Jenks

All rights reserved under International and Pan-American Copyright
Conventions. Published in the United States by Vintage Books, a
division of Random House, Inc., New York, and simultaneously in
Canada by Random House of Canada Limited, Toronto.

Owing to limitations of space, acknowledgments of permission to
publish journal passages and other material
will be found following the index.

Library of Congress Cataloging-in-Publication Data

The writers life: intimate thoughts on work, love, inspiration, and
fame from the diaries of the world's great writers/
edited by Carol Edgarian and Tom Jenks.
p. cm.
Includes index.
ISBN 0-679-76957-9
1. Life—Literary collections. 2. Authors—Diaries.
I. Edgarian, Carol. II. Jenks, Tom.
PN6071.L6W75 1997
808.8'3—dc20   96-6949

Author photograph © 1997 by Christopher Irion

Random House Web address: http://www.randomhouse.com/

Editors' Web address: http://narrativemagazine.org/

Printed in the United States of America
10 9 8 7 6 5 4 3 2 1

Contents

THE WRITER'S LIFE

Editors' Note

When we began working on this book, we decided that our essential organizing principle would be to make the collection a book of life. After all, what are diaries if not life stories, and we were initially drawn to them, and especially to their intimacy, as a way of knowing ourselves and our lives more clearly. It seems to us that nothing is more natural than to want to make an account of one's experiences, and nothing is more universal than, in making such an account, to want to arrive at truths that will endure. This impulse, this desire for insight, is a reason not only for reading diaries but for writing them.

Taking a hint from the diary form itself, we decided to organize *The Writer's Life* as a narrative, moving across the stages of life from youth to age, so that the many lives of the authors collected here represent, as it were, a span of life common to all. The book is in chapters: Talent; Inspiration; Ambition; Love, Marriage, and the Sexes; Business and Money; and so on. Our guidelines were that we would limit ourselves to poets, short story writers, novelists, dramatists, influential critics, several well-known spouses and siblings of writers, and a few authors whose reputations rest solely on their diaries. In short, we limited ourselves to literary artists and their intimates. This isn't to say that there are not plenty of remarkable diaries written by dancers, scientists, farmers, or others. There are, to be sure. But it was poetry, fiction, and drama that first aroused our interest in being writers ourselves, and poems and stories have always been for us a primary means of understanding and connection, a way of explaining what often seems inexplicable.

In our reading and research, we were interested in diary passages where the effects of language, situation, and insight were intense and total. The reader we imagine for this book is someone who is quickened and moved, perhaps delighted, but in any case deeply affected, by the shock of recognition and sympathy that good writing produces. Time and again, as we pored over hundreds of diaries, we found passages that exhilarated us, and in the end, there was simply not enough room to include in one book all the interesting passages we found. Yet we believe that we have chosen the best and that readers will find much of personal interest in the selections from the more than two hundred writers collected here.

The oldest quotes, dating from the sixteenth century, are from Montaigne; the most recent are from contemporaries; and readers will perhaps see the collection, in part, as a story of change. The preponderance of European white males, who dominated literature in previous centuries, has given way to diversity. No single worldview or attitude prevails in the book. Indeed, human contradiction provides some of the spark and humor.

Within each chapter, and from section to section, we have juxtaposed quotes to create a conversation among the authors. The quotes are aphoristic, epigrammatic, anecdotal, gossipy; some tell complete stories. Consequently, the book can be opened at random or read all the way through as a narrative.

In drawing together authors from twenty-three countries, we relied on material available in English. We did our research in bookstores, with rare book dealers, on the Internet, and in libraries around the world, turning up some important and all-but-forgotten volumes, such as Flaubert's teenage note-book and Joseph Conrad's diary of a trip up the Congo River. Part of our task was to sift through pages of detail to cull passages that would speak to readers today. Our goal was not to create a scholarly book or one of interest only to writers or lovers of great writing, but rather to create, as has been noted, an engaging book in which readers can find aspects of their own experiences revealed through the lens of art.

In addition to researching the diaries of notable writers of the past, we contacted hundreds of contemporary writers and asked for entries from their own diaries. Some wrote back immediately, others eventually; some never responded at all. To our amazement, we received a letter from May Sarton the day after her death was announced in the newspapers. Her handwriting was tiny; it took time to decipher that she was granting permission to quote from her diaries. We were also fortunate to receive unpublished material from pocket notebooks that Raymond Carver carried in his bathrobe the month or two before his death. And we are grateful to have an unpublished passage of personal writing by Peter Taylor, a mentor and friend, who died while we were in the early stages of assembling this book.

Overall, the letters we received from writers were encouraging, and as piquant as the diary passages themselves. One writer responded, "You've created a monster. I had no idea I'd kept so many journals and notebooks over the years, but a showery Saturday and your letter combined to kick me into gear and send me into the basement. . . . I had fun seeing who I was and who I am." Another writer told us, in words that seemed rueful and comic, "Thanks for asking . . . but I'm afraid I don't keep a notebook, diaries, etc. My handwriting is too poor." And with one submission, we received this enthusiastic note: "Thanks for the invite. To be under covers with Dorothy Wordsworth!"

Of course the tension in that joke is between mortality and

xii 𝕏 Editors' Note

immortality. Despite the certainty of death, it is the hope for survival, for continuity and wholeness, that readers instinctively follow and that writers call on in their work. Accordingly, we have included a section containing diary passages on aspects of the writer's art in order to provide a glimpse into how writers do what they do: how, in the words of Joyce Carol Oates, they transcribe and make permanent in art—in mere finite *words*—the unfathomable mystery of personality.

The personalities gathered here are abundantly rich in talent, and we hope readers will find their insights, as we did, variously diverting, amusing, memorable, and wise.

C.E. AND T.J.

Introduction

THE DIARIST'S ART

As readers, we come to diaries seeking answers to the human condition. Who am I? How am I to live? How am I to manage with these burdens, these gifts? We come—with humble intentions perhaps, but with the fervency of voyeurs—eavesdropping on the lives of others. Diaries attract because they allow us to see with heartbreaking accuracy inside another naked soul—warts and passions, all—and in so doing to learn something of ourselves. In reading someone else's life, we ask: Do you have the answer? Can I use it?

Wisdom. Companionship. Wit. Passion. Human folly. These are the treasures of the diary, and our response to them is often immediate and visceral. Nathaniel Hawthorne observes in his journal, "All men feel themselves akin, and on terms of intimacy, with those whom they know, or might have known, in books." So we feel we know William Blake, as he confesses, "Grown old in Love from Seven till Seven times Seven, / I oft have wish'd for Hell for ease from Heaven." Or Robert Frost, as he observes, "Seeking out your own advantage is something to rise to." Or Dawn Powell, as she casts a cold eye on New York society: "I am still so amazed at the brazenness of people who only remember you when you've gone into your fourth printing."

There is delicious surprise and comfort in discovering that others, even the famous, *especially* the famous, find life just as difficult and unwieldy as the rest of us do. All the money and talent and fame imaginable have not bought one living soul a ticket out of the worries. There are always love and sex to fret over, and children and family; not to mention the aging body; the flagging spirit; the work never done; the failures and successes; and always, always, there are the bills. For daily drama, diaries have it in spades. And in this era of self-reflection, the diary—the ultimate book of Self—may be more compelling than ever. So we come, as Edgar Allan Poe once put it, with "heart laid bare," and many of us come early.

The diary, mass-produced as a toy, we've all seen. From childhood memories, it is a red- or white-bound book, with gilt-edged pages and a gold-embossed title: "My First Diary." It has a clasp lock, a gold key. The toy makers have made the symbolism overt: the rich binding and gold connote that recorded life is precious; the lock suggests that what is precious is best kept secret. And what is the secret if not of life's essence?

Robert Frost says in his journal, "Culture is to know things at first hand (at the source)." Such is the diarist's intent. To understand his life, he watches it with the fascination of a meteorologist studying satellite images for signs of weather. No detail is too small or large. Meals eaten, money earned, slights suffered, crops ruined, babies born, marriages ended and begun, conversations, letters, lists, moods, are all duly recorded. In how many attics across the land is there a dusty, forgotten book that was Aunt Edna's or Uncle Joe's loopy-penned confession?

But it is to the diaries of known writers that we have turned. What can they teach us? First, we can say (having read hundreds of journals from writers past and present) that writers are obsessed with pretty much the same things as everyone else is. The difference is that the talented writer brings gifts of discovery, quickening the ordinary, seeing what others overlook. For many writers, the journal is a laboratory in which to test theories, anecdotes, lines of dialogue, notes on craft, that later, in the fiction, poetry, and plays, will be refined. The diary is the writer's vision in raw, and the details he records and how he records them reveal, often with startling candor, his character and heart.

Leo Tolstoy observes in his journal, "Art is a microscope which the artist fixes on the secrets of his soul, and shows to people these secrets which are common to all."

To write of secrets, one must *know*; so the diarist prays for inspiration and laments his limitations: "All your aggression is directed toward discovering new perceptions," Jim Harrison writes, "and consequently against yourself when you fail to come up with anything new."

Failure and success; despair and grief—common themes in the journals. On one particularly bleak day, Tolstoy notes, "I'm doing nothing and thinking about the landlady. Do I have the talent to compare with our modern Russian writers? Decidedly not." Society, always keeping score, judges the writer—while the writer, witness to the world around him and inside him, judges both. Thus, with wrenching acuity, John Cheever confesses, "I dream that a lady, looking at my face, says, 'I see you've been in the competition, but I can't tell by your face whether or not you've won.' "

At moments the author's self-torment turns to envy; rivalry and petty emotions take hold. Jean Cocteau, finding himself slighted in Gide's published diaries, complains, "Will the monstrous stupidity of [his] *Journal* ever be discovered?" Syliva Plath is sickened when other poets receive a prize: "Jealous one I am, green-eyed, spite-seething." Cheever admits to getting "the heaves" every time he reads a review of a book by Saul Bellow.

But where there's ugliness in human nature, with it lies the sublime. Henry James's personal incantations, jotted in a notebook, speak to the artistic soul: "To live *in* the world of creation—to get into it and stay in it—to frequent it and haunt it—to think intensely and fruitfully—to woo combinations and inspirations into being by a depth and continuity of attention—this is the only thing."

Whether a writer succeeds or fails in his lifetime, it is axiomatic that he must write: he cannot help himself. Franz Kafka admits that writing for him is a form of prayer. "I won't give up the diary again. I must hold on here, it is the only place I can." The diary serves as a repository of burdens, a safe haven, an ever-constant friend. It is what thirteen-year-old Anne Frank turns to when she is locked in an attic, hiding from the Jew-hunting Nazis, and feels herself "different" from the family hiding with her: "Yes, there is no doubt that paper is patient and as I don't intend to show this cardboard-covered notebook bearing the proud name of "diary" to anyone, unless I find a real friend, boy or girl, probably nobody cares. And now I come to the root of the matter, the reason for my starting a diary; it is that I have no such real friend."

In his journal André Gide observes, "Whoever starts out toward the unknown must consent to venture alone." But not all writers are unhappy about their solitude. Jean Cocteau: "To write is an entertainment I put on for myself." Donald Hall: "The pleasure of writing is that the mind does not wander, any more than it does in the orgasm—and writing takes longer than orgasm."

Yet for all the pleasure a writing life brings, the daily rigor and isolation take a toll. This should not be surprising, but somehow it is. Virginia Woolf, the titan diarist of modern times, speaks for many when she summarizes, with remarkable detachment and understatement, the existential struggle that plagues, and ultimately subsumes, her life: "I think the effort to live in two spheres: the novel; and life; is a strain."

It is just such strain that the diary soothes. As it proceeds from solitude toward communion, the book of self offers readers a timeless conversation between souls. Certain figures, like muses, appear and reappear—Ralph Waldo Emerson, Leo

Tolstoy, André Gide, Henry James, Virginia Woolf—their words resonating in the pages of diarists who succeed them. It is the diary's power, its art, to create a community where none exists. F. Scott Fitzgerald, pondering his habits, writes, "When anyone announces to you how little they drink you can be sure it's a regime they just started." Humorous, audacious, and true enough, yet consider John Cheever's response, years later, as he wrestles his demons: "I sit on the terrace reading about the torments of Scott Fitzgerald. I am, he was, one of those men who read the grievous accounts of hard-drinking, self-destructive authors, holding a glass of whiskey in our hands, the tears pouring down our cheeks."

It is usually assumed that literary artists who keep journals intend them to be read. Posterity leans over the shoulder of the famous novelist; she writes with a sense of her reader, just as the undiscovered poet, dreaming of recognition, addresses the page as though it were an audience. "To record," F. Scott Fitzgerald remarks, "one must be unwary." But for some, the idea of being seen is appalling. In her adolescent diary, Beatrix Potter was obsessed with privacy, writing in a complex, coded alphabet of her own invention. She warns, "No one will ever read this," and, indeed, years passed before cryptographers unlocked the secrets of her journal. Franz Kafka left instructions for his friend and literary executor Max Brod to burn the diaries; instead, Brod edited and published them, believing the worth of the diaries outweighed the writer's wishes.

We read diaries for the confession, the revelation, the dramatic scene. And if emotions are what inflame the diary, relationships are the kindling. Where there is sex in the life, in the diary it abounds, be it tender, brutal, or comic—what E. M. Forster wryly refers to as "toppings and bottomings." In his journal, Delmore Schwartz observes, "In petting there is no Mason Dixon line." William Matthews advises, "The purpose of sexual intercourse is to get it over with as slowly as possible." That goes for the diary, too. One thinks of Anaïs Nin, whose succession of lovers, including her father, seems a prolonged autoerotic act. Anton Chekhov, whose love affairs were intermittent, observes: "Women deprived of the company of men pine, men deprived of the company of women become stupid." And Edward Hoagland, with a veteran's appreciation, recalls, "If two people are in love, they can sleep on the blade of a knife."

The diary tracks sex as it tracks everything else, and when passion leads to domesticity, the writer records that too. "Marriage," Stephen Spender writes, "is ultimately an agreement—or conspiracy—between two people to treat each other as having each the right to be loved absolutely." Certainly one of the most extensively documented literary marriages is that of the Tolstoys, Leo and Sophia, who kept separate, conflicting diaries throughout their long, stormy union. Sophia writes, "Today he shouted at the top of his lungs that his dearest wish was to leave his family. . . . I long to take my life, my thoughts are so confused. . . . Everyone envies our happiness, and this makes me wonder what makes us happy and what that happiness really means." Years later, Leo will write the famous first words of *Anna Karenina:* "All happy families are like one another; each unhappy family is unhappy in its own way."

Wary as any other prospective spouse, some writers pull up shy. Kafka lists the arguments for and against his marriage: He fears the burden; he wants a wife like his sisters, before whom he always shines. He ends up a bachelor. Sylvia Plath agonizes: Will marriage and childbirth sap her creativity or enhance it? She steels herself for the test and presses on.

Diarists by definition are chroniclers of their times. They consider themselves independent thinkers, and conventional values, in the guise of formal education, organized religion, or party politics, are viewed skeptically. "What does education often do?" Henry David Thoreau asks. "It makes a straight-cut ditch of a free, meandering brook." Lord Byron emphatically states, "I have simplified my politics into an utter detestation of all existing governments. . . . riches are power, and poverty is slavery . . . and one sort of establishment is no better, nor worse, for a *people* than another." Men's voices, these, speaking from prerogatives, whereas women's leadership and independence are hard-won. Susan Griffin turns the issue of power on its head when she wisely counsels, "It is perhaps a choice each of us makes over and over, even many times throughout one day, whether to use knowledge as power or intimacy."

The best writers are prescient and guide the way for the rest of us. Gerald Early pricks the bubble of political correctness when he writes: "I personally am sick of being a 'minority,' sick of seeing meaningless statistics lumping me with Asians, Native Americans, Hispanics, and other folk on the idiotic basis of not being white (why not lump us together on the basis of not being birds or reptiles?). . . . I cannot even recall God naming me man. If He or She did, I have forgotten because it happened so long ago."

In times of difficulty, the diary provides a certain constancy. The record of one's life is a testament of survival. "Writing a journal," observes George Sand, "means that facing your ocean you are afraid to swim across it, so you attempt to drink it drop by drop." Perhaps by drinking life slowly, one is better able to withstand its trials. On the day Mary Shelley's infant dies, she keeps to the habit of her journal, recording not only the death but the title of the book she's reading. Later, she writes, "Stay at home; net, and think of my little dead baby. This is foolish, I suppose; yet whenever I am left alone to my own thoughts, and do not read to divert them, they always come back to the same point—that I was a mother, and am so no longer."

Eventually, infirmities or age close in, bringing shades of denial and acceptance. Observes H. L. Mencken, "The seat of my office chair, in use for twenty-five years, is wearing out, my office rug is wearing out, and I am wearing out. As the Chinese say, 'It is later than you think.' " May Sarton regards fate with an unsentimental eye: "So let me turn away and toward old age, the Fourth Season, as it has been called. How many times lately someone my age or older has said 'If they told us what it would be like we would have opted out.' "

For those who have lived their lives moment by moment on the page, posterity looms and questions remain. How will we be remembered? And what, if anything, will we encounter after death? Our most profound sense is of our own mortality, the breaths and heartbeats that underlie our words and give them truth. We are headed somewhere definite, we have only so much time, and the record of our sayings and doings defines us—and, after we are gone, stands in our place. So we record the date, make a note, turn the page, and look ahead. Or sometimes the view is double: forward and back. As André Gide notes: "A man's life is his image. At the hour of death we shall be reflected in the past, and, leaning over the mirror of our acts, our souls will recognize *what we are.*"

CAROL EDGARIAN AND TOM JENKS

Beginnings

———❖———

Talent

Talent is a long patience.

GUSTAVE FLAUBERT (AS QUOTED IN GIDE'S DIARY)

❧

Talent is a question of quantity. Talent does not write one page: it writes three hundred. . . . The strong do not hesitate. They settle down, they sweat, they go on to the end. They exhaust the ink, they use up the paper. This is the only difference between men of talent and cowards who will never make a start. In literature, there are only oxen. The biggest ones are the geniuses—the ones who toil eighteen hours a day without tiring. Fame is a constant effort.   JULES RENARD

❧

The true amateur moves the heart, because, for an inch of progress, he has the patience of an ant, yet has no jealousy for those able to travel with ease through the air like angels. . . . I've never known a professional who was not propelled by ambition. . . . But the amateur has a blind faith in us, a respect for our natural responsibility that we deceive in ways he'll never be aware of. That's why I'm touched by the layman's love: he sees creation as a magic world, and *I* know it's not.

NED ROREM

Every man has the philosophy of his own aptitudes.

CESARE PAVESE

❧

I have one outstanding trait in my character . . . and that is my knowledge of myself. I can watch myself and my actions, just like an outsider. The Anne of every day I can face entirely without prejudice, without making excuses for her. . . . This "self consciousness" haunts me, and every time I open my mouth I know as soon as I've spoken whether "that ought to have been different" or "that was right as it was."

ANNE FRANK

❧

If you're strong enough there *are* no precedents.

F. SCOTT FITZGERALD

❧

A mistake often made in foretelling young men's careers: that a given amount of brain power will result in a proportionate success; so many units, so much product.

THOMAS HARDY

❧

Like a young thief thinks he has a license to steal, a young writer thinks he has a license to write.

WILLIAM S. BURROUGHS

❧

. . . unfortunately talent and originality do not always attend nobility of character.   W. SOMERSET MAUGHAM

A man succeeds in completing a work only when his qualities transcend that work.   CESARE PAVESE

❧

Our gifts are not gifts, but paid for terribly.   NED ROREM

❧

Nothing is easier than the flight of an eagle—he soars up to heaven without an effort & sails about in the clouds without labor. . . .

Any one may do as much as either the poet or the eagle—provided he has the genius of the one & the wings of the other.   WASHINGTON IRVING

❧

Only the mediocre writer is always at his best.

J. D. McCLATCHY

❧

Genius goes around the world in its youth incessantly apologizing for having large feet. What wonder that later in life it should be inclined to raise those feet too swiftly for fools and bores.   F. SCOTT FITZGERALD

❧

Only intensity matters. Talent—you have it or you don't.

JEAN COCTEAU

The Writer's Youth

I don't pronounce judgment on Mummy's character, for that is something I can't judge. I only look at her as a mother, and she just doesn't succeed in being that to me; I have to be my own mother. I've drawn myself apart from them all; I am my own skipper and later on I shall see where I come to land.

ANNE FRANK

⚜

I suspect that the child plucks its first flower with an insight into its beauty and significance which the subsequent botanist never retains.

HENRY DAVID THOREAU

⚜

The power of marveling makes up the genius of childhood, so quickly blunted by habit and education, and no one will ever be able to fit words together in an acceptable order unless he knows a little how to see creation through Adam's eyes. In art, truth lies in surprising.

JULIAN GREEN

⚜

Shadows: try to remember how magical my shadow was when I was a child.

C. K. WILLIAMS

Such faint sweet signs of life as Nature shows
A sleeping infant or the breathing rose;
And in that eye where others gladly see
Earth's purest light Heaven opens upon me.

WILLIAM WORDSWORTH

✤

My dad going around at night unplugging lamps, toasters, etc., as if they might mysteriously switch on at night and burn us up.

RAYMOND CARVER

✤

I can barely see over the dashboard. . . . Riding with Daddy is fun. . . . But I'm scared. Sometimes Daddy changes to a nervous, mean man with a tight face. He gives me a white tablet with red, sweet, sticky stuff in a paper cup to drink. Tastes good. We go to a house. It is empty. Daddy takes me up the stairs. The sunlight is shiny and bright on the pretty wood floors. . . .

. . . He pulls me into the middle of the room, presses me down on the floor and pulls my underpants off. He unzips his pants. . . .He pushes his floppy thing between my legs. What is he trying to do? His smell climbs up my nose, his whiskers feel like needles. His thing is hard now. He pushes his thing, *pushes* his thing and my pelvis cracks in half when his thing goes in my body. I can't breathe. I hear Daddy say, "Your mama says it's all right. Be a good girl now." My head rolls to the side and falls off into the black. My eyes close and I float up to the ceiling and from far away I see a child's bones come loose and float away in a river of blood as a big man plunges into a little girl.

I float down from the ceiling back into my body and open my eyes. My legs feel like broken glass. . . . Where's Daddy? . . . My body burns like a knife has been stuck into me.

SAPPHIRE

It pained me this morning to think of my father carrying the image of me as a child. BILL BARICH

❦

A child's prescience—for which he/she gets no credit—i.e., the way we pick people to love, who years after, are still loved by us. . . . By age six, I knew everything I know now. By age twelve, I had loved seriously, two men whom I still love now. GRETEL EHRLICH

❦

Jessie (age three): "Don't read me a story, tell me one with your mouth." C. K. WILLIAMS

❦

In my childhood women mended stockings in the evening. To have a "run" in one's stocking was catastrophic. Stockings were expensive, and so was electricity. We would all sit around the table with a lamp in its middle, the father reading the papers, the children pretending to do their homework, while secretly watching the mother spreading her red-painted fingernails inside the transparent stocking. CHARLES SIMIC

❦

I thought it . . . my duty, when I left school, to become a governess. In that capacity I find enough to occupy my thoughts all day long, and my head and hands, too, without having a moment's time for one dream of the imagination. In the evenings, I confess, I do think, but I never trouble any one else with my thoughts. I carefully avoid any appearance of preoccupation and eccentricity, which might lead those I live amongst to suspect the nature of my pursuits.

CHARLOTTE BRONTË

❦

Like my father, I loved comic books. I think he must have introduced me to them. He knew a man, a white man, in Savannah, who ran a wholesale house specializing in comic books. . . . Sometimes, my father would take my brother and me there, and the man would let us climb into a huge bin full of remaindered comic books. We would "swim" in the bin full of old comics. The man would let us take as many as we wanted. . . . At one time, I had well over seven hundred comic books. . . .

[At school] we were required to demonstrate artificial respiration techniques. Our grades depended on our learned skills in the exercise. But during this time our mother was buying all our clothes from the Salvation Army, and there were holes in my shoes. For this reason, I refused to kneel down and demonstrate how much I knew about artificial respiration. I knew that the other kids would laugh at the holes in my shoes. . . . The teacher kept demanding that I kneel down. I kept refusing. I finally flunked the course.

But during this same time, I discovered the Colored Branch of the Carnegie Public Library less than a block away from where we lived on East Henry Street. I liked going there to read all day.

At first the words, without pictures, were a mystery. But then, suddenly, they all began to march across the page. They gave up their secret meanings, spoke of other worlds, made me know that pain was a part of other people's lives. After a while, I could read faster and faster and faster and faster. After a while, I no longer believed in the world in which I lived.

I loved the Colored Branch of the Carnegie Public Library.

JAMES ALAN McPHERSON

I have at last got the little room I have wanted so long, and am very happy about it. It does me good to be alone, and Mother has made it very pretty and neat for me. My work-basket and desk are by the window, and my closet is full of dried herbs that smell very nice. The door that opens into the garden will be very pretty in summer, and I can run off to the woods when I like.

I have made a plan for my life, as I am in my teens, and no more a child. I am old for my age, and don't care much for girl's things. People think I'm wild and queer, but Mother understands and helps me. I have not told any one about my plan; but I'm going to *be* good. I've made so many resolutions, and written sad notes, and cried over my sins, and it doesn't seem to do any good! Now I'm going to *work really*, for I feel true desire to improve, and be a help and comfort, not a care and sorrow to my dear mother. LOUISA MAY ALCOTT

❧

In 1952 I did not smoke, and abhorred jovial adolescent farting. I seemed even to myself barely to eat. I studied both alone and with a blind friend, Matt Tierney. I worked, ran races and did my best to be everywhere at once—an undiscriminating blob of European yearning.

. . . At night, by the railway line in Homebush, I slept as lightly as the teenage eighteenth-century prodigy of poetry, Thomas Chatterton, whose work I had found in the Mitchell Library in Sydney. He was one of my heroes because he proved you could become immortal by seventeen years of age. At five years, said his biographer, Chatterton ordered a cup to be made with an angel blowing a trumpet, so that it might blow his name throughout the earth. And the angel did a great job, since Chatterton's poetry, much of it in "bogus Middle English" and supposed to have been written by a medieval priest called Rowley, was hugely praised, even though people objected to the deception. When Chatterton took arsenic in London in 1770, Wordsworth called him "the Marvelous Boy," and Keats dedicated *Endymion* to him.

> Arise, good youth, for Sacred Phoebus' sake!
> I know thine inmost bosom, and I feel
> A very brother's yearning for thee steal
> Into my own . . .

As I slept in the Eastern Australian nights of 1952, in Tennessee, Elvis—soon to be discovered—was scowling and thrusting his way towards fame. Rock was imminent. But I went against the age, and Chatterton was my rocker. I too wanted to be a marvellous boy without having to take arsenic. I was a very strange little bugger.   THOMAS KENEALLY

⚜

1955 Summer. When my father, on his vacation, drove north to Baltimore with his wife Mona, to "rescue" me from my life . . . My father, whom I had not laid eyes on since I was eight . . . said in his musing, never-far-from-sarcastic voice, "I'm glad you're good-looking." . . .

I don't know what my father felt, don't know what he expected. But surely, a man who had little to do with young people, who had a well-deserved reputation for being selfish, he must have found me scarifying: both in the sense of my being selfish like him, and in the sense that I was not the malleable, appreciative daughter I am sure he thought he had the right to expect.

I had no idea that his disappointments were accumulating like waves, which, in three years, would drown him in the high tide of his despair. I do wonder what he hoped for—from me. . . .

. . . That I would be made happy and fine by coming to live with him and that I would let him know I owed my sheen to him. That we would look good together and people would say: "Look at Mose and his daughter. He went and found her and gave her what nobody else could in the way of style."

GAIL GODWIN

❧

"That's the chair you were nursed in," my mother tells me one day, disconcertingly. Speaking of an old flame of hers, she pumps her dress over her heart with two fingers to show how it had throbbed.

EDWARD HOAGLAND

❧

My dad squatting / down that time, / taking aim with / his shotgun, and / blasting a sitting / dove . . .

RAYMOND CARVER

❧

There was a maid in our house who let me put my hand under her skirt. I was five or six years old. I can still remember the dampness of her crotch and my surprise that there was all that hair there. I couldn't get enough of it. She would crawl under the table where I had my military fort and kept all my weapons. I don't remember what we said, if anything. Just her hand, firmly guiding mine.

CHARLES SIMIC

❧

You lose your innocence more than once.

BILL BARICH

❧

I was eighteen. My friend S. and I excused ourselves from our boyfriends at intermission and went to comb our hair. We stood side by side, shoulders touching in the mirror, and S. began to cry. Stupidly I tried to comfort her. I wish I were you, she said. You are everything I would want to be if I could. You . . . me . . . you . . . I wanted to jam the words back in her mouth. No one has ever said anything that frightened me so. I wanted her to say them again. I was abject. Euphoric. The only thing that disturbed me was that their truth or falsity was not to be my problem but hers. She would not simply give the words to me as a gift, they were eating at her. The evil eye, still big with tears, stared back at me from the mirror.

ROSELLEN BROWN

❧

We walked into the wood constrainedly. . . .

The Old Boy sat down on a tree-stump and said awkwardly, "There doesn't seem to be anywhere else, you'd better sit here." He smiled shamefacedly and patted his knee.

I held my breath and sat down. He held me very gingerly, as if I were a ventriloquist's doll. My body was taut. I could not relax. I didn't know what it was all about. I didn't want to be a prig. I wanted to be nice, but I also wanted to escape.

. . . I was nervously fluttering my eyelids. He saw this, and putting his face close to mine he said, "Don't be frightened of me, dearest." This endearment shocked and thrilled me. I could feel his eyelashes tickling my face and the extraordinary damp warmth of his cheek. . . .

. . . we made our way back to the car, through the corn and potato crop. I thought once, as I looked up at the high white clouds in the blue sky, "I will remember this day always." And I have.

DENTON WELCH

❧

In my memory, my parents are neither young nor old, but hover in an indeterminate space as abstractions, composites, not quite likenesses, but not unrecognizable. It is a space they forged for themselves, a space clouded with emotion, with gestures only partially embodied, with responses tangled into contradiction, into webs of affirmation and denial. I recall my mother as tall, but then I remember her shorter than me. I remember certain articles of clothing she wore, her preference for tailored tweed suits. I recall my father as a big man with a large belly. I recall the heavy blond hair that covered his arms, and the baldness of his legs, their combination of muscular firmness and delicacy at the ankles. But to know what my parents looked like I must meditate over the evidence of snapshots; I must take those frozen, isolated gestures and connect them to a time and to other gestures or actions recalled dimly in their wholeness, and I must hope that some trajectory of being suggests itself. My parents belong increasingly to a dominion that forms the near shore of nothingness. Only my sister and I and a few others carry the evidence of their having existed, and my attempts at retrieval seem more and more like stages in a prolonged farewell.   MARK STRAND

❧

There is a golden age: the age of childhood, of ignorance; as soon as one knows one is going to die, childhood is over.

EUGENE IONESCO

Education

The things taught in colleges and schools are not an education, but the means of an education. RALPH WALDO EMERSON

* * *

My education finished 9th. July. Whatever moral good and general knowledge I may have got from it, I have retained no literal rules. . . .

I regret German very much, history I can read alone, French is still going on, the rules of geography and grammar are tiresome, there is no general word to express the feelings I have always entertained towards arithmetic. BEATRIX POTTER

* * *

It is only when we forget all learning that we begin to know.
HENRY DAVID THOREAU

* * *

Talking of kids, I must not forget two stories of Cobb's. Elizabeth Cobb, when her parents began to spell: "Too damn much education here for me." And of another girl, when her parents began to whisper: "What's the good of being educated, anyway? When I've learnt to spell, you whisper."
ARNOLD BENNETT

Culture is to know things at first hand (at the source).

ROBERT FROST

❧

We live at the level of our language. Whatever we can articulate we can imagine or understand or explore. All you have to do to educate a child is leave him alone and teach him to read. The rest is brainwashing. ELLEN GILCHRIST

❧

Natural light passes through murky glass windows in the office doors and sinks into the brown linoleum. . . . The halls are long and wide, and have gloomy brown seriousness, dull grandeur. You hardly ever hear people laughing in them. The air is too heavy with significance. Behind the doors, professors are bent over student papers, writing in the margins, "B+," "A-." LEONARD MICHAELS

❧

Not to *teach* a class, but to *conduct* it: I punch the tickets and call out the stops along the way. J. D. McCLATCHY

❧

. . . a man or woman who publishes writings inevitably assumes the office of teacher or influencer of the public mind. . . . he can no more escape influencing the moral taste, and with it the action of the intelligence, than a setter of fashions in furniture and dress can fill the shops with his designs and leave the garniture of persons and houses unaffected by his industry. GEORGE ELIOT

What does education often do? It makes a straight-cut ditch of a free, meandering brook.   HENRY DAVID THOREAU

❧

A too explicit elucidation in education destroys much of the pleasure of learning. There should be room for sly hinters, masters of suggestion.

. . . Literalness is the devil's weapon.   THEODORE ROETHKE

❧

Nothing is easier than to accumulate facts, nothing is so hard as to use them.   OSCAR WILDE

❧

There are writers you admire, for the skill or for the art, for the inventiveness or for the professionalism of a career well spent. And there are writers—sometimes the same ones, sometimes not—to whom you are powerfully attracted, for reasons that may or may not have to do with literary values. They speak to you, or speak for you, sometimes with a voice that could almost be your own. Often there is one writer in particular who awakens you, who is the teacher they say you will meet when you are ready for the lesson.

JAMES D. HOUSTON

❧

Tell a well-educated college boy the best thought right out of your own thinking and he accepts it with a, *Do* they say so? He is disappointed when you have to admit, No, I say so but they will say so after I show them.   ROBERT FROST

The merits of American style are less numerous than its defects and annoyances, but they are more powerful. . . .

It's fairly obvious that American education is a cultural flop. Americans are not a well-educated people culturally. . . . On the other hand they have open quick minds and if their education has little sharp positive value, it has not the stultifying effects of more rigid training. Such tradition as they have in the use of their language is derived from English tradition, and there is just enough resentment about this to cause perverse use of ungrammaticalities—"just to show 'em."

RAYMOND CHANDLER

❧

Education: "Masticate your food properly," their father told them. And they masticated properly, and walked two hours every day, and washed in cold water, and yet they turned out unhappy and without talent.   ANTON CHEKHOV

❧

The greatest and truest knowledge that can never be taught or passed over from him or her who has it, to him or her who has it not.—It is in the soul. . . . It is the consciousness of the reality and excellence of every thing.—It is happiness.

WALT WHITMAN

Inspiration

The overriding thing must be the greatness of the conception, the dark piled-up mass, the trembling light over everything and the fearlessness of the human heart which shows things as they are and likes them that way.   BERTOLT BRECHT

☩

Always surprised on those days when the mind makes her shotgun, metaphoric leaps for reasons I've never been able to trace. Remembered that Wang Wei said a thousand years ago, "Who knows what causes the opening and closing of the door?"   JIM HARRISON

☩

I finish a glass of brandy, and want to write about this month, and know that I am too sleepy. And then I wonder why I do want to write about it, because I despise talk, and the people who talk, who tell others about themselves, and the dreadful necessity that pushes them to such confessions. They must talk. They must expose themselves. It helps them, and more horribly, it helps others.

That is what bothers me. I hate this need. I've never done much of it, and I despise it in others. But I know that I am more articulate than some, and I think well. . . . My God in

Heaven! If what I've learned about pain or food or the excreta of the seasnail can help even one poor human being, I am a rat not to write. M. F. K. FISHER

❦

To live *in* the world of creation—to get into it and stay in it—to frequent it and haunt it—to think intensely and fruitfully—to woo combinations and inspirations into being by a depth and continuity of attention and meditation—this is the only thing. HENRY JAMES

❦

What matters to an artist is not experience, but inward experience. CESARE PAVESE

❦

To withdraw myself from *myself* (oh that cursed selfishness!) has ever been my sole, my entire, my sincere motive in scribbling at all. LORD BYRON

❦

I am going to write because I cannot help it.
CHARLOTTE BRONTË

❦

Inspiration: the important thing in life is to have the right kind of frustration. THEODORE ROETHKE

❦

What's the tingling across the scalp? It's what I call the literary buzz, a little signal from the top of my head that there is some mystery here, some unrevealed linkage that will have to be explored with words.   JAMES D. HOUSTON

☙

I was eating breakfast, toast & tea, when the first call came. "The clapping started in the cheap seats." The voice was familiar, but I couldn't place it. About the same time on Tuesday: "The laughter of fools is the crackling of thrones." Now I had a clue. Wednesday nothing. On Thursday I was washing up, held the phone with a towel. "The heart is a piano of displeasure." On Friday: "Sea turtles seldom call home." Nothing on Saturday. Perhaps he's Orthodox. On Sunday even earlier: "The Ford was discovered by DeSoto," & after a pause, "Ta Ta." Dialed my own number but couldn't get thru. I'd have to go back to writing.   PHILIP LEVINE

☙

Those who are willing to be vulnerable move among mysteries.   THEODORE ROETHKE

☙

One Sunday afternoon, while I was driving my young daughters to their mother's house in a nearby town, the first line of a story had come to me. I was talking with my daughters and watching cars and the road, and suddenly the sentence was inside me; it had come from whatever place they come from. It is not a place I can enter at will; I simply receive its gifts. I had been gestating this story for a very long time, not thinking about it, but allowing it to possess me, and waiting to see these characters living in me: their faces, their bodies. I do not start writing a story until I see the people and the beginning of the story. In the car with my girls I knew I must start writing the story on Monday. . . . In that space between my heart and diaphragm was the fear I always feel before writing, when my soul is poised to leap alone. . . .

I wrote the story in four days; it is very short, and I knew before starting it that it was coming like grace to me, and I could receive it or bungle it, but I could not hold it at bay; and if I were not able to receive it with an open heart and, with concentration, write it on paper, it would come anyway, and pass through me and through my room to dissipate in the air, and it may not come back. . . . It was strange, in those four days, to become one with the woman in the story, and the evil she chose, and the ecstasy it gave her and me. I called the story "The Last Moon," and in December I wrote it again, and in January I wrote it again. I did not look at it for days between drafts, and worked at not thinking about it, because it was hot and I was hot, and we both needed to cool, so I could see it clearly enough to take words away from it. But in January it was done, which truly means I had done all I can ever do with it, and it became something that lived apart from me. I started another story, and in a few weeks "The Last Moon" was a memory, much like meeting someone while you are travelling, and you eat and drink and talk with this person, feel even love, and then you go home with the memory and it does not matter to you whether you ever see the person again.

ANDRE DUBUS

❧

The poetic flashpoint comes where the meaningless meets the sublime.

LAWRENCE DURRELL

❧

I put improvisation above reflection, feeling above reason, mercy above justice, religion above philosophy, the beautiful above the useful, poetry above all. GUSTAVE FLAUBERT

The hardest thing is letting it all go. Everything you've been taught, everything useless, everything that doesn't apply. What we are about here on earth, our task, is liberation—to let the soul rise from its prison into the light.

. . . Surprise yourself and you surprise the world.

BILL BARICH

❦

All is in yourself,
Things, thoughts, the stately
    shows of the world,
    the suns and moons,
    the landscape, summer
    and winter,
    poems, endearments,
All

WALT WHITMAN

❦

Poetry brings pollen of one flower to another flower.

ROBERT FROST

❦

We traverse the fields towards Hampstead. Under an expansive oak lies a dead calf; the cow, lean from grief, is watching it. (Contemplate subject for poem.)   MARY SHELLEY

❦

An idea has to have some dirt on its shoes, or it's just air.

MARVIN BELL

When writing poetry, it is not inspiration that produces a bright idea, but the bright idea that kindles the fire of inspirations.   CESARE PAVESE

❧

Today is the first of August. It is hot, steamy and wet. It is raining. I am tempted to write a poem. But I remember what it said on one rejection slip: After a heavy rainfall, poems titled "Rain" pour in from across the nation.   SYLVIA PLATH

❧

The scar in X.'s cheek, vertical, perhaps three inches long. Not disfiguring but startling—you look quickly back to his eyes hoping he won't have noticed (but of course he has) where you'd looked. *What caused that scar,* I won't ever ask. Because the answer would be banal and the scar itself is not.
                                                                    JOYCE CAROL OATES

❧

. . . the work is not a thing that we make, but an already-made thing which we discover.   THORNTON WILDER

❧

When idiots on boats say, "Where do your ideas *come* from?" I answer that it can't be explained. When clever laymen ask, I discuss the process at length. But when other artists talk of this, I say, "Ideas? I *steal* them." And they understand. Sometimes I rob myself.   NED ROREM

❧

Poetry makes nothing happen? It makes new poems happen.

. . . The measure of a poem's "immortality" is the later life it leads in other poems. Imitation, appropriation—dismemberment and regeneration—by new poets give the old poem its purchase on life.   J. D. McCLATCHY

❧

Who w[ould] call Virgil an imitator of Homer? . . . One real Poet is to another a piece of Nature, which he studies & imitates. . . . A poet is the joint product of such internal powers as modify the natures of others, & of external influences which excite & sustain these powers; every man's mind is in this respect modified by all the objects of nature & of art, by every word & sentence which he ever admitted to act upon his consciousness. It is the mirror [upon] which many [outward] forms are [reflected], & in which they compose one form.   PERCY BYSSHE SHELLEY

❧

The heritage of art is one thing to the public and quite another to the succeeding artists. The artist's inheritance from other artists can be little more than certain enthusiasms, which usually spoil his first work; and a definite knowledge of the modes of expression, which knowledge contributes to perfecting his more mature performance. This is a matter of technique.   EZRA POUND

❧

A Scotch congregation who wanted a minister had two candidates to preach for them on the same Sunday. Their names were Adam and Low. Low who preached in the morning took for his text "Adam where art thou"! Adam who favoured the congregation in the afternoon took for his, the words "Lo here I am."   BEATRIX POTTER

Everything which isolates, such as pride, damns;
everything which associates, such as dance, saves.

DELMORE SCHWARTZ

❦

The function of art is to enthrall and in
doing so to change, to instruct, to
encourage a new deal of the old cards
which will influence in the direction
of freedom from distress, encouragement of
happiness, well-being.

LAWRENCE DURRELL

❦

What it gave us no pleasure to conceive or make . . . will
give the world no pleasure to contemplate . . .

MATTHEW ARNOLD

❦

Yesterday, happiness came in suddenly, as it used to, and remained for a moment in the great, dark, silent drawing room.
We were standing by a window, looking at the rain as it spun
its web in the lowering sky, and I felt, in spite of all the newspapers could shout at us, that happiness was close at hand,
humble as a beggar, magnificent as a king. It is always with us
(but we are unaware) knocking at the door to come in and sup
with us.

JULIAN GREEN

❦

I grow upset, angry, depressed beyond all measure at the
amount of time and effort we give to mutable things. Houses
fall into disrepair—paint peels, walls crack, dirt accumulates—
cars slowly die, clothes wear out—yet, to these we give our

greatest loyalties. All the vast mechanical resources are mobilized to produce—a can opener.

It is this despair at the mutability of all created things that links the Artist and the Ascetic—a desire to purify and preserve—to set oneself apart—somehow—from the river flowing to the grave.   MICHELE MURRAY

Ambition

Oh my God, my God, why did you cause me to be born with so much ambition? . . . When I was ten, I was already thinking of fame—I began to compose as soon as I knew how to write; I painted ravishing pictures for myself—I dreamed of a hall, brightly lighted and glittering with gold, of hands that were clapping, of shouts, of wreathes. They call "Author! Author!"—the author is myself, of course, he has my name, he is me, me; they seek me out in the corridors, in the boxes, they lean out to see me; the curtain goes up; I step forward—such ecstasy! They are looking at me, admiring me, envying me, almost loving me!   GUSTAVE FLAUBERT

⚜

I looked through *Liberation*'s questionnaire of two years ago: Pourquoi écrivez-vous?—this time to see what was the most usual answer. Very few writers claimed financial necessity as a reason for exercising their profession. Many admitted that they had no idea why they wrote. But the majority responded by implying that they were impelled to write by some inner force which would not be denied. The more scrupulous of these did not hesitate to admit that their principal satisfaction was in feeling that they were leaving a part of themselves behind—in other words, writing was felt to confer a certain minimal immortality. This would have been understandable earlier in the century when it was assumed that life on the planet would continue indefinitely. Now that the prognosis is doubtful, the desire to leave a trace behind seems absurd. Even if the human species manages to survive another hundred years, it's unlikely that a book written in 1990 will mean much to anyone happening to open it in 2090, if indeed he is capable of reading at all.   PAUL BOWLES

❧

Mr. [Samuel] Johnson's library . . . is four pairs of stairs up, in two garrets. . . . I saw a number of good books, but very dusty and confusedly placed . . . manuscript leaves scattered up and down which I looked upon with a degree of veneration, as they perhaps might be pieces of *The Rambler,* or of *Rasselas.* . . . no place can be more favorable for meditation than such a retirement as this garret. I could not help indulging a scheme of taking it for myself many years hence, when its present great possessor will in all probability be gone to a more exalted situation. This was in a strong sense "building my castle in the air."   JAMES BOSWELL

❧

Seeking out your own advantage is something to rise to.
ROBERT FROST

❧

It is only the common ambition that is satisfied with the eminence that comes from wealth or office.   WALT WHITMAN

❧

The wretched State of the Arts in this Country & in Europe . . . demands a firm & determinate conduct on the part of the

Artist to Resist the Contemptible Counter Arts. . . . To recover Art has been the business of my life to the Florentine
Original & if possible to go beyond that Original; this I
thought the only pursuit worthy of a Man. To Imitate I ab-
hor. . . . Imagination is My World. . . . I demand therefore of
the Amateurs of Art the Encouragement which is my due; if
they continue to refuse, theirs is the loss, not mine, & theirs is
the Contempt of Posterity. I have Enough in the Approbation
of fellow labourers; this is my glory & exceeding great reward.
I go on & nothing can hinder my course.   WILLIAM BLAKE

❧

If you wish to have spare time, do nothing.
                                        ANTON CHEKHOV

❧

Serious literature does not exist to make life easy but to
complicate it.   WITOLD GOMBROWICZ

❧

. . . happiness only if I can raise the world into the pure, the
true, and the immutable.   FRANZ KAFKA

❧

The rule of "nothing inessential" is the first condition of art.
                                        ANDRÉ GIDE

❧

To find my home in one sentence, concise, as if hammered
in metal. Not to enchant anybody. Not to earn a lasting name
in posterity. An unnamed need for order, for rhythm, for form,
which three words are opposed to chaos and nothingness.
                                        CZESLAW MILOSZ

Without magic, there is no art. Without art, there is no idealism. Without idealism, there is no integrity. Without integrity, there is nothing but production.

RAYMOND CHANDLER

❧

I don't try to be so very careful to limit what I write to things that I know I can do. More and more I find I'm willing to take a chance on showing bad taste and ignorance if it will allow me a new and broader expression. I try at the same time to keep an honest and intelligent eye on what are my limitations for total success in a thing. I continue to take pleasure in doing the things that are my *type*, but I get a different pleasure from trying to branch out and experiment.   PETER TAYLOR

❧

Never to be satisfied: all of art is there.   JULES RENARD

❧

There is something even sadder than falling short of one's own ideals: to have them realized.   CESARE PAVESE

❧

Writing is a process of killing off by increments that other self, the one who wanted to write.   BILL BARICH

❧

All your aggression is directed toward discovering new perceptions, and consequently against yourself when you fail to come up with anything new.   JIM HARRISON

Ambition.—What a dismal passion! STENDHAL

❧

Having to decide to be a *great* poet, to *will* it, but at the same time somehow to keep a sense of play, because without that there's just dullness, the seriousness of mediocrity. . . . There has to be laughter behind the absurdity of confronting mysteries. A *gaiety*. C. K. WILLIAMS

❧

You must stoop a little in order to jump.

F. SCOTT FITZGERALD

❧

Even something harsh and difficult is a comfort if we choose it ourselves. If it is imposed on us by others, it is agony.

CESARE PAVESE

❧

I have only to let myself *go!* So I have said all my life. . . . Yet I have never fully done it. . . . I am in full possession of ac-cumulated resources—I have only to use them, to insist, to persist, to do something more—to do much more—than I *have* done. The way to do it . . . is to strike as many notes, deep, full and rapid, as one can. All life is . . . in one's pocket, as it were. Go on, my boy, and strike hard. . . . Try everything, do everything, render everything—be an artist, be distin-guished, to the last. HENRY JAMES

❧

The art of life, of a poet's life, is, not having anything to do, to do something. HENRY DAVID THOREAU

> . . . be not cheap or
> mediocre in
> desiring. . . .
>
> EZRA POUND

❦

To be a useful person has always appeared to me something particularly horrible. CHARLES BAUDELAIRE

❦

Ambition has been at the core of everything false in my life.
LYNN FREED

❦

To be worth something or nothing. To create or not to create. In the first case everything is justified. Everything without exception. In the second case, everything is completely absurd. The only choice then to be made is of the most aesthetically satisfying form of suicide: marriage, and a forty-hour week, or a revolver. ALBERT CAMUS

❦

> The poet's desire
> Is to be consumed in his poem as fuel
> is consumed in fire
> As the sunlight vanishes in the apple . . .
>
> DELMORE SCHWARTZ

❦

Who said, "You can't do something you don't know if you keep doing what you do know." JIM HARRISON

In order to be as you should be in life, you mustn't live for yourself; in order to write sublime works, you must live for your genius, form it, cultivate it, correct it.   STENDHAL

❧

The business of the poet and novelist is to show the sorriness underlying the greatest things, and the grandness underlying the sorriest things.   THOMAS HARDY

❧

Poetry fails, in each poem, to be as good as poetry ought to be—or as I somehow think it somewhere is, somewhere I'm not looking. Every flesh is flawed and poems are flesh.

DONALD HALL

❧

To write well, to write passionately, to be less inhibited, to be warmer, to be more self-critical, to recognize the power of as well as the force of lust, to write, to love.   JOHN CHEEVER

The
Writer's Work

(THEORY AND PRACTICE)

On Keeping Notebooks, Journals, and Diaries

. . . every writer should keep a notebook, but should never refer to it.
W. SOMERSET MAUGHAM

⚜

If some indiscreet person reads this diary, I wish to deprive him of the pleasure of making fun of me by pointing out to him that this aims at being a mathematical and rigid report on my manner of being, neither too favorable nor too unfavorable, but stating purely and severely what I believe to have taken place. It is destined to cure me of my absurdities when I reread it.
STENDHAL

⚜

It makes me laugh to read my diary. What a lot of contradictions. . . . I always write in my diary when we quarrel.
SOPHIA TOLSTOY

⚜

I wonder if I shall burn this sheet of paper like most others I have begun in the same way. To write a diary, I have thought of very often at far and near distances of time: but how could I write a diary without throwing upon paper my thoughts, all my thoughts—the thoughts of my heart as well as of my head?—& then how could I bear to look on *them* after they were written? Adam made fig leaves necessary for the mind, as well as for the body. And such *a* mind as I have!—So very exacting & exclusive & eager & head long & strong & so very very often *wrong*! Well! but I will write: I must write—& the oftener wrong I know myself to be, the less wrong I shall be in one thing—the less *vain* I shall be!

ELIZABETH BARRETT BROWNING

⚜

I suppose the point of publishing such a document is to demonstrate the way in which the hours of a day can as satisfactorily be filled with trivia as with important events.

PAUL BOWLES

⚜

Sometimes I very much doubt whether in the future anyone will be interested in all my tosh. "The unbosomings of an ugly duckling" will be the title of all this nonsense.

ANNE FRANK

⚜

A diary has impact only through the accumulation of unlimited observations (of which many are obsessive and recurring), never through the development of themes (for then it would no longer be a diary). Works of art must have a plan; beginnings and ends. A diary necessarily has no form beyond the accidental one of improvisation; hence, though it cannot be a work of art (improvisation precludes this), perhaps it *can* be a masterpiece.

NED ROREM

The utter gratuitousness of the diary, as of thought in general. I shall write tomorrow of Paris. But why? For no reason, because it amuses me. And nothing here has any reason; it's all a game. Above all, I never force my thought. If I were writing a composed book I should press on, like soldiers in war who are always made to hold out a little longer than they're able. Whereas I break off as soon as I'm ready to force myself.

JEAN-PAUL SARTRE

❦

The attraction of keeping a journal is the possibility of being able to *jot*. (Interesting, in that regard, that I have xxxed and revised that sentence.) JANET BURROWAY

❦

Reread this evening Gide's old *Journals*. It is interesting to notice how certain themes hold such prominence in his thoughts that for several months or several years he can scarcely speak of anything else; slowly they regress and disappear. Thus in 1933–34 Russia reappears on every page. Later she vanishes. We are all like that. Each of us carries with him through life a few ideas, no great number. They are made incarnate, now in a man, now in a country. Then the man disappoints, the country astonishes, and the idea, freed of its incarnation, is left to seek another body. The life of the spirit is constant metempsychosis. ANDRÉ MAUROIS

❦

I have just re-read my year's diary and am much struck by the rapid haphazard gallop at which it swings along, sometimes indeed jerking almost intolerably over the cobbles. Still if it were not written rather faster than the fastest typewriting, if I stopped and took thought, it would never be written at all; and the advantage of the method is that it sweeps up accidentally several stray matters which I should exclude if I hesitated, but which are the diamonds of the dustheap.

VIRGINIA WOOLF

❧

Virginia called them "holdalls" to reflect the light of our lives. The dark, I fear, creeps in rather more, in my case.

EDNA O'BRIEN

❧

I won't give up the diary again. I must hold on here, it is the only place I can.

FRANZ KAFKA

❧

Kafka said that writing is a form of prayer. I know that he never meant it as literally as I do today, this very instant, writing this.

ROSELLEN BROWN

❧

This is not a pen, it is a prayer, one must have compassion for that.

FYODOR DOSTOYEVSKY

❧

In rereading of writers' journals on my shelves, I find in Katherine Mansfield's a note: "Perhaps it does not so much matter what one loves in this world. But love something one must." Katherine Anne Porter, in her essay on Mansfield, writes that this is "a hopeless phrase. . . . It seems to me that St. Augustine knew the real truth of the matter: 'It doth make a difference whence cometh a man's joy.' "

Reading the journals of others forces me to wonder how much truth ought to be included here. Even if I aim for what seems to me to be truth, will not the very process of putting it into words and setting it down fictionalize it? And then there is the natural reluctance to open all the sores and secret miseries of one's life, the misdoings and meannesses. Truman Capote would have required me to tell everything: "No matter what passions compose them, all private worlds are good, they are never vulgar places."　　DORIS GRUMBACH

❧

There is a saying that "paper is more patient than man". . . . Yes, there is no doubt that paper is patient and as I don't intend to show this cardboard-covered notebook bearing the proud name of "diary," to anyone, unless I find a real friend, boy or girl, probably nobody cares. And now I come to the root of the matter, the reason for my starting a diary; it is that I have no such real friend.　　ANNE FRANK

❧

I think that if I get into the habit of writing a bit about what happens, or rather doesn't happen, I may lose a little of the sense of loneliness and desolation which abides in me.

ALICE JAMES

❧

Sometimes a light hand strokes the air behind you. The streets open up county to county but you have never belonged in any of them. That's why I write in a notebook. I carry my home in a pocket through the streets of Mexico City, Cuernavaca, Tuxtla Gutiérrez. When someone's eyes say "Stranger" I return to a page familiar as the room I grew up in. The blue walls and two windows. It could be any page.

NAOMI SHIHAB NYE

[Samuel Johnson] advised me to keep a journal of my life, fair and undisguised. . . . I told him that I had done so ever since I left Scotland. . . . I put down all sorts of little incidents in it. "Sir," said he, "there is nothing too little for so little a creature as man. It is by studying little things that we attain great knowledge of having as little misery and as much happiness as possible."　　　　　　　　　　　　　　　　JAMES BOSWELL

❦

Read the Notebooks of Leonardo da Vinci. . . . I note at random:
　"Lust is the cause of generation."
　"Reproach a friend in secret, but praise him before others."
　"Courage shortens, fear preserves life."
　"There is no sovereignty greater than that over oneself."
　　　　　　　　　　　　　　　　ANDRÉ MAUROIS

❦

A writer suggested to me, on a walk, that I should be writing in my journal about divorce (rather than talking about it to strangers, I presume). Journal? Since I started the sad thing with two entries that were dislodged, Xeroxed and used against me in the divorce suit, I've stopped keeping it. Anyway, I don't enjoy talking to myself. I prefer silence.
　　　　　　　　　　　　　　　　LYNN FREED

❦

Writing about one's own life, it is only when one writes about the most intimate and seemingly idiosyncratic details that one touches others.　　　　　　　　SUSAN GRIFFIN

Art is a microscope which the artist fixes on the secrets of his soul, and shows to people these secrets which are common to all. LEO TOLSTOY

❧

Dipped into Tolstoy's diary of his old age. Find much in it strongly repugnant. Thoroughly agree with other things. ". . . Art is a microscope. . . ." Very good. THOMAS MANN

❧

In writing your journal give primary attention to detail; for it is detail which organizes and preserves experience for your future self or some other reader. General statements like "We had a wonderful time" or "It was a dismal morning" make a mockery of the whole procedure, for they evaluate experience without recreating it. I kept long journals from ages ten to twenty-two, chronicling events and describing emotional states, but again and again missing the physical immediacy of experience, the tiny hooks by which experience could have been caught and held. I failed to record how we looked, what we saw, the minor eccentricities of circumstance which gave special character to a day. I ignored these elements not only through lack of training but through misplaced priorities: I mistakenly assumed that one could discuss the heart of things without discussing the immediate details of life.

ROBERT GRUDIN

❧

Beside the Seine. These are the loveliest of moments in the notebook, for they expand. The very words I set down here are like the roots underground in winter. They look a little skimpy on this page, but they carry secret pages in them.

JAMES WRIGHT

In a panel discussion I said that I had "never made a major life decision in the service of my work. All my major decisions had to do with my personal life." I was surprised (and appalled) to hear myself say this. But I've thought about it some hundreds of times since. The personal choice *is* my material; if I were not so constituted I wouldn't know what to write about. Today at lunch Karen suggested that this journal might be the basis of a novel; but that's backwards too. The journal is in the service of life, not the other way around.

JANET BURROWAY

❧

To keep a day book, quite different from a journal—Edith Wharton copied out passages from Goethe, Poe, Pascal, Rabelais, Spenser—nothing personal, yet I'm not sure that her act of continual quotation wasn't revealing. Edith, the half-educated girl, proving to herself that she was entitled to her bookish ways, that she was desperately serious. My days do not give me time for a day book though I can't live without a small notebook stashed in my pocket or purse. Of a hunter-gatherer tribe, I scribble: "Mary had a little lamb," first words on Edison's phonograph; flamingo preserved in rum sent to Audubon in London, so large its head must curve to the ground on the folio page; Oct. 31, 1992, the Pope acknowledged the church in error regarding Galileo; in 1952 the Dept. of the Army distinguished "official knowledge" from "formal knowledge" and so on. Born in the first year of the Great Depression, everything useful must be used. "The news which is called true is so like an old tale that the verity of it is in strong suspicion."

MAUREEN HOWARD

❧

14 March 1995 10:27 a.m.

Ah: a new dateline, a date format anew. This is all I need. I will add of course the *place* my precious things are written. I note that Leslie Fiedler wrote his introduction to John Hawkes's *Lime Twig* in O*shen* Vermont in *June* of whenever— a relief to have that known. Otherwise we might have . . . not known. We might have thought he wrote it in a lesser place than Walden, dashed it off in a subway. It might not have occurred to us to care. We might have just really been asleep, critically speaking. "Writing this on a wheelbarrow in a coal bin, boys!" "Putting this down on Kilamanjaro, ladies!" "Patmos!" "Ho Chi Minh City, amid the din of helicopter whump n' whirrrr!"

PADGETT POWELL

❧

. . . writing a journal implies that one has ceased to think of the future and has decided to live in the present. It is an announcement to fate that you expect nothing more. It is assertion that you take each day as it comes and make no connection between to-day and other days. Writing a journal means that facing your ocean you are afraid to swim across it, so you attempt to drink it drop by drop. It means that you count the last leaves of a tree whose trunk has lost its sap.

When you are in the mood to write a journal the passions have cooled, or else they have so far frozen that they may be examined as safely as ice-bound mountains are explored in the season when no avalanches fall. No one should allow himself to solidify to this extent unless he is in such a state of upheaval that all the fires of his being are in danger of eruption. Then indeed it may be necessary to harden the outer crust in order to check the explosion and save the inner flame from becoming extinct.

GEORGE SAND

❧

To record one must be unwary.　　　　F. SCOTT FITZGERALD

The problem lies in the very nature of the journal. If I tell the truth the truth *is* likely to be petty. If not demoralizing, comical in all the wrong places, crushing in its dullness. If I don't tell the truth I lose all interest in writing.

JOYCE CAROL OATES

❧

I finished my play today. . . . Three acts, six scenes, a masterpiece completed in a few weeks. . . .

. . . The play only exists as a tiny scrawl in my notebooks—things I carry about in my pockets.

GEORGE BERNARD SHAW

Tools of the Trade

VOICE, LANGUAGE, AND STYLE

Today I sent off another 13,000 odd words to be typed, and have my teeth well into a new chapter. English writers, at forty, either set about prophesying or acquiring a style. Thank God I think I am beginning to acquire a style.

EVELYN WAUGH

St.-Ex[upéry] talks of Baudelaire, his life, his poetry. He says that Baudelaire was great not for what he said but because he was one of those who knew best how to knot words, and he recites some of his poetry to me and goes on, about his theory of style—that the same words arranged differently became banal, did not mean the same thing. The unexpressed finds expression in style, rhythm, etc.—words carry only half the freight. Of how inverted words sometimes gave quality.

ANNE MORROW LINDBERGH

This is the work I do. If the artifact is flawed, I'd say the tools must be new, inexperienced (hammer speaks no English, chisel no Greek, etc.).

STRATIS HAVIARAS

Of course the writer depends on the fortuitous accident. One need only remember the story of Poussin impatiently dashing his sponge against his canvas, and producing the precise effect (the foam on a horse's mouth) which he has been long and vainly laboring for.   J. D. McCLATCHY

❧

I often think that the best writing is done after you've forgotten what you wanted to say, but end up putting something down anyway just as though it were the actual evidence of your original intention.   CLARENCE MAJOR

❧

[Isaac] Singer's stories sound like he is remembering them.
                                                ARTHUR MILLER

❧

Style should be like a transparent varnish . . . ; it should spread completely over the colors, make them brighter, but not alter them.   STENDHAL

❧

Writing in the present tense is like playing the harpsichord; no forte possible.   EDWARD HOAGLAND

❧

In effect, the way people talk is what they mean. It is precise and clear—more than mathematics, legal language, or philosophy—and it is not only what they mean, but also all they mean. That's what it means to mean. Everything else is alienation except poetry.   LEONARD MICHAELS

The possibility of *saying* as the possibility of *being*.

BILL BARICH

✢

If the word *arse* appears in a sentence, even in a sublime sentence, the public will hear only that one word.

JULES RENARD

✢

You can always get a little more literature if you are willing to go a little closer into what has been left unsaid as unspeakable, just as you can always get a little more melon by going a little closer to the rind.

ROBERT FROST

✢

Night Thought: Reading late at night after work I found myself correcting the sentences of the author to make them read the way I wanted mine to. To stretch them tauter than the vibrant bow.

EDMUND WILSON

✢

Emerson thought he wrote best in sentences; he called his paragraphs collections of "infinitely repellent particles."

ANNIE DILLARD

✢

It seems that severe emotional problems, neuroses, are born, thrive, multiply in areas where language never enters. The writer thinks that if he can solve these problems his quality of language will vastly improve. This is the fallacy of writing as therapy.

JIM HARRISON

A man may be said to possess a style if, upon coming across a phrase in a newspaper, you can say that it is written by him.

STENDHAL

❧

Oh for a draft of Hemingway prose! His prose is "poetic"— and all this overwriting, mine included, is not. Of course Hemingway's is a type of overwriting too. One reason the old Constance Garnett translations [of Chekhov and Tolstoy] remain the secret favorite of many, including me, is just that they *have* no style. Is that not, after all, the ideal condition?

DONALD JUSTICE

❧

Writers have no real area of expertise. They are merely generalists with a highly inflamed sense of punctuation.

LORRIE MOORE

❧

Wit & Humor—if any difference, it is in *duration*—lightning & electric light.　　MARK TWAIN

❧

The vague is more dangerous than the arid.

THEODORE ROETHKE

❧

Why must I like it when they tell me my stories are "well written"? Of course they are! Would that this were not what they found to say about them, all the same. This ugly little piece of jargon seems to have become a code word for dull. Worse of course would be to hear that they were "well crafted."

DONALD JUSTICE

I resolved to ask her [Anna Akhmatova]: now, after so many years of work, when she writes something new, does she have a sense of being armed, of having experience, of a path already trodden? Or is it a step into the unknown, a risk, every time?

"Naked, on naked soil. Every time."

After a pause, she added: "A lyric poet follows a terrible path. A poet has such difficult material: the word. . . . The word is much more difficult material than, for instance, paint. Think about it, really: for the poet works with the very same words that people use to invite each other to tea."

LYDIA CHUKOVSKAYA

❖

. . . every feeling has its word, everyone who has the feeling cannot seize the word: and yet we live in a time when expression is so universal & appears so facile that all who have the feeling imagine they can find the expression too—but it is not so. MATTHEW ARNOLD

❖

Some poets use the language as if it were a lock they had once picked accidentally—but don't know the combination of.

J. D. McCLATCHY

❖

I've had few students who can read a fresh page. Reason: this can be taught only by parents. One reason is that the exclamation point and question mark are the only devices we have for inflection. . . . What we ought to teach is the right way to use the voice. Teach them to read with their ears as well as their eyes. . . . We must teach them the sacredness of human communication. THEODORE ROETHKE

Start with something that has not been standardized or ab-
sorbed in the rush toward common denominators. Start with
the breath of Ben Webster, the breath-y, breathing end-notes
that whisper from the bell of his tenor sax in a tune like "The
Man I Love." That sound, that non-noted note, is the human
presence in the studio of sound. And in this day and age we
can't afford to forget the rare and specific originality of such
a signature, the exhaling brushstroke that can't be digitally
programmed or reproduced by synthesizer. Not yet, at any
rate. Ben is right there, his breath, his lungs, his interior, inside
the note, and telling you, "Hey! we're still MAKING this
stuff! Right here before your very ears!"

JAMES D. HOUSTON

❧

One doesn't always approach tenderness by joining the
other. Sometimes the space between *is* the tenderness. Just so
in language—you don't always get the payload of the energy
language releases simply by being frontal and "clear" or infor-
mational. In fact, poetry exists in order to remind us and to
prove to us that language, as a fabric of our communing with
each other, is enormously vibrant. Light shouts from what is
showing of its iceberg.   TESS GALLAGHER

❧

Wonderful how (a certain novelist) can drape an arm
around the reader and sort of whisper into his ear . . . while
stepping on his foot.   ARTHUR MILLER

❧

Exercising a beautiful mastery over every word, something
that only sincerity makes possible.   FRANZ KAFKA

POINT OF VIEW

It is appropriate . . . to let the reader get the advantage over me—to . . . allow him to think he is more intelligent, more moral, more perspicacious than the author, and that he is discovering many things in the characters, and many truths in the course of the narrative, in spite of the author and, so to speak, behind the author's back.   ANDRÉ GIDE

❧

The use of point of view is to bring the reader into immediate and continuous contact with the heart of the story and sustain him there. Point of view is the proscenium, the transparent window through which the reader views the story. Point of view is also the directed thinking of the story. And, finally, it is important to note that point of view is not a rigid and fixed mechanism, as it is often taught, an "I" or a "you" or a "he" or "she" that cannot be broken out of or shifted from and must be reflexively referred to; *no*, point of view is fluid and flexible, various and shifting, as in life. The first three pages of Virginia Woolf's *Mrs. Dalloway* are a textbook in the mastery of point of view, as are James Salter's short stories and novels.   TOM JENKS

❧

If you use the word "I" in a poem, then clearly you're talking to someone else.

Using "you" directed toward the self is one way of talking to one's self.   C. K. WILLIAMS

CHARACTERIZATION

It is the writer's business not to accuse and not to prose-cute, but to champion the guilty, once they are condemned and suffer punishment.   ANTON CHEKHOV

❦

The poor novelist constructs his characters, he controls them and makes them speak. The true novelist listens to them and watches them function; he eavesdrops on them even before he knows them. It is only according to what he hears them say that he begins to understand who they are.   ANDRÉ GIDE

❦

Attractive people are always getting into cars in a hurry or standing still and statuesque, or out of sight.

F. SCOTT FITZGERALD

❦

Make the people live. Make them live. But my people must be more than people. They must be an over-essence of people.   JOHN STEINBECK

❦

Never present ideas except in terms of temperaments and characters.   ANDRÉ GIDE

❦

Passing judgment on people, or characters in a book, means making silhouettes of them.   CESARE PAVESE

Essential characteristic of the really great novelist: a Christ-like all-embracing compassion. ARNOLD BENNETT

❧

Surely the test of a novel's characters is that you feel a strong interest in them & their affairs,—the good to be successful, the bad to suffer failure. MARK TWAIN

IMAGERY AND SYMBOL

T. S. Eliot came to Oxford and was asked what he meant by the line: "Three white leopards sat under a juniper tree." He replied: "Three white leopards sat under a juniper tree." By this he meant that the three leopards symbolize nothing, or that what they symbolize is not subject to prose analysis.

STEPHEN SPENDER

❧

A good writer refuses to be socialized. He insists on his own version of things, his own consciousness. And by doing so he draws the reader's eye from its usual groove into a new way of seeing. BILL BARICH

❧

I was never too interested in starting with "ideas" and applying images. I wanted the *stuff* of it all, the pillow, the mint leaf, the crust of paint. Let the little things lead. Then, if an idea came—lucky. If not—I could remember the clay flush of domed villages, the clouds of circling pigeons, as our train whipped past them, toward Alexandria.

NAOMI SHIHAB NYE

First I must look, then I must learn.   THEODORE ROETHKE

❦

The power of the symbol comes from the nature of perception and thought. The train whistle makes us see the train,
the footstep in the hall reminds us of the family relative. The
oranges bring back the breakfast table.

DELMORE SCHWARTZ

❦

Ezra Pound: "an image is the presentation of a psychological and emotional complex in an instant of time." To which he
adds a remark about the "sense of liberation, of freedom" that
follows. . . . Pound's definition explains my meaning completely. I cannot add a word to it.   ATHOL FUGARD

❦

The scar on my index finger from grasping that cornstalk—
that silk that time—and being cut all over—my blood on the
snow . . .   RAYMOND CARVER

❦

More astonishing to me than any technological achievement is the simple fact that a human hand holding a pencil or
a brush can render in a few lines or washes of color a state of
feeling, an insight, layers of history.   SUSAN GRIFFIN

PLOT AND THEME

A good rule for writers: do not explain overmuch.

W. SOMERSET MAUGHAM

❦

"A true method . . . tells its own story, makes its own feet, creates its own form. It is its own apology."—Emerson.

ANNIE DILLARD

❦

Flaubert said to us today: "The story, the plot of a novel is of no interest to me. When I write a novel I aim at rendering a colour, a shade. . . . In *Madame Bovary*, all I wanted to do was render a grey colour, the mouldy colour of a wood-louse's existence."

THE GONCOURT JOURNAL

❦

I wrote six of my close pages yesterday which is about twenty-four pages in print. What is more I think it comes off twangingly. The story is so very interesting in itself that there is no fear of the book answering. Superficial it must be but I do not disown the charge. Better a superficial book which brings well and strikingly together the known and acknowledged facts than a dull boring narrative pausing to see further into a mill stone at every moment than the nature of the mill stone admits.

SIR WALTER SCOTT

❦

The other activity the reader holds the writing and not the narrator or character accountable for is plotting. Even the unsophisticated reader is always conscious that the outcome of a story is arbitrary, that the writer is capable of making it come out differently. *(To the Lighthouse.)* The people that write in to soap operas. This relationship is one of the most curious. The reader, in that case the viewer, wants and does not want to influence the outcome. To write to a writer and implore her to change the ending is like prayer. It is dreadful hope, and at the same time reposes in the writer the power, the power of God of course, to ordain endings, and beyond that, to understand what ending is correct and impose it over the will of the reader. It is for this reason I doubt that interactive fiction will succeed.   DIANE JOHNSON

❧

Perhaps the best formula for the fabrication [of] a dramatic piece . . . is: Action which is never dialogue and dialogue which is always action.   HENRY JAMES

❧

Active speech is the secret of theater. . . . The chalk line in front of the chicken: if this line isn't there under the words, the spell is broken and the audience refuses to follow to the end.   JEAN COCTEAU

❧

A story should be like *Viva Zapata*—one good thing after another and the whole of some consequence.
                                                                                                    JAMES SALTER

❧

Huck comes back, 60 years old, from nobody knows where—& crazy. Thinks he is a boy again, & scans always every face for Tom & Becky &c.

Tom comes, at last, 60 from wandering the world & tends Huck, & together they talk the old times; both are desolate, life has been a failure, all that was lovable, all that was beautiful is under the mould. They die together.   MARK TWAIN

❦

Woe is unlimited, cruelty also. Tragedy captures this unlimitedness as in a net; it is necessary that it should remain unlimited and yet cease to be so. Relationships of force have got to appear in lightning fashion in the midst of which man loses himself, God, the universe, everything. *Phèdre* is like this. . . . *Lear, Othello.*   SIMONE WEIL

❦

The narrative line is to me like a Mexican mural: flattened in perspective so all is present; cramped by detail, erotic, various, the flat depth held up in the imagination, its transience and impermanence nakedly apparent. The narrative does not lead from one place to another, from the past to the future, but more deeply into the present and its sense of time is in tune with the human heart rather than the chessman's calculating mind; present moves are a means to the future. The narrative line, then, is at rest and jostling at the same time. Like a sonogram of a pregnant woman's belly: the fetus' tiny heartbeat jostled by gas.   GRETEL EHRLICH

❦

One of the great rules of art: do not linger.   ANDRÉ GIDE

❦

I'm not yet mature enough to write a novel. The first essential is maturity of the backside: to sit glued to one's chair. Great orgies of consumption have to be staged for all the senses; eyes, fingers, nose have to be fed. The main foundations however are straightforward descriptions of events and conditions, excavating their innermost core, together with an enjoyment of objects (rather than problems). Nothing there for impatient sweet-addicts and hawkers of plots.   BERTOLT BRECHT

❧

Because one has written other books does not mean the next becomes any easier. Each book in fact is a tabula rasa; from book to book I seem to forget how to get characters in and out of rooms—a far more difficult task than the nonwriter might think.   JOHN GREGORY DUNNE

❧

I admit to myself that I have now brought the book to the same point at which *The Confidence Man* came to a halt, and not by chance. Actually I have emptied my bag. Fiction must now take over. *Incipit ingenium*.   THOMAS MANN

❧

If you attempt to create and build a wholly imaginary incident, adventure or situation, you will go astray, & the artificialty of the thing will be detectable. But if you found on a *fact* in your personal experience, it is an acorn, a root, & every created adornment that grows up out of it & spreads its foliage & blossoms to the sun will seem realities, not inventions. You will not be likely to go astray; your compass of fact is there to keep you on the right course.   MARK TWAIN

❧

At moments like this, the meagerness of my imagination overcomes me. James Joyce is said to have written to an aspiring author: "Young man, you have not enough chaos in you to write a novel."   DORIS GRUMBACH

Tolstoy to Rilke, who was pestering him about techniques in writing: "If you want to write, write!"   EDWARD ABBEY

❦

Technique alone is never enough. You have to have passion. Technique alone is just an embroidered pot holder.

RAYMOND CHANDLER

❦

Two types of writers fall short: those who write well about unimportant things, and those who write badly about important things. Then there are the experimenters, who never get their bags unpacked, just try out techniques for when they'll begin.   EDWARD HOAGLAND

❦

As writers we all know that the ending is the hardest part. Getting it right. If editors interfere, it is likely to be there, at the ending. If we are unsatisfied with a narrative it is likely to be there, at the ending. We wish for happy endings but sometimes we reject them as unrealistic, therefore trashy, and we feel cheated and pandered to. Stern, sadistic endings may not please us either. Endings dictated by a morality not or no longer our own are less than satisfying. In this respect, I might mention my own experience with Henry James, a writer I revere in every detail except the endings, which always have seemed to me unnaturally punitive in accord with a nineteenth-century conception of morality that does not and perhaps never did conform with actual events. But maybe that's his game?   DIANE JOHNSON

❦

Short stories tend to be boat-shaped, with a lift at each end, to float.   EDWARD HOAGLAND

Each Day's Work—
Composition, Drafting, Revision

Flaubert: "What a heavy oar the pen is and what a strong current ideas are to row in."

GRETEL EHRLICH

❧

Novel, beginning one: any subterfuge seems preferable . . .

E. M. FORSTER

❧

The best thing is to write anything, anything at all that comes into your head, until gradually there is a calm and creative day.

STEPHEN SPENDER

❧

I'm in good form, taking no interest in things, neglecting clothes, meals, company, and feeling calm and stable as I write. Each word has broken out of its shell; sentences come thrusting up straight from my breast. I just copy them down.

BERTOLT BRECHT

❧

In writing, habit seems to be a much stronger force than either willpower or inspiration. Consequently, there must be some little quality of fierceness until the habit pattern of a certain number of words is established. There is no possibility . . . of saying, "I'll do it if I feel like it."

. . . You start out putting words down and there are three things—you, the pen, and the page. Then gradually the three things merge until they are one and you feel about the page as you do about your arm. Only you love it more than you love your arm.   JOHN STEINBECK

❧

The poet is a man who lives by watching his moods. An old poet comes at last to watch his moods as narrowly as a cat does a mouse.   HENRY DAVID THOREAU

❧

Ultimately, as the evening breeze begins to blow over the darkening hills of the desert, you pick up your pen and start writing again, working like an old-fashioned watchmaker, with a magnifying glass in your eye and a pair of tweezers between your fingers; holding and inspecting an adjective against the light, changing a faulty adverb, tightening a loose verb, reshaping a worn-out idiom. This is the time when what you're feeling inside you is far from political righteousness. It is, rather, a strange blend of rage and compassion; of intimacy with your characters, mingled with utter detachment. Like icy fire. And you write. You write, not as someone struggling for peace, but more like someone who begets peace and feels eager to share it with the reader; writing with a simple ethical imperative: Try to understand everything. Forgive some. And forget nothing.   AMOS OZ

❧

Training to be a writer is a slow and continuous process, with time off for human behavior.   MARIE-ELISE

To write is to become disinterested. There is a certain renunciation in art. Rewrite—the effort always brings some
profit, whatever this may be.   ALBERT CAMUS

❧

Work every day in the reading room at the British Museum. . . . When I lay too late in the mornings (which was
most often the case) I did not go to the Museum until after
dinner. . . .

. . . I made a stand against late rising by using an alarm clock
and actually succeeded in getting up regularly at 8 every
morning until the end of the year, when the clock broke and
I began immediately to relapse. I got a new clock, but did not
quite regain my punctuality, which by and by, made me so
sleepy in the afternoon that I got into the habit of taking a nap
in the Museum over my books.   GEORGE BERNARD SHAW

❧

I now spend most of my time copying out Lyova's novel
[*War and Peace*] (which I am reading for the first time). . . .
As I copy I experience a whole new world of emotions,
thoughts and impressions. Nothing touches me so deeply as
his ideas, his genius. . . . I write very quickly so I can follow the
story and catch the mood, but slowly enough to be able to
stop, reflect upon each new idea and discuss it with him later.
He and I often talk about the novel together, and for some
reason he listens to what I have to say (which makes me very
proud) and trusts my opinion.   SOPHIA TOLSTOY

❧

Finish each day before you begin the next, and interpose a
solid wall of sleep between the two. This you cannot do without temperance.   RALPH WALDO EMERSON

Up at 8:30 ... and at work before 10. I found my mind stiff and my diction stilted but by dinner-time I had finished 1,300 words all of which were written twice and many three times. ... The hotel is full of elderly women who do not distract me from my work. Carolyn has given me the room they call "the middle lounge" for a private sitting-room but the fire smokes so badly that I must choose between freezing or going blind.   EVELYN WAUGH

❦

Teatime—Trying to write—God! I have a brain like a peanut. ... "Found a peanut, found a peanut" echoes in my head the insane song.   JOHN DOS PASSOS

❦

Who would write, who had any better thing to do?
                           LORD BYRON

❦

I seldom try to probe the mystery of my sloth. ... Because of it, I have squandered a gigantic fortune of workhours. Now, with a life-expectancy of 8.5 years, it seems likely that I'll go on squandering till the very end. ... Instead of deciding either to rest or to do one single job, I neither work nor rest. For example, I'll start writing in this book, then break off because I remember someone I should call on the phone; then, as I reach for the phone, I decide that I'll first go into the kitchen and fix a cup of coffee; then, on the way to the door, passing the bookshelves, I wonder what the name was of the boy who was employed for a while at the Hogarth Press and, later in life, wrote a book about his experiences there, so I take down Quentin Bell's biography of Virginia Woolf and turn its pages until I've admitted to myself that I'm not curious enough to go on looking. At this point, maybe, I become aware of what all this fussing around really amounts to—nothing. Upon which, I feel acutely uneasy and, at the same time, indignant. I tell myself that I'm behaving like this because I am being pressured—too many people are making demands on me, tormenting me with compliments or criticism, expecting me not to disappoint them. And therefore I exclaim to myself with sincere fury and self-pity: *why* won't they let me *work*?

CHRISTOPHER ISHERWOOD

❧

A moderate blessing-counting mood. I sit hour after hour, reading snippets of myself and others, not knowing (as Auden accurately observed) whether I am procrastinating or must wait for it to come, but not wanting to avoid the desk.

JANET BURROWAY

❧

I must again remind myself that the feeling that I have made an advance these two days is the result of three things: (1) That I immersed myself in the play by working on the dialogue of some already stable portions; (2) That I dropped everything else to take a long walk; (3) That I bent my attention not on the action of the play, but on the basic ideas from which it originally sprang.

THORNTON WILDER

❧

. . . it is not always by plugging away at a difficulty and sticking at it that one overcomes it; but, rather, often by working on the one next to it. Certain people and certain things require to be approached on an angle.

ANDRÉ GIDE

The pleasure of writing, in practice, is that of eating a nice juicy steak with loose teeth.   ROY BLOUNT, JR.

❧

The pleasure of writing is that the mind does not wander, any more than it does in the orgasm—and writing takes longer than orgasm.   DONALD HALL

❧

. . . racking my brains from ten in the morning till four in the afternoon trying to write two and a half lines . . .   STENDHAL

❧

I snarl at my writing. Who would ever read *that* drivel? I ask myself with the greatest disrespect.

"Stay with the Group!" my brain shrieks. It shrieks across its wiring, "Stay with group tradition! Don't think! Do ritual instead! Plan celebrations of the stale! Avoid pain!"

Most of my brain's in-use circuitry seems to cry against innovation, not for it.

But there are Planck and Gould and Jesus and Woolf and other innovators. Their brains, too, must have been trembling with convention, with the electricity bullying its way around the dendrons and synapses. Planck and Gould and Jesus and Woolf were not yellow.

I want to hold my D-battery against a huge magnetic field. The magnetic field shrieks, "Select all and then Delete! Delete! Do not save!"

This is worse than a so-called inner critic. This is 100,000 years of *homo sapiens timensque*. Human species, both reflective and chicken.   CAROL BLY

"Oh that my words were now written! Oh that they were printed in a book!"—Job XIX, 23.　　　　ROY BLOUNT, JR.

❦

I remember that the BBC interviewed E. M. Forster when I was an undergraduate at Cambridge. The interviewer asked him whether he'd found writing easy or hard. I enjoyed it, he said blandly. But when an undergraduate he'd taken to asked him why he never wrote another *Passage to India*, he said, Oh, it was too hard.　　　　JANET BURROWAY

❦

Hard days, lots of work, no money, too much silence. Nobody's fault. You chose it.　　　　BILL BARICH

❦

Found this in an old journal of mine—Humphry Trevelyan on Goethe: "It seems that two qualities are necessary if a great artist is to remain creative to the end of a long life: he must on the one hand retain an abnormally keen awareness of life, he must never grow complacent, never be content with life, must always demand the impossible and when he cannot have it, must despair. The burden of the mystery must be with him day and night. He must be shaken by the naked truths that will not be comforted. This divine discontent, this disequilibrium, this state of inner tension is the source of artistic energy. Many lesser poets have it only in their youth; some even of the greatest lose it in middle life. Wordsworth lost the courage to despair and with it his poetic power. But more often the dynamic tensions are so powerful that they destroy the man before he reaches maturity."　　　　MAY SARTON

What happens when a writer doesn't want to write anymore? When the progression of fingers across the keyboard is like an old dry horse hitched to the millstone, blinders and yoke lashed, the only path between day and nightfall one's own scoured rut of circling footsteps? This is of no use to anyone, if anything is of use, if utility is to be more than what one suspects it is—the plank across the mudhole. RITA DOVE

❧

I would love to have a house by the sea. There is more than a bit of foolishness in this notion, and I hope I have not been too much influenced by seeing Jane Fonda in the movie "Julia" playing Lillian Hellman and typing furiously in a little room in a beach house while the ocean roars away below. I believe at one point she threw her typewriter out the window, and perhaps it is only some such grand gesture I am longing for.

LINDA PASTAN

❧

Two days of blank misery; incapable of work; feeling almost ready for suicide. This evening a little light comes to me. Will it be credited, that I must begin a new novel? I am wholly dissatisfied with the plan of what I have been writing. This terrible waste of time. I dare not tell anyone the truth; shall merely say that I am getting on very slowly. GEORGE GISSING

❧

The blackness continues, quite hellish, as I work—and, curiously, the sound of the railway twice louder than usual in the stillness of it. JOHN RUSKIN

I write in the dark, late at night. . . . I walk about my rooms, sit at my table, and work against the night. . . . I welcome the burning sensation on the surface of my eyeballs which begins at one or two A.M. I pull my shirtsleeves down as the room grows colder. I flex my fingers. . . . I lower my head and swing it from side to side to restore the muscles of my neck. And then little or nothing is left of the demands of will to prevent the opening up of the skull. Images of feeling shake free of their origins to line up in the matrix of an idea which did not exist during the earlier part of the evening. This goes on until a limit has been reached, by which time I am without words and can barely make it into bed. I have succeeded in stamping out my mind. In the morning, the evidence of the page smells like a baby.   MARVIN BELL

❦

I stake my destiny upon hours of uninterrupted work.
                                                      CHARLES BAUDELAIRE

❦

Again and again I threaten myself that I will not write anything for a year. It is an interesting habit: I indulge the thought only when the writing is going terribly, and I do consider it an earnest attempt at help. Perhaps if all the words are bottled up, they will finally explode under pressure—an orgy of creativity! But the very idea is a punishment, never a cure, and it frightens me back to work. I know that for me writing has something in common with nursing the baby. I can't do it if I don't do it all the time. Put it aside to build up strength, the flow will dwindle and finally disappear. When the baby was at my breast ten times a day, I had the rare secret feeling that we were violating a law of nature, defying a form of entropy. . . . One cannot hoard some things. The more I gave the baby, the more I had to give her, and had I tried to conserve myself, I would have found that I conserved nothing.

ROSELLEN BROWN

❦

And this is the way a novel gets written, in ignorance, fear, sorrow, madness, and a kind of psychotic happiness as an incubator for the wonders being born.   JACK KEROUAC

❦

I think the day to day continuity helps one to see the larger movement and pay less attention to each damned day in itself.   C. S. LEWIS

❦

Whatever becomes of the work, the occupation of writing has been a real boon to me. It took me out of dark and desolate reality into an unreal but happier region . . . imagination lifted me when I was sinking. . . . I am thankful to God, who gave me this faculty.   CHARLOTTE BRONTË

❦

In every poet I think lurks the secret writer of prose. . . . It is not just the possibility of fame and fortune that poets miss, the silence with which we greet editors and friends when they insist we have at least one novel inside us. . . . it is the security I imagine a prose writer must feel at the prospect of months, even years, of continuous work. In contrast, a poet must start absolutely from scratch over and over again. I long to have work to return to the way a man or woman may long for marriage after years of love affairs.   LINDA PASTAN

A bright warm day and I returned again to the long story. It was my birthday but I had forgotten.   SHERWOOD ANDERSON

❦

Another silent period broken. . . . Although I suffer writing blocks, I do not believe in them. No, blocked writing is not this loss of language. I suffer *value* blocks. I write to undo or evade the specious and to find the forms for values. Thus, my "writing blocks" are places where the path goes under the brush, where my thinking dead-ends for a while. I have run out of form, or I have run out of values: the consequences are the same.   MARVIN BELL

❦

The necessity for patience, especially now. At the museum a troubled woman destroys a sand painting meticulously created over days by Tibetan monks. The monks are not disturbed. The work is a meditation. They simply begin again.   SUSAN GRIFFIN

❦

Someone will always ask, "How long does it take you to write a novel?" I hardly ever give them the real answer. "It depends," I will say. "A year. Sometimes three or four." The real answer, of course, is that it takes your entire life. I am forty-four, and it took me forty-four years to get this novel finished. You don't mention this to too many people, because it can fill their hearts with sadness, looking at you and thinking, Jesus, forty-four years to come up with *this*? But it's always the truest answer. You could not have written it any sooner. You write the book when its time has come, and you bring your lifetime to the task, however few or many years you have behind you.   JAMES D. HOUSTON

If thou art a writer, write as if thy time were short, for it is indeed short at the longest. HENRY DAVID THOREAU

❧

Here in the few minutes that remain, I must record, heaven be praised, the end of *The Waves*. I wrote the words O Death fifteen minutes ago, having reeled across the last ten pages with some moments of such intensity that I seemed only to stumble after my own voice . . . and I have been sitting these fifteen minutes in a state of glory, and calm, and some tears. . . . How physical the sense of triumph and relief is! Whether good or bad it's done. VIRGINIA WOOLF

❧

Melville in a letter to Hawthorne, after finishing *Moby-Dick:* "Am I not now at peace? Is not my supper good?"
ROY BLOUNT, JR.

Books and Publication

The manuscript sample has now been at ——— [publishers] for six weeks—two weeks beyond the amount of time they were supposed to need. I wait; I approach my mailbox as though it contained a bomb. . . . I feel at times that the book is very bad and at times that it is very good; an ambiguity complicated by the fact that, if very bad, it may still be successful; if very good, still rejected. Chiefly for reasons of self-defense, I expect a rejection.   ROBERT GRUDIN

❧

Still no response from my editor in New York. Almost two months now since I sent back the manuscript. There are problems, I saw today, but nothing insurmountable. It's the other thing, this silence, that sits on my chest and crushes the breath out of me.   BILL BARICH

❧

My novel [*An Unsuitable Attachment*] is with Faber, but surely not for much longer. . . . Last night it came back but with a nice letter. . . . Now I feel as if I shall never write again, though perhaps I will eventually. Rather a relief to feel that I

don't have to flog myself to finish the present one since probably nothing I write could be acceptable now.   BARBARA PYM

※

Finished the novel in July and have since driven 27,000
miles to get over it. Perhaps it is easier to write a novel than
survive it.   JIM HARRISON

※

To walk around the day your book appears, to cast side
glances at the stacks of copies as though you were afraid of
the salesman, to hold as a mortal enemy the book merchant
who has not put it in the window and who has simply not received it yet, to be like one painfully flayed. Such cakes of
soap as books have become!   JULES RENARD

※

My new book sells faster, it appears, than either of its fore-
goers. This is not for its merit, but only shows that old age is
a good advertisement. Your name has been seen so often that
your book must be worth buying.   RALPH WALDO EMERSON

※

Yesterday I was talking on the phone to a writer, and she
asked, "Are you writing anything?" And I said, "Of course not."
And she said, "Well, that's publication."   ELLEN GILCHRIST

※

I believe we are living and writing in the last epoch of
human endeavor in which anyone will attend to style. A big
snowplow behind us will bring a horde of plainspoken medi-

ocrities utterly indifferent to the things we prize Proust, Nabokov, Beckett for. The advance guard of this horde has already taken up roost in the publishing houses.   PAUL WEST

❦

A thick steady snow providentially canceled The Lunch.

The *New York Times* did not include *Mr. Bedford* in its list of notable books, although small fry like ———— and ———— got included. But I wasn't hurt and stunned as I used to be. I thought: well: I am not one of their favorites and I will exist in spite of them. I may even outlive the *New York Times*. And I feel—it is difficult to express—less and less of their world and more of my own. Maybe this is part of the cantankerous pleasure of getting older and skilled at what you do. You rejoice at thick snow so you don't have to have lunch with an ass who happens, at the moment, to be an important somebody in publishing.   GAIL GODWIN

❦

Beside the pool between swims I am reading a new first novel by a very young woman whose story is anguished, self-pitying, revealing the disturbed state of her mind. I remember Simone de Beauvoir writing: "In one way or another, every book is a cry for help."   DORIS GRUMBACH

Readers, Reviewers, and Critics

Gertrude Stein, asked by Virgil Thomson what a writer wants most, is reported to have flung up her great hands and cried, laughing, "Oh, praise, praise, praise!"

THORNTON WILDER

꧁

A disaster of a reading! . . . In an auditorium seating five hundred we pulled maybe eighty. . . . I couldn't have picked a worse bunch to read new poems to. They sat there like dandelions on a lawn. So I went to the Tried and True, and I still fell flat. . . .

Afterward they told me I was great. With one of them . . . I argued, which is stupid; it begs for praise. Imagine the reasonable discussion: "You were great." "Actually I was ghastly." "Ah, yes, I see. You have a point. I must have been mistaken."

DONALD HALL

꧁

If ever you write something, and it is reviewed, and the review includes a photo of you, and both the photo and the review are bad, you will find that the photo is the more painful.

DIANE JOHNSON

It isn't given to us to know what is good, only what is popular.

JAMES SALTER

✤

Criticism is the science of discovering the beauties and defects in works of art and literature. It is based (1) on an absolute knowledge of the rules by which the artist or writer has been guided in his work, (2) on a study in depth of examples, and on the alert observation of contemporary phenomena.

ALEKSANDR PUSHKIN

✤

Again there is the shaking of heads over not writing about "nice people—people one likes." *Who* likes? *I'm* doing the work. I write about people *I* find interesting. . . . My readers and critics never recognize themselves. I find this country monstrously hypocritical—absolutely unable to stand the truth. A sort of ignorant belief in Party Manners for book people.

DAWN POWELL

✤

Success in writing, versus painting, means that your work becomes *cheaper,* purchasable by anybody.

EDWARD HOAGLAND

✤

The public really loves in art that which is banal and long familiar, that to which they have grown accustomed.

ANTON CHEKHOV

Oh what venom is flowing through my veins. . . . When I was young, I could cry; now I can't! I can only be proud, hate, despise, give my soul to the evil powers to find a moment's comfort! Here, in this big, strange city, Europe's most famous and noble personalities fondly surround me, meet me as a kindred spirit; and at home boys spit at my heart's dearest creation! Indeed, even if I am judged after my death as I have been while I lived, I will have my say: the Danes are evil, cold, satanic. . . . But I am probably expressing myself characteristically for a playwright who has been booed off stage.

HANS CHRISTIAN ANDERSEN

❦

Why book reviewers hate my books:
Because the books are really no good? Perhaps. But I think I've got a better explanation. Almost all reviewers, these days, are members of and adherents to some anxious particular sect or faction. I.e., they are lesbians or New Agers or fem-libbers or (even Worse) male fem-libbers or technophiles or Negroes or female Negroes or third-world lesbian militant maniacs or Negro poetesses or closet Marxists (Marxoids) or futurologists or academical specialists or Chicano ideologues or ballerinas or Kowboy Kiltists or Kerouac Kultists or Henry James Minimalist Perfectionists or one-tenth Chippewa "Native American" Indians or a very least and all-inclusive Official Chickenshit Correct-Thinking Liberals etc. etc.

EDWARD ABBEY

❦

A rule or two invariable in personal and literary demeanor.—
Never to complain of any attacks or harsh criticism upon myself, or my writings—never to defend either by a single word or argument—never to deprecate any one's enmity or opposition—nor vindicate myself.— Not to suppose or recognize

as a possible occurrence, that it can be necessary for me to *prove* I am right or clean.—   WALT WHITMAN

❧

Published work becomes for the writer a second face: people can gaze upon it and say it is ugly or pretty, and you yourself can sometimes look in horror at its imperfections, but it is a face nonetheless and it is yours, and at the end of the day when you bring it home, if you know you've done your best—know your standards have been met—you can say without shame, Mine.   CAROL EDGARIAN

❧

The path you must take, none but you must know. The critic can never tell you.   RALPH WALDO EMERSON

❧

Critics understand very little. They have to be taught the long hard way.   JOHN STEINBECK

❧

I do not speak of disinterestedness—but anyone who is guided in his criticism by anything other than a pure love of art debases himself to the level of the mob, which is slavishly controlled by the lowest mercenary considerations.

Where there is no love of art, there is no criticism. "If you wish to become a connoisseur in the arts," says Wincklemann, "try to love the artist and seek for beauties in his works."
                    ALEKSANDR PUSHKIN

❧

My books are water; those of the great geniuses is wine. Everybody drinks water.   MARK TWAIN

Saw Steve Canady in the post office. Asked him how he liked my book. He said, "Well, hell, I haven't finished it yet. . . . where'd you get all them eight-cylinder words?"

GRETEL EHRLICH

❧

The dilemma of the critic has always been that if he knows enough to speak with authority, he knows too much to speak with detachment. RAYMOND CHANDLER

❧

There's nothing like ignorance to engender wild enthusiasm. THEODORE ROETHKE

❧

I like to write for a reader I would enjoy talking to. I like to read things that are better than I could write myself. Of course, I can't write such things, but they make one want to try. JAMES SALTER

❧

. . . sometimes our works encounter people who would have liked to write them or paint them, and this creates a kind of family for us out there in the world. Art's only excuse is that it makes friends for us. JEAN COCTEAU

❧

All men feel themselves akin, and on terms of intimacy, with those whom they know, or might have known, in books.

NATHANIEL HAWTHORNE

Success and Failure

To flourish is to become dangerous.　　　ROBERT FROST

⚜

Success is paralyzing only to those who have never wished for anything else. Similarly, when the envious arrive at the position of being enviable their envy is redoubled and they become murderous toward others and whip themselves into being murderous toward themselves.　　　THORNTON WILDER

⚜

Every time I read a review of Saul Bellow I get the heaves. Oh this big, wild, rowdy country, full of whores and prize-fighters, and here I am stuck with an old river in the twilight and the deterioration of the middle-aged businessman.

JOHN CHEEVER

⚜

There are no second acts in American lives.

F. SCOTT FITZGERALD

... most writers are bipolar. ... this characteristic blood chemistry is compounded by the volatility of reputation, or even by the melodrama of the daily mail. Independent (largely) of the writers' bipolarity are the extraordinary ups and downs of book reviews, like the good luck or bad of the *NYTBR* assignment. And in the mail a young editor of an old house in New York introduces herself and wants to reprint two out-of-print books in a new series. In the same mail an old friend screams that my new work is a total disaster. The telephone rings and I have won a prize I never thought about, $10,000. A week later the young editor has eloped to Syracuse and abandoned her projects. Next day I am included in an anthology, seven poems, and my name goes unnoticed in a history of my own generation.   DONALD HALL

⚜

This evening ... Colonel Goldsworthy marched up to my tea-table, and hastily saying, "There, ma'am," he put a newspaper on the table and hurried out of the room with the greatest speed.

I read this paragraph:—"The literary silence of Miss Burney at present is much to be regretted. No novelist of the present time has a title to such public commendation as that lady; her characters are drawn with originality of design and strength of coloring, and her morality is of the purest and most elevated sort."

You will say, perhaps, Why be vexed? Why, my dearest friends, because every mention alarms me; I know not what may follow. ... Indeed the more and the longer I look around me, the greater appears the danger of all public notice! Panegyric is as near to envy as abuse is to disgrace.

FANNY BURNEY

Every ounce of acknowledgment of one's worth, however little, by the outside world, each endorsement of what I have become (no matter how insignificant), puts me in danger. In order to move forward in my work and deeper into the chambered nautilus of the mind that produces it, I need to retreat from praise from the world, from the arena of critical recognition.　　　　　　　　　　　　　　　　　　　　DORIS GRUMBACH

❧

What exactly do I think about *prizes?* . . . it makes me really uneasy to imagine all the furor of applause . . . around a Goncourt winner. . . . Furthermore, the idea that one owes one's worth to the *judgment* of certain people is intolerable. . . .

Yet . . . there's an agency or manner whereby the *prize* appears as a social phenomenon, quite independently of those who give it—rather like the annual return of some sun festival, which arrives to settle capriciously on a chosen head. . . . And . . . as the beneficiary for one year of such an honorific institution—I shouldn't dislike it all that much. My cynicism thus masks a dubious taste for consecration.

　　　　　　　　　　　　　　　　　　　　JEAN-PAUL SARTRE

❧

The Americans collect other people's past because they have none. They dream of instantaneous tradition. . . . The immediate museum. You astonish; they consecrate you; they kill you.　　　　　　　　　　　　　　　　　　　　JEAN COCTEAU

❧

Today I awakened in the delight of not knowing what a literary award is, that I do not know official honors, the caresses of the public or critics, that I am not one of "ours," that I entered literature by force—arrogant and sneering. I am the self-made man of literature! Many moan and groan that they had difficult beginnings. But I made my debut three times (once before the war, in Poland; once in Argentina; and once in Polish in emigration) and none of these debuts spared me one ounce of humiliation.   WITOLD GOMBROWICZ

❦

Most defeats are profitable. Most victories costly.
                                                STRATIS HAVIARAS

❦

I suppose one has to be desperate, to be a successful writer. One has to reach a rock-bottom at which one can afford to let everything go hang. One has got to damn the public, chance one's living, say what one thinks, and be oneself. Then something may come out.

But I am afraid to do this. . . . I try to write "proper" books, which fizzle out for their propriety, when all the time there are other things that I should like to say and honester ways to say them. I was lamenting this to a friend of mine who is a burglar, but he answered: "You can't starve. All you have to do is try burglary. If you get away with it you have money; and if you are caught they give you food in prison."   T. H. WHITE

❦

I am 34 and know that life is short. I have accomplished nothing of what I wished to accomplish. And what was that? Really, I wanted the impossible. A man could do it, perhaps, but not a woman. I wanted to *become somebody*, an artist entire, beginning with nothing, nothing at all—no roots, no money, no parental help, no culture, no father—to create myself from scratch through language only, to see my face without a mirror. And I have failed, naturally. Everything else that I have—and it is a lot—has lost its savor because of that failure. Praise is empty. I have accomplished nothing of what I intended and never shall. The children do not make up for that. They have their own destinies and I have just a succession of days.   MICHELE MURRAY

❧

The disappointment of hope leaves a scar which the ultimate fulfillment of that hope never entirely removes.

THOMAS HARDY

❧

We have sold 650, I think; and have ordered a second edition. My sensations? as usual—mixed. I shall never write a book that is an entire success. This time the reviews are against and the private people enthusiastic. Either I am a great writer or a nincompoop. "An elderly sensualist," the Daily News calls me. Pall Mall passes me over as negligible. I expect to be neglected and sneered at. And what will be the fate of our second thousand then?   VIRGINIA WOOLF

❧

. . . the public is very critical of my Pugachev and, what is worse, is not buying it.   ALEKSANDR PUSHKIN

I dream that a lady, looking at my face, says, "I see you've been in the competition, but I can't tell by your face whether or not you've won." JOHN CHEEVER

❦

You don't think of those who haven't, you think of those who have. JAMES SALTER

The
Writer's Life

❖

Business and Money

When a writer tells you that he's never written anything for money, it means that the livelihood is already provided.

TOM JENKS

❧

How much easier it is to rusticate when there's money in the bank!

BILL BARICH

❧

Sometimes wealth seems to me as amazing as genius.

JEAN COCTEAU

❧

"You have a million-dollar personality," said delicatessen store man to me.

"I'll trade it for a million dollars," I said.

DELMORE SCHWARTZ

❧

I simply *must* try . . . to produce half a dozen . . . plays for the sake of my pocket. . . . Of how little money the novel makes for me I needn't discourse. . . . The theater has sought me out. . . . The field is common, but it is wide and free—in a manner—and amusing. And if there is money in it that will greatly help: for all the profit that may come to me in this way will mean real freedom for one's general artistic life: it all hangs together (time, leisure, independence for "real literature" . . .).

HENRY JAMES

❧

We're going to be experiencing cash-flow problems at some point fairly soon if something unexpected doesn't come through. I saved up a bunch of money while I was pregnant, mostly by doing nonfiction pieces for various publications. Plus I get a thousand a month for a food review. Maybe we've got enough to last through the end of the year. But then, well, I don't know. I'm not too worried yet. I know God hasn't brought me this far to drop me on my head now.

ANNE LAMOTT

❧

Whenever you receive a letter from a creditor write fifty lines upon some extra-terrestrial subject, and you will be saved.

CHARLES BAUDELAIRE

❧

"What I want is the income that really comes of itself, while all you have to do is just blossom and exist and sit on chairs." —Robert Louis Stevenson, letter to Henry James.

ANNIE DILLARD

❧

My father's death in April put a stop to the 30/- a week he had been sending us, but we got nearly £100 by a policy of insurance on his life. With this we could do little more than pay off our debts and replace our worn-out clothes. . . . My mother suddenly struck a new vein of work as the teacher of singing in the High Schools. . . . I also slipped into paid journalism; but this put a stop to my life's work.

GEORGE BERNARD SHAW

⁂

The dollar as a god is even more enervating than the Holy Trinity.   NOËL COWARD

⁂

I must abandon again this whole metaphysical urge that leads me further each month back to an uncreated world of bliss of my own making in my own head—bliss which I do not even remember any more, is just an idea—while the real world passes me by.

I must find a small cheap comfortable apartment of my own.

I must stop putting off looking for *any* kind of job—and go out to get what I can. I think maybe a totally non-literary job. . . . Place in society. I have no function in the world I live in. I am oppressed by my own inaction and cowardice & conceit & cringing, running away from life.

What will I *make* happen to my life?   ALLEN GINSBERG

⁂

This is the last month of my money from Farrar & Rinehart or from anywhere—from now on, nothing—and the morbidity has set in that invariably has its base in finance. I am appalled at this secret, iron determination to make money—to win the artistic esteem its possession automatically confers.

By this time next year I will have a fortune, have cut the throats of my best friends, have kicked my inferiors in the pants, have refused to be connected with any strangers except properly identified ones, and be loved and respected by all.

DAWN POWELL

❦

From the 19 January to the 2d February inclusive is exactly fifteen days during which time . . . I have written a volume. . . . A volume at cheapest is worth £1,000. This is working at the rate of £24,000 a year, but then we must not bake bunns faster than people have appetite to eat them. They are not essential to the market like potatoes.

SIR WALTER SCOTT

❦

Young American at the next table says, "I just send it back until it comes as I want it. That's the American method." Is my fury because I am totally cut off from money-making and efficiency? I want some elementary things—three cups of tea for breakfast. I believe it easier to think that all good things come by chance.

ANGUS WILSON

❦

Again we had twelve louis; Fedya took five and went to the tables. After he left, I became terribly sad; I was quite sure that he would lose again and torment himself again. I cried bitterly. My apprehensions came true: Fedya returned home in the greatest despair. He said he had lost all, and began begging me to give him two more louis, saying he must play on. . . . He fell on his knees before me, imploring me. . . . Seeing him in such despair, I could not help agreeing. . . . off he went. A rather long time passed, and I was sure that he could not remain there so long with so little money. At last he returned, and said that he had pawned his wedding ring and that he had lost all he had. He asked me to give him three more louis to redeem the ring; for it might be lost. . . . There was nothing to be done but give him the money; thus we were left with two louis and one gulden. ANNA DOSTOYEVSKY

❖

Sickly and neurotic as he is, Zola works every day from nine until half-past twelve and from three until eight. That is what is necessary nowadays, with talent and something of a reputation, in order to earn a living. *THE GONCOURT JOURNAL*

❖

The novel, hanging about
waiting to be cinematized.

LAWRENCE DURRELL

❖

A young American has found one of my books of poems in the MGM library in Hollywood with this file card: "Unusable." JEAN COCTEAU

❖

H. Freedman, my agent, came up for the final performance tonight. Heavens, to pay a man ten percent of your earnings to bore you! What a life! CLIFFORD ODETS

❖

Saw Bentley. Very polite. Gave me his note for 100 pounds at 60 days for "Redburn"—Couldn't do better, he said. He expressed much anxiety & vexation at the state of the Copyright question. Proposed my new book—"White Jacket" to him & showed him the Table of Contents. He was much pleased with it. And not withstanding the vexations & uncertain state of the Copyright matter, he made me the following offer:—To pay me 200 pounds for the first 1000 copies of the book (the privilege of publishing that number). And as we might afterwards arrange, concerning subsequent editions. A liberal offer. But he could make no advance.

HERMAN MELVILLE

❧

Axiom: all editors that are not by nature & intention essentially base, do by continued practice of their trade become so.

Axiom: there is not & never can be a truce between the living art & the magazines, tho there may under exceptional circumstances be a lull of hostilities. EZRA POUND

❧

When authors quarrel with their publishers I usually sympathize with the publishers, for they are nearly always in the right.

H. L. MENCKEN

❧

No—Editors don't care a button
What false & faithless things they do—
They'll let you come and cut their mutton,
And then they'll have a cut at *you*.

THOMAS MOORE

❧

If you enter a bookstore or a publisher's office your life again becomes incomprehensible. Fear refreshes. Luckily you can head immediately for a good restaurant. JIM HARRISON

. . . in a lunch between an editor and an author, each makes mistakes and successes, and when it is done one hardly knows what has happened and whether it has been for one's good or for one's bad, but an "experience" has taken place.

NORMAN MAILER

❦

Commerce is, in its very nature, *satanic.*

CHARLES BAUDELAIRE

❦

All men in New York insult you. . . . I am speaking of all persons who are clothed in a little brief authority.

MARK TWAIN

❦

Received a check for £400 from Blackwood, being the first installment of the payment for four years' copyright of "Adam Bede." . . . Blackwood writes very pleasantly—confident of its "great success." Afterwards we went into town, paid money into the bank, and ordered part of our china and glass towards house-keeping.

GEORGE ELIOT

❦

The wealth—the immense display of wealth along Avenue Louise—the rich houses, and the expensive cars—with my brief case beside me I felt like pauper.

THOMAS WOLFE

❦

Wealth is just one of the most important ways of getting your self importance.

ROBERT FROST

Fame

I dream that my face appears on a postage stamp.

JOHN CHEEVER

❧

"I have a hundred clippings," I say, "testifying to the success of *Plaisir de Rompre*." Why do I say a hundred, when I know quite well there are not over seventy?　JULES RENARD

❧

If I valued fame, I should flatter received opinions.

LORD BYRON

❧

At the end of my siesta came a rather rat-like man, a Fleming and a teacher in a Protestant school. He had written a novel in English and wanted my advice about an agent. Is there any part of the world, in the most remote corner, where an author who is known will not encounter very soon one who wishes to be a writer? Do doctors encounter middle-aged men who still have the ambition of becoming doctors?

GRAHAM GREENE

At my appointment with the ob/gyn. Dr. N has bought my novel, read the articles and reviews, though I doubt she's read the book. (She told me last time she prefers to read happy books.) Anyway, I slip off my clothes, don the paper smock and, climbing onto the table, assume the position—legs spread, feet in the stirrups. In the space of a minute, Dr. N says hello, glances at my chart, snaps on a pair of rubber gloves and coats them with goo.

Without further introduction, she plunges her hand inside me and, seizing my ovary, asks, "Did you ever think of writing plays?"

I gasp or, more precisely, grunt, and somehow this utterance is understood by the doctor as affirmative.

"I wondered," she nods, smiling pleasantly, withdrawing and ripping off the gloves, "with the Tony Awards and all coming up."   CAROL EDGARIAN

❧

You are not what you are, you are what the perception of you is. This lack of authenticity invades every part of our lives.
                                                                            JAMES SALTER

❧

I take A. to Barnetby. He leaves his Mackintosh. I write A. Tennyson & ask the Book-keeper to pack it for me. He sees the address and says what! the great Poet Alfred Tennyson.
                                                                            LADY TENNYSON

❧

The most intolerable people are provincial celebrities.
                                                                            ANTON CHEKHOV

We stopped at Voltaire's château, and walked in his garden. . . . In the court of the château, a person was ready to
conduct us to the philosopher's bed-chamber, where he died;
the tattered curtains, elbow chairs, pictures, prints, remaining
as he had left them. I say *tattered* curtains; for in that condition they *must* be, as more devoted visitors than we not in-
frequently purloin a slip of the material, carrying it home as
a precious relic.   DOROTHY WORDSWORTH

❧

The bookseller showed me to-day several books attributed
to me, that I had never even read.   JAMES FENIMORE COOPER

❧

The condemnation which a great man lays upon the world
is to force it to explain him. (Hegel).   OSCAR WILDE

❧

I am still so amazed at the brazenness of people who only
remember you when you've gone into your fourth printing.
                                            DAWN POWELL

❧

His biceps and shoulders were like silky balls melting together. How I longed to be strong and lusty, not ill!
And being ill made me think of being great and famous.
They are always linked together in my mind. I must not be so
ill that I cannot be famous.   DENTON WELCH

Great men are generally more anxious to have the reputation of talents which they do not possess, than to be extolled for those on which their greatness is founded.

WASHINGTON IRVING

❧

The desire for publicity throws me back into some former self, a long way back, to stage-mother era, doing pieces for KOY, auditioning for the Little Theatre, getting my name in the paper, later auditioning despairingly for modeling jobs that I was not pretty enough, not thin enough to get, always I suppose believing that if somebody (mom wasn't going to do it) told me I *was* thin enough and pretty enough, why then I would be, and she would have to believe it.

JANET BURROWAY

❧

Fame: why is it so addictive to the writer? I read a biography a few years ago which posed the question: What became of Ernest Hemingway in his later years? The tragic reply was the title of the book: Fame became of him.

DORIS GRUMBACH

❧

They will find me or not find me. There is no certainty in these things. I am no longer interested in glory.

JAMES SALTER

❧

Paris . . . Our hotel is small but comfortable. There's a place for Ray [Carver] to smoke so we need only one room. The area of Paris where we've located is on the Left Bank. Many bookstores nearby. Ray goes into one to see if they have his book. They don't. At the Café Bonaparte I say: "Well it doesn't look like you're going to be mobbed here." Ray: "Well, it's only Sunday." TESS GALLAGHER

❧

The only pleasure of fame is that it paves the way to pleasure. LORD BYRON

❧

Lenny Bernstein once said . . . , "The trouble with you and me, Ned, is that we want everyone in the world to personally love us, and of course that's impossible: you just don't *meet* everyone in the world." NED ROREM

❧

The crush of minor literary men whom one sees at funerals, distributing handshakes and trying to catch the eye of the writer of the *obituary* notice. CHARLES BAUDELAIRE

❧

By Fame . . . I mean anything rather than "Reputation"—I mean, the desire of working on the good & great permanently, thro' indefinite ages—the struggle to be promoted into the rank of God's Fellow-labourers. For bold as this expression is, it is a quotation from Scripture—& therefore justified by God himself: for which we ought to be grateful, that he has deigned to hold out such glory to us!

SAMUEL TAYLOR COLERIDGE

❧

National Public Radio is still airing tapes of reviews I did last month. In the market I meet a chap who is behind me in line. He hears me speak to a clerk, and recognizes my voice.

"Are you Doris Grumbach?" he asks.

"I am."

"Well, I want to tell you. I listen to you in the morning on the radio while I pee."

I thank him, thinking that this must be as much fame as I will ever achieve. What greater recognition can come to me? I pay the clerk, who is now staring at me, for the cooking sherry and ginger root I have bought, and leave, quickly.

DORIS GRUMBACH

Travel

The early raptures of reading are the first travel.

WILLIAM MATTHEWS

❧

A traveller! I love his title. . . . Going from ——— toward
———; it is the history of every one of us.

HENRY DAVID THOREAU

❧

It is always depressing the first day in a very strange region
knowing that weeks are to go by before one returns to the
familiar, but after a few days (hold on and wait till they have
passed) one has constructed the familiar in the very heart of
the strange.

GRAHAM GREENE

❧

[In the Congo, 1890.] Put up at the Gov[ernment] shanty.
Row between the carriers and a man stating himself in
Gov[ernmen]t employ, about a mat. Blows with sticks raining
hard. Stopped it. Chief came with a youth about 13 suffering
from gunshot wound in the head. Bullet entered about an

inch above the right eyebrow and came out a little inside. The roots of the hair, fairly in the middle of the brow in a line with the bridge of the nose. Bone not damaged apparently. Gave him a little glycerine to put on the wound made by the bullet coming out. . . . Beastly. Glad to see the end of this stupid tramp. Feel rather seedy. Sun rose red. Very hot day . . .

JOSEPH CONRAD

❦

Little sleep last night. Ship rolling heavily, and foghorn early morning.

Steward's attempt to regularize my life.

"What time would you like to be called?"

"I'll ring."

"What time will you ring?"

"At different times. It depends how I have slept."

"Will you want tea, coffee, cocoa, or fruit?"

"Sometimes one, sometimes another. I will tell you when I ring."

"What time will you want your bath?"

"Sometimes evening, sometimes morning."

Despair lightened by present of cigar.   EVELYN WAUGH

❦

I seem to spend half of my life arriving at strange hotels. And asking if I may go to bed immediately.

"And would you mind filling the hot water bottle? . . . Thank you that was delicious. No, I shan't require anything more."

The strange door shuts upon the stranger, and then I slip down in the sheets. Waiting for the shadows to come out of the corners and spin their slow, slow webs over the Ugliest Wallpaper of All.   KATHERINE MANSFIELD

We drift together in another strange bed, this one so low to the ground, yesterday's high and hard, inscribing generous messages with tongue, finger, lip. No one on the whole continent of South America knows us but if anyone knocks, they will say we weren't at home.   NAOMI SHIHAB NYE

❧

To travel is to engage the fantasy that one can be at home anywhere.   WILLIAM MATTHEWS

❧

I reached Herning. . . . A room had been reserved for me . . . off the garden—I worked out how I could get out in the event of an assault—for someone had told me that people here were hard up. I went to bed early but got almost no sleep; lay feverish, waiting to be attacked.

HANS CHRISTIAN ANDERSEN

❧

Every family is a conspiracy of heartbreak, and thus a family traveling together becomes a small band of smugglers. You wait and wait. One of you smokes and another of you hates it. The people who go by probably belong here and have ordinary lives. Then the train stutters and rolls off. Customs agents pass through the train like a combine through a field. Instead of a heart you have a rabbit in your chest. But it's no use. They come and go. You'll never be discovered. It will always be this way.   WILLIAM MATTHEWS

❧

Strange position of the postponed traveler. He has packed his baggage, made his farewells, and suddenly finds his time empty of all engagement. This should be a joy, this total lack of obligation of which one dreams on crowded days. But it comes as a surprise, one is not prepared to take advantage of it; and like a bird who, when his cage is opened, stays on his perch, dazzled by freedom, the postponed traveler does not see that his cage, with its bars of anxiety, is open.

ANDRÉ MAUROIS

❧

Vienna . . . Taken by Dr. Haas to find Freud's house. He was not sure of the number and stopped at one point on the Berggasse to ask a woman who is sweeping the sidewalk, "Could you please tell us which of these houses was Freud's?" She had no idea. "*Doctor* Freud?" No, sorry. She went on sweeping. "I'm sure it's along here somewhere," Dr. Haas told me. We were about to return to the car when he had a bright idea. "Actually," he said to the woman, "it was *Professor* Freud." "*Ja!*" said she. "Professor Freud lived just there," pointing.

THOMAS BERGER

❧

As the crowded joyous ferry-boat was nearing Messina, I was seized by an ailment perhaps confined to myself and which I have isolated and named. I call it "Xenodochiophobia." It makes me sweat with anxiety about what I shall find in the hotel that I approach. If the room should be of the wrong shape, too high or too low, too narrow, with furniture out of proportion, dusty, grimy, with torn wallpapers, without a reading lamp by the bed, without a waste paperbasket, I know I shall feel utterly miserable in it. . . . My fears with regard to the hotel here at Messina were not groundless. Entrance hall magnificent with double grand staircase leading up to rooms I shall not praise, and the price charged for them is not in proportion to the rooms but to the splendour of the staircase.

BERNARD BERENSON

Nantucket: beloved of tourists and natives, of photographers and youth hostlers, of travel agents, bird watchers, fishermen, and of just about everyone who sets foot here. I might as well have fallen for a rock star.   LINDA PASTAN

❧

Checked into a motel in Manhattan, Kansas, and got the last room. Though it was midnight, people were still arriving. The highway was loud throughout the night. American refugees seek the road, the road.   LEONARD MICHAELS

❧

Stones of Judea. We read a good deal about stones in Scriptures. Monuments . . . are set up of stones; men are stoned to death; the figurative seed falls in stony places; and no wonder that stones should so largely figure in the Bible. Judea is one accumulation of stones. . . . The toes of everyone's shoes are all stubbed to pieces with stones.   HERMAN MELVILLE

❧

We eat like oxen, fried potatoes and five tumblersful of coffee each. We sweat, they keep serving us, all this is terrible, I tell them fairy tales about Bolshevism—the blossoming, the express trains, Moscow's textile mills, universities, free meals . . . and I captivate all these tormented people. . . . The old woman sobs, sitting on the floor, and her son, who worships his mother and says he believes in God just to please her, sings in a pleasant, light tenor, and tells the story of the destruction of the Temple. The terrible words of the prophet—they eat dung, their maidens are ravished, their menfolk killed, Israel subjugated, words of wrath and sorrow. The lamp smokes, the old woman wails, the young man sings melodiously, girls in white stockings, outside—Demidovka, night, Cossacks, all

just as it was when the Temple was destroyed. I go out to sleep
in the yard, stinking and damp. ISAAC BABEL

❦

"The word travel is the same as the French *travail*," writes
Bruce Chatwin. "It means hard work, penance and finally a
journey." WILLIAM MATTHEWS

❦

The *patron* has demanded payment in advance—"This is
Africa," he says. He is right.

At dinner. There is a negress *habillée en rose* with her hair
piled up as a cathedral bell and her legs gleaming black like
the shining black of her shoes and hard as steel. Her heart of
steel I imagine too. . . .

> They are black here
> Mica black
> Obsidian black
> And their mouths are stone hard
> When you pay for their mouths
> Stone hard and pink at the edges.
> But the African back
> Expanse of volcanic dunes
> Black and rippling
> And the rump
> And the walk
> Both sexes are irresistible.

BRUCE CHATWIN

❦

I am convinced that it is better for a writer to know a little
bit of the world remarkably well than to know a great part of
the world remarkably little. THOMAS HARDY

Quaint old hotel—Ropes up the passages for bannisters—
not otherwise remarkable. T.H. [Thomas Hardy] cross at finding we are not on the Grand Canal & our Jerusalem friends
are at Hotel Swiss.   EMMA HARDY

❧

I had climbed but a short distance when I was overtaken by
a young man on horseback, who soon showed that he intended to rob me if he should find the job worth while. After
he had inquired where I came from, and where I was going,
he offered to carry my bag. I told him that it was so light that
I did not feel it at all a burden; but he insisted and coaxed
until I allowed him to carry it. . . . At a turn of the road . . .
when he thought he was out of sight, I caught him rummag-
ing my poor bag. Finding there only a comb, brush, towel,
soap, a change of underclothing, a copy of Burns' poems, Milton's Paradise Lost, and a small New Testament, he waited for
me, handed back my bag, and returned down the hill, saying
that he had forgotten something.   JOHN MUIR

❧

I stayed at the Conference Center as long as I could, listening to one broken story after another, some told as though by
rote, others too fragmented to be entirely comprehensible,
though the gist was always the horrors Pol Pot had brought to
his people and the hope that I might help in getting the
speaker out of that camp and into a third country. I didn't
have the heart to explain that I was just an observer. . . . The
one succinct version I got was at the far end of the barracks
rows, where a kid who couldn't have been more than twelve
and who had been tugging at my sleeve so that I couldn't get
set for the long-view picture I wanted of that god-forsaken
camp, got me to stop: "Hey Mister," he said. "You take me
home now, we buy a car, we go to California, OK?" I was try-

ing to smile—"OK," I said, "OK"—but he could see that there was something wrong with my face, and then I couldn't look at him, so he just shrugged and turned away.

EDMUND KEELEY

✤

Tonight the moon is invisible, darkness itself has nearly vanished, and the known world, which we map with families, routines, and newspapers, floats somewhere beyond the horizon. Traveling to a strange new landscape is a kind of romance. You become intensely aware of the world where you are, but also oblivious to the rest of the world at the same time. Like love, travel makes you innocent again. The only news I've heard for days has been the news of nature. Tomorrow, when we drift through the iceberg gardens of Gerlache Strait, I will be working—that is, writing prose. My mind will become a cyclone of intense alertness, in which details present themselves slowly, thoroughly, one at a time. I don't know how to describe what happens to me when I'm out in "nature" and "working"—it's a kind of rapture—but it's happened often enough that I know to expect it.   DIANE ACKERMAN

✤

The commonest practice of the Romans is to promenade through the streets; and ordinarily the enterprise of leaving the house is undertaken solely to go from street to street, without having any place in mind to stop at. . . . To tell the truth, the greatest profit that is derived from this is to see the ladies at the windows, and notably the courtesans, who show themselves at their Venetian blinds with such treacherous artfulness that I have often marveled how they tantalize our eyes as they do; and often, having got off my horse immediately and obtained admission, I wondered at how much more beautiful they appeared to be than they really were. They know how to present themselves by their most agreeable feature; they will show you only the upper part of the face, or the lower, or the side, and cover themselves or show themselves in such a way that not one single ugly one is seen at the window. All the men are there taking off their hats and making deep bows, and receiving an ogling glance or two as they pass.

MONTAIGNE

❧

On to Sare, a much visited village even on a Monday in September—mainly French, though a sprinkling of Belgians, Germans and English. Ponies graze the mountainsides, youths play pelota. Hotel Arraya, and a nice picture in our room: print of "the Portrait of the famous horfe Old Partner" (published 11th March, 1735). Good-looking, frisky animal with jockey in pale blue with long-peaked cap. (It says on another wall that the Hotel Arraya was formerly a resting place for the Compostela pilgrims.)

Notable encounter in the hall: two ageing academics surprised to find one another here (Hotel Arraya no doubt mischievously recommended, for the pair are clearly enemies). Polite handshaking failed to disguise a surge of infectious fury. What stealing of thunder has there been? What moments of High Table fury, what scorn exchanged? "A sherry before dinner?" came a reluctant invitation, obligatory on foreign soil. The wives stumped off, dreadfully uneasy, preceding their chaps to the bar.　　　　　　WILLIAM TREVOR

❧

The rigorous discipline of a Motel 6. Bare white walls, stripped-down furniture, a mirror without a frame, seventy-five cents extra to turn on the TV—you're on the road to travel, buster, not to have fun.　　　　BILL BARICH

Impossible to read "The New York Review of Books" in Elko, Nevada.   BILL BARICH

❧

Until I visited Egypt in my early sixties, I believed that small is just as good as big. But after seeing Abu Simbel and Karnak, I buried this idea without regret.

Another delusion I discarded is that you must be a superior person if you're happier in the country than you are in the city.   ANNE BERNAYS

❧

Impression of Santa Fe as having become largely a sucker town. Many Indians and Mexicans on the street. 10 gallon hats everywhere. We went to dine at a Mexican restaurant run by two eastern college girls.   SHERWOOD ANDERSON

❧

There isn't *any*thing in the whole wide world that a body can't buy in London except a good potato.   MARK TWAIN

❧

French woman dips into love like a duck into water, tis but a shake of the feathers & wag of the tail & all is well again but an English woman is like a headless hen venturing into a pool who is drowned—   WASHINGTON IRVING

❧

When you are an old woman you should be able to say of Paris, "My dear, that was fucking. That was fucking in its hey-day."   JAMES SALTER

Love, Marriage,
and the Sexes

To love another: the riskiest, most profound choice: . . . obviously the ground of all real ethics, the most terrifying, the one that demands the most commitment and energy, the most potentially annihilating, the most demanding of both identity and non-identity.   C. K. WILLIAMS

❧

If two people are in love they can sleep on the blade of a knife.   EDWARD HOAGLAND

❧

Desire. In the midst of people—relatives, children, spouses, he took my hand and said, Let's go to Lake Tahoe (where I've never been). I said yes. We went to a whorehouse built out over the water. The view of the lake was astonishing—black water like lacquer and a huge silhouette of a heron looming close. X told the madame that we wanted a room for a few hours. She laughed at us, our desperation and innocence, and showed us a tiny space: a mattress fit into a glass cube cantilevered way out over the water—fifty feet or so. When she left we crawled under the comforters and made love over and over and over. There was no stopping it. But once I looked down at the water and asked why it was so black.

GRETEL EHRLICH

❧

Experience is in the fingers and the head. The heart is inexperienced.   HENRY DAVID THOREAU

❧

Waiting in line at our Army P.O., hoping for a letter from Asya, I find that I am of some interest to a large handsome girl with brilliant black hair who is standing right behind me. . . . she is so sophisticated that she takes me in hand and without my quite knowing how all this got started so fast, I find myself in bed with her and enjoying her directness. Caroline says with a smile, "Isn't it amazing? A nice girl like me can end up having as many men as . . ." When I tell her that I am about to leave for Paris, she replies with the total self assurance with which she regards everything, "I'll see you when you return."

How right she was.   ALFRED KAZIN

❧

I left her virtue intact, but it was quite a struggle. She nearly won.   RAYMOND CHANDLER

❧

A laugh at sex is a laugh at destiny.   THORNTON WILDER

❧

I called Deb to take pen, ink, and paper and write down what things came into my head for my wife to do, in order to her going into the country; and the girl writing not so well as she would do, cried, and her mistress construed it to be sullenness and so was angry, and I seemed angry with her too; but going to bed, she undressed me, and there I did give her good advice and beso la, ella weeping still; and yo did take her, the first time in my life, sobra mi genu and did poner mi mano sub her jupes and toca su thigh, which did hazer me great pleasure; and so did no more, but besando-la went to my bed.

SAMUEL PEPYS

❧

Only in books can you be married to them all.

JAMES SALTER

❧

How unbearable, for women, is the tenderness which a man can give them without love.

For men, how bittersweet this is.   ALBERT CAMUS

❧

Love is hard—when you love it takes your breath away, you lay down your life and soul for it, and it's with you as long as you live.   SOPHIA TOLSTOY

❧

Long before
I look'd upon her, when I heard her name
My heart was like a prophet to my heart,
And told me I should love.

ALFRED, LORD TENNYSON

After tea I went shopping and when I came back there was a light in my room. I went in and saw someone standing in a camel hair coat with his back to me. He turned and faced me and held out his hands to me. I scarcely knew him as we had only met once before. Soon I was talking rather nervously and rapidly and found out that he was writing for a newspaper called *Oxford Comment*, that he hadn't been well and was going to Spain [to war] in March. He thought perhaps that I was disappointed in meeting him again but soon our arms were around each other and I knew it wasn't so.

BARBARA PYM

⚜

Sexual acts divide into (i) congress in the hope of producing a child (ii) everything else.—Which is on reflection the R.C. point of view, though they further limit theirs by insisting on a solemnised marriage. For me (ii)—i.e. all toppings and bottomings—can only be estimated in terms of response. Human beings could be mutual and so respond best, human being and animal less well, human being and hairbrush not at all.

E. M. FORSTER

⚜

Can a man really know the nature of the female orgasm? Yes, and no—but the simple answer is no.

CLARENCE MAJOR

⚜

If you keep people's blood in their heads it won't be where it should be for making love.   F. SCOTT FITZGERALD

I became more and more lucid the later it got. Everybody was already asleep. I tried to wake J., but she drew me down on her breasts sleepily. We made love, and then I talked to her about philosophy, to my heart's content, while she slept.

CHARLES SIMIC

❧

Nothing indeed comes closer to a frenzied lunatic than a man in a paroxysm of desire. We are bound to earth by the middle of the body.

JULIAN GREEN

❧

"Do you think it's possible to have fifteen sincere relationships?"

"Not even one," she says. "Let me tie you to the bed."

"No."

"Why not?"

"Because I don't want you to."

"But I'll stop when you tell me. Just don't say 'stop.' That only excites me. Say 'tomato' or something."

LEONARD MICHAELS

❧

In petting there is no Mason Dixon line.

DELMORE SCHWARTZ

❧

. . . we love what is *above* us more than what is under us.

SAMUEL TAYLOR COLERIDGE

❧

. . . we talked about the state of mind that follows on the satisfaction of physical desire. . . . "With me something very peculiar happens," said Turgenev. "After it is all over I enter into communication again with the things around me. . . . Things take on again a reality which they lacked a moment before. . . . Yes, the relations between myself and Nature are restored and re-established." *THE GONCOURT JOURNAL*

❦

A man's amours and his maladies are generally the most interesting topics to himself & the most tedious to the rest of the world. WASHINGTON IRVING

❦

The purpose of sexual intercourse is to get it over with as slowly as possible. WILLIAM MATTHEWS

❦

Home at 11 & Helen & I talk in bed until 3. Another delicious round with her. Has the full forward, lavender lids and bluish white eye lids of a sex extremist. Uses the most coaxing & grossly enervating words of any girl I know. (Theo & Helen are between the sheets & no one sees what they are doing. No one, No one. Theo is between Helens thighs—Helens soft white thighs. Theo is fucking her and Helen is taking it—giving herself to him—her belly—her tittys—her thighs—oh—oh.) So on to orgasm. THEODORE DREISER

❦

This being in love is great—you get a lot of compliments and begin to think you're a great guy. F. SCOTT FITZGERALD

❦

Sensual pleasure is pleased with itself. . . . Love, on the contrary, demands sharing. GUSTAVE FLAUBERT

I loved her body, which I had first seen in a bathing suit. . . . there was nothing about it that displeased me—her breasts were low, firm and white, perfect in their kind, very pink out-standing nipples, no hair, no halo around them, slim pretty ta-pering legs, feet with high in-steps and toes that curled down and out. . . . Reactions quite different from those of any other woman I had known. She would look at me fixedly, her eyes becoming gray and as if somehow out of focus or differently focused, a little wolfishly, as if she too has a strain of the Ger-man police dog.   EDMUND WILSON

❧

I do not know of a single relationship in my life in which I wasn't eating or being eaten.   ATHOL FUGARD

❧

Father asked me to move nearer. He was lying on his back and could not move.

"Let me kiss your mouth." He put his arms around me. I hesitated. I was tortured by a complexity of feelings, wanting his mouth, yet afraid, feeling I was to kiss a brother, yet tempted-terrified and desirous. . . . He smiled and opened his mouth. We kissed, and that kiss unleashed a wave of desire. I was lying across his body and with my breast I felt his desire, hard, palpitating. Another kiss . . . He so beautiful—godlike and womanly, seductive and chiseled, hard and soft. . . .

"We must avoid possession," he said, "but, oh, let me kiss you." He caressed my breasts and the tips hardened. I was re-sisting, saying no, but my nipples hardened. . . .

Ecstatic . . . and I now frenzied with . . . desire . . . undu-lating, caressing him, clinging to him. His spasm was tremen-dous, of his whole being. He emptied all of himself in me . . .

and my yielding was immense, with my whole being, with only that core of fear which arrested the supreme spasm in me.   ANAÏS NIN

❧

Vice can be depicted, but love can no more be described than light itself. The idea we give ourselves is always simplified and contradictory.   JULIAN GREEN

❧

The most commonplace kind of love is fed by what one does not know about the loved one. But what can surpass a love based on what one does know?   CESARE PAVESE

❧

When Fedya came to bid me goodnight he was in an agitated state. He said that he loved me passionately . . . that he was not worthy of me, that I was his guardian angel . . . that he must correct his ways; that, although he was forty-five, he was still unfit for family life; that he must prepare himself for it; that at moments he still had his fancies. I do not know what he meant by the last phrase; can it be that he wants to be unfaithful to me?   ANNA DOSTOYEVSKY

❧

Grown old in Love from Seven till Seven times Seven,
I oft have wish'd for Hell for ease from Heaven.
                                        WILLIAM BLAKE

When I tell people I have been married for 38 years, faces crunch up, eyes widen, as if I am a mummified dinosaur come to life, bearing some secret potion. "To the same man?" they say. I have learned to answer, "No, to five different men." My husband has changed at least that many times—as I have, too.

JEANNE WAKATSUKI HOUSTON

❧

Someone asked me about the long marriage to Joe—42 years—and I reflected that he was the only person in the world I found it always a kick to run into on the street.

DAWN POWELL

❧

She felt that when she was talking to him she was in prime time.

CHARLES BAXTER

❧

When we grow old, we won't look back upon our famous books, on the flattery we have had, but to our early loves, to our real *enjoyments*, perhaps often those in which the intellect has had little part. I shall never forget the charm of these days—not only for the awakening of my intellect—delightful as it is to begin to think freely—but because Bernard looked in such and such a way, and spoke in sweet deep tones. . . . ah how happy, how happy I am.

MARY BERENSON

❧

B.B. got into an awful rage and behaved like a naughty child: so I took the key and went off into the woods. It was *un jour entre les jours*, and I grew calm and happy. I think I should have been very agreeable on coming in, but it is not right for a man to be so disagreeable, and so I told him at lunch that his way of taking things made it extremely unpleasant for me to take the practical burdens off his shoulders as I try to do. I said it made me loathe that kind of work (if only he were nice about it I shouldn't mind *anything*!) at which he got furious and pushed away his plate and rushed out of the room saying "Well; go on loathing it" like a bad boy. MARY BERENSON

❦

We see different truth and we know different truth.
JAMES SALTER

❦

In a world of men you have not been afraid. In a world of men and women—yes. THOMAS WOLFE

❦

Lord Chesterfield on sex: "The pleasure is momentary, the expense exorbitant, the position ridiculous." EDWARD ABBEY

❦

Love: looks and sounds like murder. THEODORE ROETHKE

❦

In *Lovers and Tyrants* du Plessix Gray strikes a strong note, says that what men dislike most in women is what they fear in themselves: hysteria, breakdown, not coping. Struck me that what women dislike in men is what they fear in themselves: violence, brutality, hatred, contempt.

JANET BURROWAY

The worst of all duperies that may result from the knowledge of women is never to fall in love for fear of being betrayed.   STENDHAL

⚜

Women deprived of the company of men pine, men deprived of the company of women become stupid.

ANTON CHEKHOV

⚜

She's unmarried. She told me in her opinion marriage was bound to be a failure if a woman could only have one husband at a time.   W. SOMERSET MAUGHAM

⚜

One can run away from women, turn them out, or give in to them. No fourth course.   E. M. FORSTER

⚜

We are neither male nor female. We are a compound of both. I choose the male who will develop and expand the male in me; he chooses me to expand the female in him. Being made "whole" . . . And why I chose one man for this rather than many is for safety. We bind ourselves within a ring and that ring is as it were a wall against the outside world. It is our refuge, our shelter. Here the tricks of life will not be played. Here is *safety* for us to *grow*.

Why, I talk like a child!   KATHERINE MANSFIELD

⚜

Summary of all the arguments for and against my marriage:
1. Inability to endure life alone . . .
2. Everything immediately gives me pause. Every joke in

the comic paper, . . . the sight of the nightshirts on my parents' beds, laid out for the night. . . .

3. I must be alone a great deal. . . .

4. I hate everything that does not relate to literature. . . .

5. The fear of connection, of passing into the other . . .

6. . . . the person I am in the company of my sisters has been entirely different from the person I am in the company of other people. Fearless, powerful, surprising, moved as I otherwise am only when I write. If through the intermediation of my wife I could be like that in the presence of everyone!

7. Alone, I could perhaps some day really give up my job. Married, it will never be possible.   FRANZ KAFKA

⚜

People are bachelors or old maids because they rouse no interest, not even a physical one.   ANTON CHEKHOV

⚜

I wonder if art divorced from normal and conventional living is as vital as art combined with living: in a word, would marriage sap my creative energy and annihilate my desire for written and pictorial expression, which increases with this depth of unsatisfied emotion . . . or would I achieve a fuller expression in art as well as in the creation of children? Am I strong enough to do both well? . . . That is the crux of the matter, and I hope to steel myself for the test.   SYLVIA PLATH

⚜

All things come to him who mates.   F. SCOTT FITZGERALD

⚜

We fall asleep hard, tired, holding each other. We may have twenty years left, or three months, or forty years, or more: but it is a finite unit, like the quantity of anything in the world, and I do not take it for granted, but rather, try to be surprised at its continued presence, and thankful that, at the surface, anyway, its waning is not apparent.   RICK BASS

❧

Love is passion recollected in tranquillity.
                                    ROBERT OLEN BUTLER

❧

A. [Alfred Tennyson] often brings me flowers and one day digs up a large root of primroses and plants them in the big Terra Cotta vase which was tumbled on my arm from its stand before my marriage & has made [it] I fear less useful for life. Now I have the happy primrose memory instead of the unhappy accident one.   LADY TENNYSON

❧

She died at nine in the morning. . . . Charlotte—my thirty years' companion— . . . that yellow masque with pinched features which seems to mock life rather than emulate it, can it be the face that was once so full of lively expression? . . . I wonder how I shall do with the large portion of thoughts which were hers for thirty years. I suspect they will be hers for a long time at least. But I will not blaze cambrick and crape in the publick eye like a disconsolate widower, that most affected of all characters.   SIR WALTER SCOTT

❧

Marriage is ultimately an agreement—or conspiracy— between two people to treat each other as having each the right to be loved absolutely. If there is not this understanding, there is no marriage; if there is this understanding all the things that are supposed to go with marriage—children, sex, etc., are secondary. For this reason, whereas marriage between two people of the opposite sex who are physically attached to one another fails if there is no such bond of understanding, marriage between two people of the same sex may be immensely binding, and marriage in which there are no children, perhaps even sex, may be extremely real.   STEPHEN SPENDER

❧

Homosexuality is a couple of hairy old males sitting on each other's knees and liking it.
—Brigadier Terence Clark, M.P. for Portsmouth West, as quoted by Encounter for May 1961.   E. M. FORSTER

❧

. . . my first marriage had been spent at the movies and I had gotten married the second time in the way that, when a murder is committed, crackpots turn up at the police station to confess the crime.   DELMORE SCHWARTZ

❧

At my parents' wedding in Michigan, one of Mother's uncles leaned over before the cake cutting and whispered to her, "Feed the brute and flatter the ass."   EDWARD HOAGLAND

❧

Today he shouted at the top of his lungs that his dearest wish was to leave his family. . . . I long to take my life, my thoughts are so confused. . . .
. . . Everyone envies our happiness, and this makes me wonder what makes us happy and what that happiness really means.   SOPHIA TOLSTOY

Fet used to say, every husband gets the wife he needs. She was—and I can see now in what way—the wife I needed. She was the ideal wife in a pagan sense—in the sense of loyalty, domesticity, self-denial, love of family. . . .

. . . I'm sorry that she's depressed, sad and lonely. I'm the only person she has to hold on to, and at the bottom she's afraid I don't love her, don't love her as much as I can, with all my heart. . . . Don't think that. . . . I am with you . . . I love you, love you to the very end with a love that could not be greater. LEO TOLSTOY

❧

X calls his wife "The Sea Hag" and "The War Department." CHARLES BAXTER

❧

Passionate love at its most romantic and demanding has already the seeds of death in it. . . . At best it changes and grows into friendship. MAY SARTON

❧

What is beyond Desire, but Desire? GRETEL EHRLICH

❧

Desire is attention, not gratification of the self. The ego is the enemy of love. Happiness is always a return. It must have been out of itself to be anything at all. GUY DAVENPORT

❧

When I had told my mother that I was going to get married, she went to see my fiancée, and when the latter opened the door to her, my mother looked at her for a moment, although she had known her for quite a long time, as though she had an unfamiliar person in front of her. . . . It was a silent communication. . . . At that moment my mother gave up her place, and gave me up, too, to my wife. This was what my mother's expression said: he is no longer mine, he is yours. What silent injunctions, what sadness and what happiness, what fear and hope, what renunciation there was in this expression!

—EUGENE IONESCO

⚜

This love—perhaps I over-rate it,
And make my god an any woman
With lovely hair and teeth,
Praising an empty gesture as a world of meaning,
Thinking a smile meant faith,
And a word so lightly uttered
Immortality.
I am too gay perhaps,
Too solemn, insincere,
Drowned in too many thoughts,
Starved of a love I know
True and too beautiful.
But too much love, I know
Will make me weak,
I spend my great strength so
In every motion
To your hand, or lip, or head.

DYLAN THOMAS

⚜

One loves a husband, a wife, etc., all things *for oneself.* Fundamental idea:

To restrict one's love to the pure object is the same thing as to extend it to the whole universe. SIMONE WEIL

Love. He is our deepest self. Mysterious, actual, delightful and sorrowful at once, full of gentility and imprudence, a beneficent spirit, a god acting thru human masks. He is the same in all, neither man or woman. We all have the same sense of bottom self.

Thus love others as the self. We are incorruptible. . . . The god survives. Love is complete. There is more than can be given. None is wasted and no love is amiss none goes astray none perishes. . . . it never lacks because it is All. It comes on the mind in visions. Watch for it coming! It enters the house of the body without your seeking.   ALLEN GINSBERG

❧

. . . love involves a kind of divinity instinct.

JEAN-PAUL SARTRE

Home and Family

. . . kinship is one of the most primitive of tyrannies. Our real kin are those we have chosen.   GUY DAVENPORT

✣

N. Marries. His mother and sister see a great many faults in his wife; they are distressed, and only after four or five years realize that she is just like themselves.   ANTON CHEKHOV

✣

Mother and Hitler's birthday. Worked a bit and lay in the sun.   NOËL COWARD

✣

Lisa. How important she has become! . . .

Her birth has settled some of the problems, finally. I have a family—for the rest of my life, a home. These two realities will, between them, determine the pattern of 90% of my living.

And then there is also the thought: one day she will evaluate me—as a father, as a man, as a writer. Maybe this thought covers 9 of that remaining 10%. I will keep that remaining 1% for the fool in me. I'll be making an arse of myself up to the moment of my death. . . .

The best of me she will find in my writing—even to an understanding and compassion for the mistakes I will make as a father.   ATHOL FUGARD

❧

Jamie hanging on my elbow as I write: "You're *always* writing, I hate it when you're always writing."

After several more interruptions, I finally lose all patience and yell, "Jamie, I'm *working*. This is how I *work*." He stares at me for a long time, then goes into his room and plays/reads quietly until I'm done.

I used to think that being a writer would be compatible with motherhood. Instead, I find my child is one more person I have to reaffirm my space with.   MARIE-ELISE

❧

My children afford me no pleasure.   EVELYN WAUGH

❧

She is tall, with traces of rustic beauty, rummages around among 5 children sprawled out on the bench. Curious—each child looks after one of the others, "Mama, give him your titties." The mother, shapely and red-faced, lies with dignity in that heaving heap of children. The husband is a good sort. Sokolov: these whelps should be shot, why keep breeding them? Husband: they're little now, but they'll get bigger.

ISAAC BABEL

❧

The men make great jabber, but they are awfully incidental parts of the machine of reproduction. It's on the women that the men to come, as well as the women to come, depend.

JOHN DOS PASSOS

[Mary] is in labour, and, after a few additional pains, she is delivered of a female child. . . . The child is not quite seven months; the child not expected to live.

PERCY BYSSHE SHELLEY

❧

Find my baby dead. Send for Hogg. Talk. A miserable day. In the evening read "Fall of the Jesuits." . . .

. . . Shelley and Clara go to town. Stay at home; net, and think of my little dead baby. This is foolish, I suppose; yet, whenever I am left alone to my own thoughts, and do not read to divert them, they always come back to the same point— that I was a mother, and am so no longer. MARY SHELLEY

❧

He's so fine all day, so alert and beautiful and good, and then the colic kicks in. I'm okay for the first hour, more or less, not happy about things but basically okay, and then I start to lose it as the colic continues. I end up incredibly frustrated and sad and angry. I have had some terrible visions lately, like of holding him by the ankle and whacking him against the wall, the way you "cure" an octopus on the dock. . . . I have four friends who had babies right around the time I did, all very eccentric and powerful women, and I do not believe that any of them are having these awful thoughts. Of course, I know they're not all being Donna Reed either, but one of the worst things about being a parent, for me, is the self-discovery, the being face to face with one's secret insanity and brokenness and rage. Someone without children, who thinks of me as being deeply spiritual, said the other day that motherhood gave me the opportunity to dance with my feelings of inadequacy and anger, and my automatic response was to think, Oh, go fuck yourself, you New-Age Cosmica Rama dingdong head—go dance with *that* one. ANNE LAMOTT

C. [Charles] talks to me in the morning about what I am going to do when he is away. . . . he worries about me, he wants me to be satisfied, he wants me to write, and he knows the burden of two unfinished books is a terrible blot on my conscience. He tries to encourage me: Couldn't I get the anthology finished by the time the baby is born? . . .

But you ask too much, I want to cry out. . . .

. . . Once the baby starts to move and you are physically conscious of what you are creating you can no longer create in another line, at least *not* to your best capacity. . . . it is really what keeps me from writing. I know it will *not* be the best writing. The *best* writing is going into that child.

ANNE MORROW LINDBERGH

⚜

Hopeless evening with the family today. My brother-in-law needs money for the factory, my father is upset because of my sister, because of the business, and because of his heart, my unhappy second sister, my mother unhappy about all of them, and I with my scribblings.   FRANZ KAFKA

⚜

An hour ago I was sitting on the side porch, nothing but a little peaked roof to keep the rain away, going through a ritual of the blues. . . . I will never be able to write anything again, good or bad; L. was speaking at dinner about her prolific friend who tosses off every form of brilliant work—I despise L. (who doesn't know how I happen to be feeling today); despise the friend; disparage, thus discredit, L.'s taste in writing; despise myself (which I should have begun with); then all around again. I also despise the baby, who has spent the whole day hanging on me (reluctantly—she too can think of better fun but she is teething and very sad) so that I couldn't even read. Why didn't I wait to have a baby till I had *done* something . . .

. . . I blow my nose with histrionic vigor, and feel my small self-conscious funk being ignored so loudly by my husband that he is telling me what he thinks of my indulgence without even having to look up from his book. . . . Defeated I stand, let the screen door slam behind me like a backfire, and—never to write again—sit down in this chair and begin . . .

ROSELLEN BROWN

❦

A poet told me that when her little boys were small she used to put her typewriter in the playpen and sit there and work while they tore up the house around her. Of course, she is an exceptionally energetic and resourceful person.

ELLEN GILCHRIST

❦

I was getting worried about becoming too happily stodgily practical: instead of studying Locke, for instance, or writing— I go make an apple pie, or study *The Joy of Cooking*, reading it like a rare novel. Whoa, I said to myself. You will escape into domesticity & stifle yourself by falling headfirst into a bowl of cookie batter. And just now I pick up the blessed diary of Virginia Woolf . . . and she works off her depression over rejections from *Harper's* (no less!—and I can hardly believe that the Big Ones get rejected, too!) by cleaning out the kitchen. . . . Bless her.   SYLVIA PLATH

❦

Before lunch I took a walk up to the village. I felt peaceful, bought a packet of cigarettes, thought how lovely the autumn was. After lunch I came upstairs, sat and read a little. . . . Kit came and lay down on the settee. I resented her presence. My head began to ache. I must go away, I thought. I'll go to Germany. I'll borrow money. When Kit, feeling my resentment, went and sat downstairs, I asked her to come back. I insisted she should rest while I took the children out. They came with me, and I sawed logs, and cut some with an axe. As I wielded the axe I thought I might murder the two children. Then I'd be mad, I thought. Shall I, perhaps, go mad? I took the two children with me to fetch drinking water. Kit came out with her coat on. I told her to go back, and took the children up to the little church. Val cried, and I let her cry, and then harshly wiped her face. When I came in I went up to my room and lay down on the sofa, planning to go away, to borrow money and go to Germany. MALCOLM MUGGERIDGE

⚜

I have not the slightest capacity for happiness. Woe to my wife! Good night. CLIFFORD ODETS

Society and Solitude

The bore is meeting people who say the usual things.

VIRGINIA WOOLF

⚜

Remember this—if you shut your mouth you have your choice.

F. SCOTT FITZGERALD

⚜

[In the Congo, 1890.] Feel considerably in doubt about the future. Think just now that my life amongst the people (white) around here cannot be very comfortable. Intend to avoid acquaintances as much as possible.

JOSEPH CONRAD

⚜

The truly free man is the one who will turn down an invitation to dinner without giving an excuse.

JULES RENARD

⚜

(How "food" is associated in my mind sheerly with "talk"— "companionship"—the ritual of love/friendship. And what would food taste like, otherwise. Bitter? Satirical? Delicious? Or like nothing at all?)

JOYCE CAROL OATES

Eating is primal aggression. Beneficent interference is the ultimate aggression.   ROBERT FROST

☙

Eheu!—Papa has sent me word that I must not stay at home tonight!—

Curling hair & dressing to meet a crowd of people whom I know nothing of, & care for less than I know.

ELIZABETH BARRETT BROWNING

☙

In the society of many men, or in the midst of what is called success, I find my life of no account, and my spirits rapidly fall. I would rather be the barrenest pasture lying fallow than cursed with the compliments of kings.

HENRY DAVID THOREAU

☙

So many things that you would think go without saying, don't.   ROY BLOUNT, JR.

☙

One evening, at the house of an acquaintance, [Ezra] Pound was silent. He heard his mistress, Olga Rudge, say that they ought to go home. "We'll never get there," he replied. He said good-bye to his host and asked him: "Why is it that one always happens to be where one does not want to be?"

DORIS GRUMBACH

☙

Chief among the activities that bore me—because I cannot give sufficient attention and my mind wanders and I want to

be doing something else—is talking with other human beings. . . . As I am sitting in my living room talking to my friend
Z., with whom I enjoy a correspondence, after twenty or
thirty minutes I become bored and restless. I want to go off
into my study, close the door, and be alone—where I would
be perfectly happy to write a letter to Z.   DONALD HALL

❧

To write is an entertainment I put on for myself.

JEAN COCTEAU

❧

In order for a genius to be a genius, he must have a selfless
slave between him and the world so that he may select what
tidbits he chooses from it and not have his brains swallowed
up in chaff. For women this protection is impossible.

DAWN POWELL

❧

I think the effort to live in two spheres: the novel; and life;
is a strain.   VIRGINIA WOOLF

❧

The world is in my head. My body is in the world.

PAUL AUSTER

❧

I have always been a coward: afraid of things that hurt, body
or soul. At school I was horribly afraid of being beaten. Before
I fractured my leg I was terrified at the idea of a broken bone,
imaginatively terrified. And now . . . I am afraid of people, of
personal contacts. Some of my friends, who suffer from the

same fear, have had the natural sense to give in to it and become happily shy. Unfortunately I didn't do this. I had to go
out to meet the personal contacts in armour: a shell like the
protection of the hermit crab. One can understand a lobster
wanting to pinch a hermit crab behind.   T. H. WHITE

※

It's hard not to exaggerate the happiness you haven't got.

STENDHAL

※

And how much I want to be carried away by play,
to have a conversation, to speak the truth,
to blow my depression to the mist, the devil and to hell,
to take someone by the hand and say to him "Be kind—
we're on the same road."

OSIP MANDELSTAM

※

This inescapable duty to observe oneself: if someone else is
observing me, naturally I have to observe myself too; if none
observes me, I have to observe myself all the closer.

FRANZ KAFKA

※

No, I don't despise myself much. I have so many magnani-
mous ideas, that cleanse me so. Funny ones. One laughs by
oneself.   FYODOR DOSTOYEVSKY

※

Anyone, provided that he can be amusing, has the right to
talk to himself.   CHARLES BAUDELAIRE

Leo Tolstoy once said to a lizard in a low whisper: "Are you happy, eh?"

The lizard was warming itself on a stone among the shrubs that grew on the road to Dulber, while he stood watching it, his hands thrust inside his leather belt. Then, cautiously looking around, the great man confided to the lizard: "As for me— I'm not!"   MAXIM GORKY

❦

Solitude. In what does its value actually consist? For we are in the presence of ordinary matter (even the sky, the stars, the moon, trees in flower), of things of lesser value perhaps than a human spirit. Its value consists in the superior possibility of attention. If one could be attentive to the same degree in the presence of a human being . . . (?)   SIMONE WEIL

❦

Whoever starts out toward the unknown must consent to venture alone.   ANDRÉ GIDE

❦

I don't belong here, and I've had to turn my not belonging into a triumph.   LYNN FREED

❦

Even if I should, by some awful chance, find a hair upon my bread and honey—at any rate it is my own hair.

KATHERINE MANSFIELD

❦

Why must we know so many people? Because any single person has his limits. One will begin to repeat himself after ten minutes, another after ten days, a third after three months, and a very sly one after a year. Sooner or later we know them all, and all their secrets. Each goes in his orbit, a cycle of subtleties which are our own and which we have known since the age of two. Each of our *clichés* becomes new insofar as we expose it to a new person. But we stay the same. Therefore no two people are sufficient unto themselves.

NED ROREM

❧

Our friends coming to the house that time—me forgetting their names and going into the bathroom.

RAYMOND CARVER

❧

I have often noticed how people laugh and cry when they are by themselves. A writer, a perfectly sober man, who rarely indulged in drink, used to cry when he was alone, and whistle the old hurdy-gurdy tune. . . . He whistled badly, like a woman, and his lips trembled: tears rolled slowly out of his eyes. . . .

This, however, is not so queer: laughter and tears are the expressions of sane and natural states of mind: they do not puzzle one. Neither do solitary nocturnal prayers of people in the fields, in the woods, in the plains, and on the sea. Masturbation always gives the impression of being crazy—this, too, is natural, almost always distasteful, but sometimes funny, too. And very weird. A medical student—a rather unpleasant young woman, conceited, a boaster, who had read Nietzsche and been driven insane by him, pretended in a coarse and naïve way to be an atheist, but masturbated in front of Kramskoi's picture of Christ in the desert.—Come on,—she moaned softly and languorously—My dearest, my misery, come on, come on! Then she married a rich merchant, bore him two sons and ran away with a wrestler.   MAXIM GORKY

❦

I only go out to get me a fresh appetite for being alone.

LORD BYRON

Friends and Enemies

We cherish our friends not for their ability to amuse us but for ours to amuse them—a diminishing number in my case.

EVELYN WAUGH

✣

I have often observed that most people grow bold and hard when they are treated with gentleness and consideration. But as soon as they meet harshness and violence, they lose all self-assurance and become conciliatory and soft. This trait of human nature is almost always apparent in love, and unhappily it often appears in the personal conflicts between friends.

GEORGE SAND

✣

On George Sand . . . She has never been an artist. She has that celebrated *flowing style,* so dear to the bourgeois.
She is stupid, she is clumsy, and she is a chatterbox. . . .
Sand represents the *God of decent folk,* the god of concierges and thieving servants.
She had good reasons for wishing to abolish Hell.

CHARLES BAUDELAIRE

Thy friendship oft has made my heart to ake:
Do be my enemy for friendship's sake.

WILLIAM BLAKE

❧

Jealous one I am, green-eyed, spite-seething. Read the six women poets in the *New Poets of England and America*. Dull, turgid. Except for May Swenson and Adrienne Rich, not one better or more-published than me.

SYLVIA PLATH

❧

It's best to win, but worst that your enemies win.

WILLIAM MATTHEWS

❧

On television I see Mary McCarthy talking about her Vassar friend, the poet Elizabeth Bishop. I notice Mary's instant, icy smile, so often present when I interviewed her in Paris in 1966 for a book. George Grosz saw the same smile on Lenin's face. "It doesn't mean a smile," he said. I am fascinated by it. It represents, I think, an unsuccessful attempt to soften a harsh, bluntly stated judgment. Last summer, twenty-two years after the book I wrote about her, which she so disliked, appeared, I encountered Mary for the first time in an outdoor market in Blue Hill.

"Hello, Mary," I said. "Do you remember me?"

Her smile flashed and then, like a worn-out bulb, disappeared instantly.

"Unpleasantly," she said.

It didn't mean a smile.

DORIS GRUMBACH

. . . men of business being (from their habits of speculation, I suppose) the greatest of all castle-builders—we poets are nothing to them. Told . . . this to Wordsworth. . . . This led to Wordsworth telling me . . . of the very limited sale of his works, and the very scanty sum, on the whole, which he had received for them,—not more I think than about a thousand pounds, in all. I dare say I must have made by *my* writings at least twenty times that sum; but then I have written twenty times as much, such as it is. . . . On the subject of Coleridge as a writer, Wordsworth gave it as his opinion (strangely, I think) that his prose would live and deserved to live—while of his poetry he thought by no means so highly.

THOMAS MOORE

❧

W[illiam] W[ordsworth] &c
It is not in nature to love those, who after my whole man-hood's service of faithful self-sacrificing Friendship have wan-tonly stripped me of all my comfort and all my hopes—and to hate them is not in *my* nature. What remains?—to do them all the good, I can; but with a blank heart!

SAMUEL TAYLOR COLERIDGE

❧

When you begin to get good, you'll arouse the haters of life.

THEODORE ROETHKE

❧

People I liked have changed. Thinking there is money, they want it. And even if they don't want anything, they watch me and they aren't natural anymore. . . . "Seen about your luck." I got me luck. "Send one hundred dollars." Luck! He thinks it is luck. He is poor and I am rich. . . . The Greeks seem to have known about this dark relationship between luck and destruction. It is so hard to know anything. So impossible to trust oneself. Even to know what there is to trust. . . . The time passes. The thoughts race.   JOHN STEINBECK

❧

Went with Ted Lilienthal, by car to spend the day with John Steinbeck for whose Grapes of Wrath there is a great rage just now. He has a ranch in the mountains near Los Gatos, California. A big man physically with a big wife. I didn't like [her] as I did him. She may push him too much. There was a lot of talk of the danger he was in from money and popularity that has done such evil things to so many writers.

SHERWOOD ANDERSON

❧

Let the subconscious run riot. It will reveal all, as Kerouac used to say—still think so, Jack? I still hold that trust fund against you.   WILLIAM S. BURROUGHS

❧

"Madman" I have been call'd: "Fool" they call thee.
I wonder which they Envy, thee or Me?

WILLIAM BLAKE

❧

Let us do what Whitman dreamed—let us stick to each other as long as we live—and let us find out who and what and why we are!   THOMAS WOLFE

❧

What is wonderful for me is to be with someone whose vision of life is so like mine, who reads avidly and with discrimination, who goes deeply into whatever is happening to her and her family and can talk about it freely, so it feels a little like a piece of music in which we are playing different instruments that weave a theme in and out, in almost perfect accord.

MAY SARTON

❧

Now after fifty years we're in
Touch again. You've had four
Husbands and I'm on my third
Marriage. You say that you
Can hardly remember our love-
Making on the flowering desert.
How can that be? For me it's
As fresh as if it only happened
Yesterday. I see you clear with
My garland in your hair. Now we
Are two old people nursing our
Aches. What harm can there be
In remembering. We cannot hurt
One another now.

JAMES LAUGHLIN

❧

When I was young, I expected people to give me more than they could—continuous friendship, permanent emotion.

Now I have learned to expect less of them than they can give—a silent companionship. And their emotions, their friendship, and noble gestures keep their full miraculous value in my eyes; wholly the fruit of grace.

ALBERT CAMUS

Gossip Through the Ages

To luncheon with the Huntingtons to meet James Joyce . . .
. . . "Are you," I say to Joyce, hoping to draw him into conversation, "are you interested in murders?" "Not," he answers,
with the gesture of a governess shutting the piano, "not in the
very least." The failure of that opening leads Desmond to start
on the subject of Sir Richard and Lady Burton. . . . "Are you
interested," asks Desmond, "in Burton?" "Not," answers Joyce,
"in the very least." In despair I tell him, not him but Desmond,
that I have not been allowed to mention *Ulysses* in my wireless talks. This makes Joyce perk up. He actually asks, "What
wireless talks?" I tell him. He says he will send me a book
about Ulysses which I can read and quote. . . . He is not a rude
man: he manages to hide his dislike of the English in general
and of the literary English in particular. But he is a difficult
man to talk to. "Joyce," as Desmond remarked afterwards, "is
not a very *convenient* guest at luncheon."

HAROLD NICOLSON

❧

There is a new biography of Joyce which has confirmed
what everybody probably suspected: that his personal life has
been dreary and rather uninteresting. I suppose he has been
too much whipped. His pictures show him to be a slight,

skinny, small-boned Irishman; blind, grey, sharp-nosed, sharp-chinned, a bit arrogant. . . .

He is fastidious-looking too. He has long fingers, small feet. In a lot of ways he reminds me of a missionary. . . . He also looks more like a bookkeeper than a writer. That he happens to be the best writer in this century is quite apart from this, and nobody ever said that his looks had anything to do with what he wrote.   THOMAS MERTON

❧

Edith Sitwell . . . had a letter from some silly woman saying, ". . . As an admirer of your poems I am nevertheless greatly disturbed by a poem containing a line about the mating of tigers. I have a daughter . . . and a son. . . . I wish to entreat you dear Dame Edith when you write your poetry, to consider the disturbing effect that lines like those about the mating of tigers may have on the young." Edith wrote back: "Tell your dirty little brats to read *King Lear*."

STEPHEN SPENDER

❧

Byron, a 110-proof lush and sexsmith, sex-cessful.

DELMORE SCHWARTZ

❧

Henry James at Pinker's. Very slow talker. Beautiful French. Expressed stupefaction when I said I knew nothing about the middle class, and said the next time he saw me he would have recovered from the stupefaction, and the discussion might proceed. Said there was too much to say about everything—and that was the thing most felt by one such as he, not entirely without—er-er-er-er—perceptions. When I said I lay awake at nights sometimes thinking of the things I had left out of my novels, he said that all my stuff was crammed, and that when the stuff was crammed nothing more could be put in, and so it was all right. He spoke with feeling about his recent illness. "I have been very ill." . . . An old man, waning, with the persistent youthfulness that all old bachelors have.

ARNOLD BENNETT

❧

Read the third volume of George Eliot's letters and journals, at last. . . . what a monument of ponderous dreariness. . . . What a lifeless, diseased, self-conscious being she must have been! Not one burst of joy, not one ray of humor. . . . And when you think of what she had in life to lift her out of futile whining! But the possession of what genius and what knowledge could reconcile one to the supreme boredom of having to take one's self with that superlative solemnity? What a contrast to George Sand, who, whatever her failings, never committed that unpardonable sin; it even makes her greasy men of the moment less repulsive.

ALICE JAMES

❧

Will the monstrous stupidity of Gide's *Journal* ever be discovered? What a mountain of hypocrisy and lies concealed by the pretense of telling a truth limited to the picturesque. . . .

Of course, it's not because he speaks ill of me and lies about me that I find Gide's *Journal* ridiculous.

JEAN COCTEAU

❧

Lunched with Coco Chanel. Not a good word spoken about anyone but very funny.

NOËL COWARD

Whenever Picasso is interested in something, he denigrates it. This he has in common with Goethe. Whatever does not disturb him he praises to the skies.   JEAN COCTEAU

❀

Yesterday I met Man Ray. . . . For twelve years I've admired his pictures of the French Great. . . . These things nourished the legend that we Americans are raised on, that celebrities are of different flesh than others. Yet Man Ray himself is a meek little man, not particularly interesting despite his myriad contacts. In fact all the great people I've met have disappointed me: they are too concerned with their work to be personally fabulous. They are like anyone, they are like me.

NED ROREM

❀

Turgenev's brain was the heaviest ever recorded, 4.7 lbs.; 3 is average.   EDWARD HOAGLAND

❀

I can't stand Balzac. His work, him. Everything in him is exactly what I don't like and don't want to like. I can't stand it! He is too contradictory and somehow repulsively, stupidly contradictory! A wise man—and such a dolt! An artist—and how much bad taste from the most distasteful of epochs there is in him! A fatso—yet a conqueror . . .

WITOLD GOMBROWICZ

❀

Balzac entertains me hugely. He belongs among the titans of the novel. I cannot follow the financial affairs, and yet he has a breadth of sympathy like Tolstoy's, though not so humane. The French fascination with society puts me off, but is nevertheless amusing. He spawns characters; he is irresponsible both as an artist and as thinker, and in fact may be quite unimportant.

THOMAS MANN

❧

Herman Melville came to see me . . . looking much as he used to do (a little paler, and perhaps a little sadder), in a rough outside coat, and with his characteristic gravity and reserve of manner. . . . He is a person of very gentlemanly instincts in every respect, save that he is a little heterodox in the matter of clean linen.

. . . he has a very high and noble nature and is better worthy of immortality than most of us.

NATHANIEL HAWTHORNE

❧

Grace Paley; short stocky woman who at first sight on the Sarah Lawrence campus I mistook for the cleaning woman; asked her where the men's room was.   EDWARD HOAGLAND

❧

. . . in the evening went to dine with Max Perkins and Tom Wolfe. . . . Wolfe a huge man 6 ft 4—very alive and sensitive—too easily hurt. He is one of the few real ones.

SHERWOOD ANDERSON

❧

Mr. Thoreau dined with us yesterday. He is a singular character—a young man with much of wild original nature still remaining in him. . . . He is as ugly as sin, long-nosed, queer-mouthed, and with uncouth and rustic, although courteous manners, corresponding very well with such an exterior. But his ugliness is of an honest and agreeable fashion, and becomes him much better than beauty.

NATHANIEL HAWTHORNE

❦

Flaubert said to us: "When I was young my vanity was such that when I went to a brothel with my friends I always picked the ugliest girl and insisted on making love to her in front of them all without taking my cigar out of my mouth. It wasn't any fun for me: I just did it for the gallery." Flaubert still has a little of this vanity left, which explains why, though perfectly frank by nature, he is never wholly sincere in what he says he feels or suffers or loves. *THE GONCOURT JOURNAL*

❦

Flaubert smoked a cigar, wrote a letter, and copulated with a prostitute before his friends and on a bet. When this story was told to the Circle, one of the Freudians remarked, "I bet that what he really enjoyed was the cigar!"

DELMORE SCHWARTZ

❦

Went into town again on various businesses. Saw Burroughs & Ginsberg again, this time by accident. We were all in high spirits. I mention this for some obscure reason. It always amazes me to find myself acting furtively like a Dostoevsky character. I remember saying to myself, "Don't tell them too much about your soul. They're waiting for just that." Which of course they weren't, or they would have to be raving mad, and probably are, as I am. "We were all in high spirits . . ." Yet there's a lot of peculiar emotional energy always at work between us and we all know it. Life is a tremendously furtive thing. JACK KEROUAC

Dined with Bernard Berenson. . . . He used to dine regularly with Oscar Wilde. He said that when alone with him the mask slipped off. But in public he posed deliberately. Mrs Berenson says that having met him five nights in succession, he said to her, "Now you have exhausted my repertory. I had only five subjects of conversation prepared and have run out. I shall have to give you one of the former ones. Which would you like?" They said they would like the one on evolution. So he gave them the one on evolution. HAROLD NICOLSON

Poor Oscar Wilde, what a silly, conceited, inadequate creature he was and what a dreadful self-deceiver. It is odd that such a brilliant wit should be allied to no humour at all. . . . The trouble with him was that he was a "beauty-lover."

Read Maugham's *Writer's Notebook*. So clear and unpretentious and accurate after that poor, podgy pseudo-philosopher [Wilde]. NOËL COWARD

. . . why should a female protagonist be good only for bed? . . . where are those intellectually prominent women of the century, able to stir the imagination of a chronicler? Undoubtedly the most famous was Simone de Beauvoir, yet she does not bring honor to the promoters of feminism and the sooner she is forgotten, the better. . . . When she published her novel *Les Mandarins*, gossipy, with "a key," in a Parisian provincial mode, I asked Albert Camus whether he intended to answer. He shrugged: "One does not answer a gutter." He was right. CZESLAW MILOSZ

[Willa] Cather handles herself very skillfully, and has made a good deal of money. She lives simply and is thus rich. Knopf gets on with her amicably and thus likes her, but she bothers him with all sorts of business and is something of a nuisance. When she visits him at his office she expects him to drop all other work and give her undivided attention. Some time ago she called up his father, Samuel Knopf, and asked him to get her a bottle of gin and another of brandy. She was giving a party and didn't know any bootlegger. The old man sent her two bottles out of his own stock.　　H. L. MENCKEN

❦

[At the Olivet, Michigan, writers' conference] Went to hear Robert Penn Warren on poetry. Liked him, the cut of his jaw, his quality. . . . Katherine Anne Porter cold woman. Too many middle aged women about.　　SHERWOOD ANDERSON

❦

[Philip] Roth a man who wears his heart on his sleeve, thus rather vulnerable to insult and injury; part of his exceptional generosity. Tells story of man bleeding in front of God but trying to hide blood from His sight apologetically.

EDWARD HOAGLAND

❦

Coghill came for dinner. He told me what Gertrude Stein's "gift of repartee" . . . was really like at the meeting in her honour the other night. Cecil of Wadham rose to ask her what she meant by the same things being "absolutely identical and absolutely different" to which Stein (she is a dowdy American) replied "Wall, you and the man next to you are abso-o-lute-ly identical the way you both jump up to ask questions, but abs-o-lute-ly different in character." This nonsense was greeted with rounds of approving laughter by the crowd.

C. S. LEWIS

W. tells an anecdote of Gertrude Stein, who was asked at a lecture why it was that she answered questions so clearly and wrote so obscurely. "If Keats was asked a question would you expect him to reply with the 'Ode on a Grecian Urn'?"

GRAHAM GREENE

Race, Gender, Politics, and Power

It is perhaps a choice each of us makes over and over, even many times throughout one day, whether to use knowledge as power or intimacy.
SUSAN GRIFFIN

❧

The misery of the present age is not in the intensity of men's suffering—but in their incapacity to suffer, enjoy, feel at all.
MATTHEW ARNOLD

❧

. . . lunch with Tomás Borge, Minister of the Interior. Tortured for years in Somoza's prisons, after the Sandinista takeover he recognized one of his torturers in a prison lineup, and he is reported to have said, "My revenge is to have you shake my hand."

He's a tough little number . . . the only one of the three original founders of the Sandinista movement still alive. His face shows it, it's hard, it's been through it. . . . When we go with him to the public market for lunch, he drives his big van, with a couple of trucks of soldiers before and after.

. . . I sit down on a bench with Borge as the people crowd around. . . . He calls me *poeta* whenever he has a chance to speak to me, which isn't often. He says *poeta* with a mixture of respect and realism, as if he didn't expect much from me.

. . . One fishwife corners him and pours out her complaint. He takes her by both arms, almost embracing her, and looks in her face close up, listening intently. . . .

Back in the driver's seat, he tells me, "These people really aren't *with* the Revolution. They're putting themselves first. The Revolution is for the consumer, not the merchant." When he drops me off in town, I look at the finely printed card . . . he gave me: his name without title, under a single silver star with red and black olive branches crossed beneath it.

LAWRENCE FERLINGHETTI

&

I am Nicaraguan. I am Salvadoran. I am Grenadian. I am Honduran, I chant to myself. It has almost become a mantra.

And yet, this year I paid more in taxes than my parents and grandparents together earned all the years they worked the land of the gringos of the South. And over half that money will go to buy weapons that will be shipped from the Concord Naval Weapons Station at Port Chicago, California, thirty miles from my home, and used against these people that I think of as myself.

These were my thoughts a few days before I was arrested for blocking one of the gates to the Concord Naval Weapons Station.   ALICE WALKER

&

The artist cannot be concerned with politics, for a regime may change each year, but a work of art remains.

NED ROREM

. . . instead of talking about the wicked German, or Japanese, or Russian, or the wicked bourgeois, or the criminal incendiary, or the horrible militarist, or the treacherous deserter, etc., if instead of all that I strip man of the inhumanity belonging to his class, his race, his bourgeois—or other—status: when I look behind all this, and speak of what is an intimate part of myself, of my fear, my longings, my anguish, my delight in being . . . I no longer belong to any class or race or to this army or to that army.

. . . This is the sphere of profound identification, this is the way to attain it.   EUGENE IONESCO

❧

I have simplified my politics into an utter detestation of all existing governments. . . . riches are power, and poverty is slavery all over the earth, and one sort of establishment is no better, nor worse, for a *people* than another.   LORD BYRON

❧

To be ever ready to fight, to die even for an opinion—not to be cowardly, passively pacifistic—not united with others against "the enemy," which changes from day to day at behest of stupid leaders. And to sacrifice one's home, one's own, everything precious, rather than give in to the vile low instincts of the mob, the dream-passion, is not cowardly, but the quintessence of courage and heroism. A more difficult and thankless sort of courage.

. . . The artist's position to a T. The most precious thing is one's self—how it concerns me—*not* brother & sister, *not* humanity. Exactly the position that Christ took, that every great leader, thinker, lover of man, has taken. *Self-responsibility!* Out of the swarm—out of nullity and nightmare!   HENRY MILLER

I did nothing to beat Hitler. I saved no one.

"Grandpa, what did you do during the war? What was your worst experience?"

"Surviving the martinis at the Hotel Connaught as I sat facing the monumental portrait of Victoria, Queen and Empress, and her 'immortal' words during the South African War. 'There is no pessimism in this house and there will be none.' "

ALFRED KAZIN

❧

Mankind has conceived history as a series of battles; hitherto it has considered fighting as the main thing in life.

ANTON CHEKHOV

❧

Poetry makes nothing happen? It should be noted that between 1942 and 1944 the BBC aired a nightly 15-minute broadcast in French, narrated by Pierre Holmes and called "The French Speak to the French." Holmes would often broadcast coded messages to the Resistance by this means. The D-Day invasion at Normandy on June 6, 1944, was signaled by a line from one of Paul Valery's poems: "Long violin sobs rock my heart in monotonous anguish."

J. D. McCLATCHY

❧

Everyone confidently refers to a time when this country still had its cherry. The time when America was innocent is always twenty to fifty years ago. Lately it's mostly before 1945—before victory, before Hiroshima. But sometimes it's before Kennedy was killed, before Chicago in 1968, before Watergate. I'm old enough to remember people saying that it was before the Depression, before Prohibition, before the Great War. There are always fine reasons, always fatuous. . . .

. . . go read Henry Adams about Jefferson's lies and Madison's chicanery. What innocence? We imported black captives . . . then we turned Virginia and Maryland into breeding farms exporting forty thousand black slaves every year to work in the deep south. Some Eden. No nation was ever innocent.   DONALD HALL

⚜

The function of a newspaper in a democracy is to stand out as a sort of chronic opposition to the reigning quacks. The minute it begins to try to out-whoop them it forfeits its character and becomes ridiculous.   H. L. MENCKEN

⚜

Every time I hear a political speech or I read those of our leaders, I am horrified at having, for years, heard nothing which sounded human. It is always the same words telling the same lies. And the fact that men accept this, that the people's anger has not destroyed these hollow clowns, strikes me as proof that men attribute no importance to the way they are governed; that they gamble—yes, gamble—with a whole part of their life and their so-called "vital interests."

ALBERT CAMUS

⚜

Do you suppose the world is finished, at any certain time— like a contract for paving a street?—Do you suppose because the American government has been formed, and public school established, we have nothing more to do but take our ease, and make money, and sleep the rest of the time?

WALT WHITMAN

The Americans are children—Yes, but children are tyrannous if they are in power.   THOMAS WOLFE

❧

The common run of men have no special gift & can be applied to anything—All work for them is merely occupation. Stupid Hobbs who digs turnips would be stupid still if he had Lord Dulls [sic] library to read in, and leisure to think in: and so the world loses nothing by his remaining where he is. And genius is seldom left digging in a turnip field without being acknowledged: it has the more chance of being acknowledged from their [sic] being a large idle and rich class to be amused by it and to protect it. So under an aristocracy with all its apparent inequalities, a nation gets perhaps all the benefit that is to be got out of its members.   MATTHEW ARNOLD

❧

I am very sorry to see my Countrymen trouble themselves about Politics. If Men were Wise, the Most arbitrary Princes could not hurt them. If they are not wise, the Freest Government is compell'd to be a Tyranny.   WILLIAM BLAKE

❧

My kids think I'm paranoid. They smile indulgently when I tell them I was advised in college to switch my major from journalism to social welfare because I was a woman AND Asian-American. No jobs for you, the advisors said. That was 40 years ago. But I still don't take freedom for granted . . . especially freedom of expression.

JEANNE WAKATSUKI HOUSTON

❧

Mr. John Blackwood [George Eliot's publisher] called on us, having come to London for a few days only. He talked a

good deal about the "Clerical Scenes" [stories composing
Eliot's first book] . . . and at last asked, "Well, am I to see
George Eliot this time?" G. [George Lewes, Eliot's compan-
ion] said, "Do you wish to see him?" "As he likes—I wish it to
be quite spontaneous." I left the room, and G. following me a
moment, I told him he might reveal me. Blackwood was kind,
came back when he found he was too late for the train, and
said he would come to Richmond again. He came on the following Friday and chatted very pleasantly—told us that
Thackeray spoke highly of the "Scenes," and said *they were not
written by a woman.* Mrs. Blackwood is *sure* they are not written by a woman. Mrs. Oliphant, the novelist, too, is confident
on the same side. I gave Blackwood the MS. of my new novel
[*Adam Bede*]. . . . He opened it, read the first page, and smiling, said, "This will do."   GEORGE ELIOT

❧

God help the weak; the strong will help one another.
                                                    WASHINGTON IRVING

❧

Stray thoughts: The man who has served a good king
treacherously will, when his mind has brooded on that until
[it] allures no more, will serve a false king truly, & the measure of his freedom will be in the measure of that service. A
man who has long truly served an ugly woman shall treacherously desert a beautiful woman & the measure of his freedom
shall be the measure of that treachery.   W. B. YEATS

❧

If we mutilated criminals instead of executing; boiled a
prisoner's blood for twenty seconds, then revived him; drilled

a hole in his elbow or guillotined a hand instead of a head . . .
would we tolerate this? Exactly why not? Because it would
reveal our mean, vengeful, cowardly cruelty to ourselves?

ARTHUR MILLER

❦

Give a person power over another person and the ease with
which he uses it to punish is staggering—hardly aware of
what he is doing—and if I use the masculine pronoun here it
is because in spite of feminism so many women lack power
because in our society money is power. I see it so clearly in my
parents' marriage—the absolute power the money he earned
gave my father when my mother was doing all the housework
and he never realized what food, clothes, etc. cost. It is hard
for me to forgive.

MAY SARTON

❦

Man does not live by bread alone. That is, a man, if only he
be a man, will not rest content even having eaten his full, but
feed a cow and she will be as serene as any liberal who had
finally bought, for his liberalism, his own house.

FYODOR DOSTOYEVSKY

❦

Men's urgency, which is imposed upon them by nature, has
become a mischief and an insult to women. It is now considered a moral failing.

JAMES SALTER

❦

I'm violently opposed to the notion, held for so long, that
women's true subject is "love and loss"—having been tagged
with that myself. Some women collaborated in that view. But

women who were intensely involved in social concerns were slotted into the old love & loss category: Ms. Browning, who wrote about child labor, slavery, Italian freedom and women's rights, is chiefly remembered for the number of ways in which she loved Mr. Browning. Ms. Millay, in addition to burning her candle at both ends, burned with indignation about the judicial murder of Sacco and Vanzetti. I want to redress the balance here—in general I am going to favor poems which are "gender-neutral." I want to prove that we can write brilliantly on the great subjects, subjects other than romance and domesticity.　　　　CAROLYN KIZER

❦

I personally am sick of being a "minority," sick of seeing meaningless statistics lumping me with Asians, Native Americans, Hispanics, and other folk on the idiotic basis of not being white (why not lump us together on the basis of not being birds or reptiles?), sick of seeing ads in *The Chronicle of Higher Education* where colleges request vita for their minority vita banks when they have no intention of hiring any blacks—the minority we're really talking about here—at all, which is why they want your vita instead of you; thus I hereby sign off and break all pledges I have in that line. I cannot even recall God naming me man. If He or She did, I have forgotten because it happened so long ago.　　　　GERALD EARLY

❦

And what is history . . . ? It is the autobiography of the human race. . . . History . . . is composed of individual creeds, passions, follies, heroisms in contrast with a universe that knows us not and goes its own way. The account of how man has managed to subdue this outerworld to his needs, to his pleasures, to his ideals, the struggle to master nature, to exploit it despite nature's utter indifference, is a great chapter of history. So is anything that has helped to humanize us, to give us command of our passions, to feel for others.

BERNARD BERENSON

❧

Only "birth" makes noble. So it follows indisputably that if Adam was noble, all are; & if he wasn't, none are.

MARK TWAIN

Virtues and Vices

The only thing that distinguishes man from the animals is that he eats when he is not hungry, drinks when he is not thirsty—free will. GUSTAVE FLAUBERT

⚜

Thoughts about the degree to which I'm a slave or lowly employee of the system I've created: cigarettes smoke me, food eats me, alcohol drinks me, house swallows me, car drives me, etc. JIM HARRISON

⚜

He that lives by the skin will die in it.

THEODORE ROETHKE

⚜

In relation to Gauguin, Van Gogh, and Rimbaud, I have a distinct inferiority complex because they managed to destroy themselves. . . . I am more and more convinced that, in order to achieve authenticity, something has to snap. . . . But I have protected myself against snapping. . . . I'm bastard enough to leave something of myself *intact*. JEAN-PAUL SARTRE

I reflected with dismay, but not without some satisfaction, at my own relative competence and health, on the tendency of the writers of my generation to burn themselves out or break down: Scott and Zelda [Fitzgerald], John Dos Passos. . . . One didn't really believe till one saw it demonstrated that fixing oneself up completely to art, to emotion, to enjoyment, without planning for the future or counting the cost, produced dreadful disabilities and bankruptcies later.

EDMUND WILSON

❧

When anyone announces to you how little they drink you can be sure it's a regime they just started.

F. SCOTT FITZGERALD

❧

I sit on the terrace reading about the torments of Scott Fitzgerald. I am, he was, one of those men who read the grievous accounts of hard-drinking, self-destructive authors, holding a glass of whiskey in our hands, the tears pouring down our cheeks.

JOHN CHEEVER

❧

It is a sign of vanity that one fails oneself perpetually.

ROSELLEN BROWN

❧

Thirst being a condition more characteristic of men than of women. What are they doing there, in bars, elsewhere, pouring beer down themselves? They are in a condition of unappeasable unquenchable thirst.

CHARLES BAXTER

I should like to write a book in praise of liquor.

T. H. WHITE

❧

Plenty leads to abstinence—Inside every ogre there is an aesthetic eager to fast.   LAWRENCE DURRELL

❧

He—took to drink, he couldn't stand it. I am a dreamer, I can stand it. I would have stood it.   FYODOR DOSTOYEVSKY

❧

There is no other medicine, no other rule or science, for avoiding the ills, whatever they may be and however great, that besiege men from all sides and at every hour, than to make up our minds to suffer them humanly, or to end them courageously and promptly.   MONTAIGNE

❧

How often have I resolved to try for a nobler life on this day, and always fallen back to the wretched one.

JOHN RUSKIN

❧

The greatest charity is to give way to an occasional inconsistency.   ROBERT FROST

❧

Repentance is one of the evils that increases with years & every day we add something to it as to a possession.

WASHINGTON IRVING

Reality has always been virtual. And so has virtue itself.

STRATIS HAVIARAS

❧

Men are admitted into Heaven not because they have curbed & govern'd their Passions or have No Passions, but because they have Cultivated their Understandings.

WILLIAM BLAKE

❧

Clemency is as different from weakness as is prudence from fear.

ANDRÉ MAUROIS

❧

Less effort, more humanity.

BILL BARICH

❧

To be, *before all else*, a *great man* and a *saint* according to one's own standards.

CHARLES BAUDELAIRE

❧

We cannot do well without our sins; they are the highway of our virtue.

HENRY DAVID THOREAU

❧

In how kind and quiet a manner the *Conscience* talks to us, in general . . . how *long-suffering* it is, how delicate, & full of pity—and with what pains, when the Dictates of Reason made impulsive by its own Whispers have been obstinately pushed aside, does it utter the sad, judicial, tremendous Sentence after which nothing is left to the Soul but supernatural aid.

SAMUEL TAYLOR COLERIDGE

In a well-loved story of Japan, a beautiful young girl who would not tell her angry parents who had made her pregnant finally pointed at an old and revered Zen master, who until now had been praised for his pure life. Accused by the parents, all the old man said was, "Is that so?" When the child was born, he accepted it into his house and took good care of it, unconcerned about this loss of reputation. Not until a year had passed did the remorseful girl admit to her parents that the good old man was entirely innocent, that the real father was a young man in the fish market. The embarrassed parents rushed to fetch the child, apologizing to the old master and begging his forgiveness for the great wrong that they had done. "Is that so?" was all the old man said.

PETER MATTHIESSEN

❧

It is hard to be simple enough to be good.

RALPH WALDO EMERSON

❧

Am thinking about integrity, which surely means that mine is being tested. CAROL EDGARIAN

❧

It is easier to hate someone for picking his nose than to love him for composing a symphony. For the trifle is characteristic and describes the person in his everyday dimension.

WITOLD GOMBROWICZ

❧

Tragedy is based on bourgeois virtues, deriving its strength from them and declining with them. There is no sense in fumigating a saint if you believe in no gods at all.

BERTOLT BRECHT

The evil in this world is immense and everlasting, but it is not personal: it controls men, but it is not controlled by them.

THOMAS WOLFE

❦

Zelda's idea: the bad things are the same in everyone; only the good are different.

F. SCOTT FITZGERALD

❦

There are moments when I think how simple it would be if we all had the same problems. We would surely be able to say "All women are faithless, all men are corruptible" if it weren't for the fact that a lot of women are cold and a lot of men cowardly or stupid about money.

BERTOLT BRECHT

❦

There are two sorts of happiness: the happiness of the virtuous and the happiness of the vain. . . . Happiness based on vanity is destroyed by it: fame by slander, wealth by fraud. But happiness based on virtue cannot be destroyed by anything.

LEO TOLSTOY

❦

Once, Maritain quoted to me what a mother superior of a convent said about a nun who was too much attached to a strict observance of the Rule: "She will remain a long time in Purgatory on account of her virtues."

JULIAN GREEN

❦

Respectability is the cloak under which fools cover their stupidity.

W. SOMERSET MAUGHAM

There are two infinities in this world: God up above, and down below, human baseness.   *THE GONCOURT JOURNAL*

❧

I expect nothing good from men. No treachery, no vileness will surprise me.   GUSTAVE FLAUBERT

❧

People will sometimes forgive you the good you have done them, but seldom the harm they have done you.

W. SOMERSET MAUGHAM

❧

Be modest! It is the kind of pride least likely to offend.

JULES RENARD

❧

Modesty is the illusion of privacy in situations where there is none.   C. K. WILLIAMS

❧

To strike a balance is everything: If a person sings quietly to himself on the street people smile with approval; but if he talks it's not all right; they think he's crazy.

EDWARD HOAGLAND

❧

Arrogance and boredom are the two most authentic products of hell.   THEODORE ROETHKE

Man will only become better when you make him see what he is like. ANTON CHEKHOV

❖

They say "Virtue is its own reward,"—it certainly should be paid well for its trouble. LORD BYRON

Self-Knowledge and Self-Love

Trust to that prompting within you. No man ever got above it.

RALPH WALDO EMERSON

❧

Do you want to know who you are? Don't ask. Act. Action will delineate and define you. You will find out from your actions.

WITOLD GOMBROWICZ

❧

When I was young I pretended to know everything. . . . One of the most useful discoveries I ever made was how easy it is to say: "I don't know."

W. SOMERSET MAUGHAM

❧

I cannot say this way, my way, is right for others. It *is* mine. It is one of the final meanings in my life.

ATHOL FUGARD

❧

Everything that takes me away from the knowledge of the human heart is without interest for me.

STENDHAL

About what is called The Dark Tone of my work: happiness is what I most know in life, but grief is what I best understand of it.   J. D. McCLATCHY

❦

I am by and large a very happy man. People and critics like to think of me in despair because they hate to think of anyone whose way of life they disapprove of as being happy.

WILLIAM S. BURROUGHS

❦

Blessed is the artist who is aware of his own limitations—his shall be the kingdom of heaven!   CLIFFORD ODETS

❦

I do think if I were to go crazy again for the *third* time I should know I was so.   JOHN RUSKIN

❦

When the story changes without us, we gasp, catching up. Bad news, on the telephone. What day was it before this call? Which careful narrative will ease us into the life that follows this news? Color drains from the room. We answer in two voices. The voice we used to have and the new, knowledgeable one that doesn't fit yet, not at all.   NAOMI SHIHAB NYE

❦

Nearly all life's misfortunes come from our false notions about the things that befall us. To know mankind thoroughly

and to judge events sanely is consequently a great stride toward
happiness. STENDHAL

❧

If a person could ever be seen truly, it would be by himself.
But that seldom happens. Or perhaps, is that rare inward vision of oneself what explains the look of rapturous amuse-
ment on a dying person's face, which is always interpreted by
good Christians as the first peer at Heaven? M. F. K. FISHER

❧

Eyes are questions. LEONARD MICHAELS

❧

I can find no more comfortable frame of mind for the conduct of life than a humorous resignation.
W. SOMERSET MAUGHAM

❧

You must make up your mind to acknowledge your limits.
JEAN COCTEAU

❧

. . . the best sentence, the one that echoed in my head long
after I had put *Monsieur Teste* [by Paul Valery] down: "One
must go into himself armed to the teeth." DORIS GRUMBACH

❧

Wisdom, when acquired, proves incommunicable and useless and goes with our learning into the grave. The edges of it

occasionally impinge on people, though, and strike a little awe into them.   E. M. FORSTER

❦

Here's the nostrum [from the Confucian Analects]. "The way out is through the door." How is it nobody remembers this method.   WILLIAM MATTHEWS

❦

In general, the man who is readily disposed to sacrifice himself is one who does not know how else to give meaning to his life.   CESARE PAVESE

❦

I didn't have the two top things—great animal magnetism or money. I had the two second things, tho', good looks and intelligence. So I always got the top girl.

      F. SCOTT FITZGERALD

❦

I don't know whether to be cheered or not by the sister of a Singhalese friend, "Mr. Angus has a face that tells me he went to a good school."   ANGUS WILSON

❦

When it comes to writing I have always had a total indifference (contempt) for my own life and its issues. . . . I *do* write about myself but never what is uniquely "self"—a self that has something in common with at least one other human being. If it concerns *him* or *me*, the chances are that it concerns *you* as well.   ATHOL FUGARD

Confidence: the belief in the person one is at the moment a poem is being executed.　　　　C. K. WILLIAMS

✲

I have had considerable pleasure in my life and have two or three times come very near being happy—which I believe is as much as most men can say.　　　　WASHINGTON IRVING

✲

What a strange life mine has been!　　　　MARY SHELLEY

Self-Doubt

I'm doing nothing and thinking about the landlady. Do I have the talent to compare with our modern Russian writers? Decidedly not.   LEO TOLSTOY

⚜

It's having no children, living away from friends, failing to write well, spending too much on food, growing old. I think too much of whys and wherefores; too much of my self. . . . Unhappiness is everywhere; just beyond the door; or stupidity, which is worse.   VIRGINIA WOOLF

⚜

I want to write and I never never will. . . . Whatever I'm doing, it's always there . . . saying, "Write this—write that—write—" and I can't. Lack ability, time, strength, and duration of vision. I wish someone would tell me brutally, "You can *never* write *anything.* Take up home gardening!"

ANNE MORROW LINDBERGH

⚜

I feel that I shall have a very ordinary life in the world, sensible and reasonable—that I shall be a good bootblack, a good stablehand, a good re-soler of sentences, a good lawyer—whereas I'd like to have an extraordinary life.

GUSTAVE FLAUBERT

❧

Instead of separating myself from pressure to write, I find myself inwardly screaming, frustrated because I'm not super-woman: the perfect mother, perfect lover, perfect poet. I'm afraid I'm going to fail at all these, or have a nervous break-down, or beat my child, or continue in some mundane exis-tence, hating myself for no longer writing.   MARIE-ELISE

❧

No appetite for lunch or for dinner almost every day. Loss of insight & loss of excitement—of almost every kind. The blear of boredom and unattractiveness over everything within and outside of me.

"Where is there an end of it?"   DELMORE SCHWARTZ

❧

I have written practically nothing yet, and now again the time is getting short. There is nothing done. I am no nearer my achievement than I was two months ago, and I keep half-doubting my will to perform anything. Each time I make a move my demon says at almost the same moment: "Oh, yes, we've heard that before!"   KATHERINE MANSFIELD

❧

I find myself now with a growing reputation. In many ways it is a terrible thing. . . . Among other things I feel that I have put something over. That this little success of mine is cheating.

JOHN STEINBECK

Do you know, I'm beginning to think you are a very ordinary fellow. You are vain, dishonest, morally lax; you are proud, you are lazy, and self-indulgent. . . . You are constantly excusing yourself for all these patent deficiencies by saying this sort of jellyfish existence is a prime requisite of the creative personality. . . . Right now, friend, you are excusing yourself by saying, "Here again is this old foolish American cry for competence and result every minute!" These are the whispered thoughts which will ruin you.   CLIFFORD ODETS

❧

I'm not sure I'm a writer. There are many things I want to write but don't know how to—I can't seem to find a way.

                                                                    JAMES SALTER

❧

. . . the creative years are slipping past me without a chance to get to my real work. . . .

I began to think again of the pleasures of death, as I used to: not melodramatically, as of suicide, but with longing for the state of an old, successful man of genius, sitting with all his work behind him, waiting to drop off.

This of course was nonsense.   C. S. LEWIS

❧

He who does not sometimes feel too much and too tenderly, he assuredly at all times feels too little.

                                                    SAMUEL TAYLOR COLERIDGE

Memories, Dreams, and Reflections

Memory is a beloved old neighborhood. In time, the wrong sort of people start moving in.   J. D. McCLATCHY

❧

I have travelled as much, I believe, in the World of My Own as I have in the Common World. My travels in both have not been without drama, but in My Own World one travels at the speed of the fastest jet.   GRAHAM GREENE

❧

A dream last night. I was in a dark place, like a museum hall after hours, and before me, in a diffuse but very bright light, was a slender canoe shaped from the trunk of a tree. All about me in the penumbra of the light were boxes, each about the size of my hand and each a different geometrical shape and pastel color. The dream was simple, an action: I was gently stacking these boxes into the bark canoe. I filled the canoe with these pastel boxes and though they had a bewildering variety of shapes, they were fitting together with great precision. At last the canoe was tightly packed, no space was left in the canoe and every box had found its place and I felt a little trill of joy. I knew what this dream was about even as I dreamed it. There was no reflection on the meaning, no sense of symbolic equivalencies. I simply knew what I was doing: I was writing a novel. ROBERT OLEN BUTLER

❧

That peculiar but very beautiful girl I saw in a dress shop in Key West ten years ago reappeared. She told me you can't give up Eros. Then, as with most of my dream women, she turned into a bird (this time a mourning dove), and flew away. . . .

. . . In another dream she ran backward nakedly into history which was an improbable maze. Another night an unpleasant visit with Herman Melville who didn't look well.

JIM HARRISON

❧

Nightmare. In a dark room dressed in black. My face, however, is clearly visible in white but no features can be made out. I think, Well, I am safe. Then the mirror image, a full-length mirror, reaches out black arms to me and I wake up groaning. WILLIAM S. BURROUGHS

❧

I pray for dreams. I pray each night for translucent colors to swirl in my head like rainbow smoke, tinting symbolically the images waiting to act out my yet unwritten dramas. Even when the dreams are murky, dark and colorless in watery undersea caverns, filling me with anxiety, I am grateful for the gift I receive when I break through the surface.

JEANNE WAKATSUKI HOUSTON

❧

There are two kinds of truth: the truth that lights the way and the truth that warms the heart. The first of these is science, and the second is art. . . . The truth of art keeps science from becoming inhuman, and the truth of science keeps art from becoming ridiculous.   RAYMOND CHANDLER

❧

I had a dream that I went to live with an elephant, a rather fractious one. I made clothes for it. At first its trainer, who was a sort of concierge, thought I wouldn't be able to handle the animal. But, in fact, the elephant and I became quite fond of each other, used to each other. The place in which the elephant lived was a castle, or a prison on top of a mountain, and shaped like an elephant's quarters in the zoo. No one else could handle this elephant, but the keeper seemed to assume I could.

The elephant is my book.   LYNN FREED

❧

Question: when we are dreaming and, as often happens, have a dim consciousness of the fact and try to wake, do we not say and do things which in waking life would be insane? May we not then sometimes define insanity as an inability to distinguish which is the waking and which the sleeping life? We often dream without the least suspicion of unreality: "sleep hath its own world" and it is often as lifelike as the other.   LEWIS CARROLL

❧

Startled to read in Jung that violently colorful dreams & psychic events occur to people in psychic flux who need more consciousness.   JIM HARRISON

❧

. . . a distinction between pleasure and joy. When one is working very hard, it may at any moment be more pleasurable to go from the work and sleep, or eat or lie in the sun. But joy, which is a different, deeper, more thrilling kind of pleasure, joy which is an experience of embodied meaning, joy may be had from working on. Even when the body complains, or the mind aches and claims it cannot go on. To find joy, even in the erotic, one must push past resistances, both in the psyche and the physical, and above all this is significant to the process of writing. But one does not intend to push past a resistance to punish oneself. Rather, one has a hunger for this joy, for this meaning that will pierce experience, and make one suddenly close to all being.   SUSAN GRIFFIN

❧

Thought is the greatest of pleasures—pleasure itself is only imagination—have you ever enjoyed anything more than your dreams?   GUSTAVE FLAUBERT

❧

We talk vaguely about which we would prefer, to live in one of these houses in town, full of the smell of Murphy's oil and history, or to have a small house by the ocean. It is amazing how such conversations can wander lazily and in seeming safety around the no man's land of possibility and somehow find that they have crossed blindly into the mined and dangerous country of intent.   LINDA PASTAN

❧

I am not sure that Fear is not a pleasurable sensation; at least, *Hope* is; and *what Hope* is there without a deep leaven of Fear?   LORD BYRON

❧

I want to think back over the moments and situations of my life and *complete* them, re-enter them and, in so doing, bring back a tenderness for them, a sentience, that they did not have. I want to occupy them again, haunt them with the love that wasn't there, bring back to those moments a measure of *glory*.   GARRETT HONGO

❧

I don't know what I want, but I want it now.

RAYMOND CARVER

❧

In listening to first-rate music there is a sense of anxiety and labour, labour to enjoy it to the utmost, anxiety not to waste our opportunity. . . . In truth we are not intended to rest content in any pleasure of earth, however intense: the yearning has been wisely given us, which points the way to an eternity of happiness, as the only perfect happiness possible—"Thou wilt keep him in *perfect peace*, whose soul is stayed on Thee."

LEWIS CARROLL

❧

Pleasure is not always at the time.   JAMES SALTER

Time and the Seasons

The present is more derived from the future than from the
past.   ROBERT FROST

✣

Is not all summer akin to paradise?
                                      HENRY DAVID THOREAU

✣

The soft surface of the earth is no more than the thickness
of a tarnish on a metal ball.   ROBERT FROST

✣

Art, sorrow, and beauty are perhaps useless, but no more so
than earth itself. What is useful? Useful for what?
                                                NED ROREM

✣

If mankind were all intellect, they would be continually
changing, so that one age would be entirely unlike another.
The great conservative is the heart, which remains the same
in all ages.   NATHANIEL HAWTHORNE

Everything which agitates man agitates him in his feeling of time. Control over oneself = control over one's manner of feeling time: e.g. the future. If one is to be shot on the morrow, to know how to alter the dimensions of duration in such a way as still to have a future to fill up. SIMONE WEIL

❧

Ours is an age which measures time most accurately by the rate of decay of radioactive matter. WILLIAM MATTHEWS

❧

The mind is given its speed of more miles an hour than even the stream of time so that it can choose absolutely how fast it will go with the stream or whether it will stand still on it or go against it. The great thing is that it can stay in one place for a while and it is probably the only thing that can.

ROBERT FROST

❧

When one subtracts from life infancy (which is vegetation),—sleep, eating, and swilling—buttoning and unbuttoning—how much remains of downright existence? The summer of a dormouse. LORD BYRON

❧

Of eternity we have a number of score of years. . . . I have had several months near joy, and of that perhaps one day doing what I most want and of that a minute of perfection.

ALLEN GINSBERG

Dawn. Lying after just waking. The sad possibilities of the future are more vivid than at any other time. A man is no longer a hero in his own eyes: even the laughing child may now have a foretaste of his manhood's glooms; the man, of the neglect and contumely which may wait upon his old age. It is a supremely safe time for deciding upon money ventures: no false high hope tempts one to run a dangerous risk. In fact, as the man who acts upon what he resolved before sleeping is the man of most brilliant successes & disastrous failures, so the man who abides by what he thought at dawn is he who is found afterwards in the safe groove of respectable mediocrity.

THOMAS HARDY

❧

Time is always short, from birth to death. Why? Because we don't know how to stop.　　　　　JULIAN GREEN

❧

Time rolls on, and what does it bring? What can I do? How change my destiny? Months change their names, years their cyphers. My brow is sadly trenched, the blossom of youth faded. My mind gathers wrinkles. What will become of me?

MARY SHELLEY

❧

Each moment in which a thought occurs has more to do with that moment itself than with anything in the past or the future. This, to my way of thinking, is actually more positive than negative, because it supports the continuous nature of life—and that of art, too.　　　　　CLARENCE MAJOR

No such thing as present sight. Hindsight and foresight.

DAWN POWELL

❧

He who clings to Pleasure, that is to the Present, makes me think of a man rolling down a slope who in trying to grasp hold of some bushes, tears them up and carries them with him in his fall.

CHARLES BAUDELAIRE

❧

There are arts that happen in "real time," like music and film, and part of their authority for heartbreak is that they do. Poetry refers by its every formal wile to our urge to go slower, and that longing is part of poetry's authority for heartbreak.

WILLIAM MATTHEWS

❧

Post literacy. A time in which reading and writing no longer matter. Books as "home enhancers," chosen for their covers or bindings. No need to be able to read the fine print in contracts because you're going to get screwed anyway. To be post-literate is to be conversant with an idiom whose components are borrowed, often haphazardly, from the incessant Now. In the post-literate world, meaning is ever-shifting, a little fantastic, never to be pinned down. Anything that's pinned down is, in an essential way, dead—movement, the ability to alter circumstances, count for everything.

BILL BARICH

❧

Great acts are irrevocable. Everything is irrevocable.

JAMES SALTER

This joke told in a cabaret in the new Germany, "A wonderful future lies behind us."   SUSAN GRIFFIN

⚜

Snow. Fire. Waves: the three great hypnotizers. I can sit in front of a window of falling snow for hours, just watching, or before the restless flames in the fireplace. Perhaps it is the incessant movement of each, or the deceptive domesticity beyond which, biding its time, waits danger.

LINDA PASTAN

⚜

It must be hard to be March, one of those adolescent months people patiently wait for the year to outgrow.

JAMES SCHUYLER

⚜

Oh, dear, angelic time—go on.
I'll try to imitate your going,
And turn my wheel round, too,
As sure and swift as yours.
Between each revolution,
(Wise time—go on,
My voice shall speed you
'though you need no strength
To make your turn, I know),
There's all my laughter smoke,
My grief a little empty sound,
And all my love a cloud
Who sails away from me.
I can't be happy.
Try to-day, try this time (sweet time),
To-morrow's never.

DYLAN THOMAS

After a while you see there's neither a right nor wrong to history, not even meaning. There are snail tracks.

JAMES SALTER

❦

After all my childhood joys and terror, and shallow adolescent anguish; the shock of October 24, 1929, when the stock market crashed and my father, "wiped out" as he said, put his head down on the dining-room table in the middle of dinner and cried, at about the same time that my best friend's father, whose name, I recall, was Robert Dince, took his life by jumping from a window of a tall building in the garment district of New York; and after the exhilaration of learning how to learn and reason in college; after the suicide (or accidental death) of my friend John Ricksecker, who jumped (or fell) from the roof of the School of Commerce on the last day of classes of our senior year, his arm catching on the no-parking stanchion, stopping his fall for a moment, and then coming off at the shoulder; after the war, in which we women served, and were served by the elevating symbol of the uniform we wore and the power of elating and irresponsible love affairs; after the short-lived postwar optimism during which I had children because I believed the world was going to be better, we would be extraordinarily successful and, someday, very rich; after the slow descent into the present, marked by the dissolution of family ties by death and divorce, by the dilatory liberation of blacks and women, by the minute beginnings of a recognition of overt sexual diversity and androgyny (what in my youth was called "perversity"), by the gradual disappearance of forms of religious belief, of hopes for peace after Korea and Vietnam and Cambodia, of faith that the forests were protected, the rainwater, springs, and water table pure, the cities safe, interesting, and clean; and after my sad loss of patriotic conviction that this is the smartest, most ethical, richest, and most trust-

worthy country on the face of the earth, of certainty that medical sciences, injections and pharmaceuticals are a sure protection against most viruses, bacteria, germs, fungi, I have
come to this age of anxiety, despair and hopelessness. All this
has happened in my lifetime, in two-thirds of a century. This
morning, listing it all as I lie on the couch, I still have no firm
answer to the question that continues to plague me:

"Who am I?" Or the question that runs parallel to it: "What
has my life meant?"   DORIS GRUMBACH

Faith

On our knees in church (even in the cathedral) we are face-to-face with the bare facts of our humanity. We praise Him, we bless Him, we adore Him, we glorify Him, and we wonder who is that baritone across the aisle and that pretty woman on our right who smells of apple blossoms. Our bowels stir and our cod itches and we amend our prayers for the spiritual life with the hope that it will not be too spiritual.

JOHN CHEEVER

❧

If there is a God, atheism must strike Him as less of an insult than religion. *THE GONCOURT JOURNAL*

❧

Last night I decided that it is totally nuts to believe in Christ, that it is every bit as crazy as being a Scientologist or a Jehovah's Witness. But a priest friend said solemnly, "Scientologists and Mormons and Jehovah's Witnesses are crazier than they *have* to be." ANNE LAMOTT

❧

No country will more quickly dissipate romantic expectations than Palestine—particularly Jerusalem. . . .

Is the desolation of the land the result of the fatal embrace of the Deity? Hapless are the favorites of heaven.

HERMAN MELVILLE

❦

Someone we have come to see as pretty superficial decides to go into retreat as a spiritual recluse: at first the fraudulence of this move is obvious, and then what seems to be the case is that something genuine is happening—the person takes on an aura of spiritual weight and alarming inner dignity.

CHARLES BAXTER

❦

As to the *Miracle* . . . of Poetry. There is truly but one miracle, the perpetual fact of Being and Becoming, the ceaseless saliency, the transit from the vast to the particular, which miracle, one and the same, has for its most universal name the word God. Take one or two or three steps where you will, from any fact in Nature or Art, and you will come out full on this fact; as you may penetrate the forest in any direction and go straight on, you will come to the sea.

RALPH WALDO EMERSON

❦

One of the problems of traditional Christianity is that it doesn't take the human body into account except as a metaphor—the Church, the body of Christ, transubstantiation. It leaves us in the darkness with all of our physical yearning, as though the spirit and soul were apart from the body, and knowledge is in heaven.   TOM JENKS

❦

Above all the act of writing calls on faith.   SUSAN GRIFFIN

Am *I* a deep philosopher, or a great genius? I think neither. What talents I have, I desire to devote to His service, and may He purify me, and take away my pride and selfishness, Oh that *I* might hear "Well done, good and faithful servant"!

LEWIS CARROLL

✣

There is no exalted pleasure which cannot be related to prostitution. At the play, in the ballroom, each one enjoys possession of all. God is the most prostituted of all beings, because he is the closest friend of every individual, because he is the common inexhaustible reservoir of love.

CHARLES BAUDELAIRE

✣

Yesterday the Frank Harrises called and took us to Saint-Raphael for lunch. He said: "God when he was young had a liking for the Jews. But when he was old he had a senile weakness for the English."

ARNOLD BENNETT

✣

How often people speak of the absurdity of believing that life should exist by God's will on one minute part of the immense universe. There is a parallel absurdity which we are asked to believe, that God chose a tiny colony of a Roman Empire in which to be born. Strangely enough two absurdities seem easier to believe than one.

GRAHAM GREENE

✣

Instead of having faith, which is a virtue, and therefore nourishes the soul and gives it a healthy life, people merely have a lot of opinions, which excite the soul but don't give it anything to feed it, just wear it out until it falls over from exhaustion.

An opinion isn't one thing or the other; it is neither science nor faith, but has a little bit of either one. It is a rationalization bolstered up by some orthodoxy which you happen to respect, which, naturally, starves the mind instead of feeding it and that is what people who have no faith imagine faith does, but they don't know what they are talking about, because faith is a virtue, an active habit which cannot even pretend to rationalize anything: it seeks what is beyond reason.

THOMAS MERTON

⚜

It is impossible to use love of humanity to make up for the absence of God, because man will immediately ask: why should I love humanity? FYODOR DOSTOYEVSKY

Aging and Death

Growing up and growing old are a continuous process of learning what one cannot do well.   EVELYN WAUGH

❧

I go to the park and play basketball with the black kids. My body knows what to do, but does less than it knows. After a bad pass and a bad shot, I overplay a kid out of exasperation and bump him too hard. "I'm sorry," I say, "I'm too old." He says, "Don't say that, man. Look at me. I'm eighteen."

LEONARD MICHAELS

❧

The forties are the old age of youth and the fifties the youth of old age.   EDWARD HOAGLAND

❧

Well, my birthday is over and I am now fifty-eight, two years off sixty and twelve years off seventy and, lord knows, I should have learnt wisdom by now but I haven't and that's that.   NOËL COWARD

"Life is a warning," says boxer Larry Holmes, when asked if Muhammad Ali's physical decline seems like a warning to him.   EDWARD HOAGLAND

❧

Every wildness plays with death. Washing your hands is a ritual to protect against death. The small correct thing you do everyday. Aren't there people who do nothing else? They have proper sentiments and beliefs. They are nice people. I wanted to do dull ordinary chores all day and be like nice people only to forget death, only to feel how I'm still alive.
                                                 LEONARD MICHAELS

❧

Life is slowly bending me, like a wrestler forcing an opponent to the floor, to the idea of the end.   JAMES SALTER

❧

God, how beastly it is when our bodies go back on us and betray us to a nest of microbes. Yet there is a certain romance about illness in the Mediaeval manner that makes you almost desire it; Arthur, faint unto death, carried away by the queens on a barge to Avilion.   JOHN DOS PASSOS

❧

People love talking of their diseases, although they are the most uninteresting things in their lives.   ANTON CHEKHOV

❧

Those who have never been ill are incapable of real sympathy for a great many misfortunes.   ANDRÉ GIDE

I must tend my body with at least as much care as I tend the compost, particularly now when it seems so beside the point. Is this pain and despair that surround me a result of cancer, or has it just been released by cancer? I feel so unequal to what I always handled before, the abominations outside that echo the pain within. And yes I am completely self-referenced right now because it is the only translation I can trust, and I do believe not until every woman traces her weave back strand by bloody self-referenced strand, will we begin to alter the whole pattern. . . . I want to write rage but all that comes is sadness. We have been sad long enough to make this earth either weep or grow fertile. I am an anachronism, a sport, like the bee that was never meant to fly. Science said so. I am not supposed to exist. I carry death around in my body like a condemnation. But I do live. The bee flies. There must be some way to integrate death into living, neither ignoring it nor giving in to it.   AUDRE LORDE

❧

So let me turn away and toward old age, the Fourth Season, as it has been called. How many times lately someone my age or older has said "If they told us what it would be like we would have opted out."   MAY SARTON

❧

At breakfast in the hotel a little girl screams at the sight of me and cannot be calmed by her parents. She is removed by the mother. Later she appeared on the hotel roof where I was writing. . . . Violent screams again and her nurse rushed out to remove her. . . . Later, the girl's father came to apologize: it seems that my white hair made the girl think of Father Christmas, and as Christmas was over, it was unseasonable and frightening of FC to appear again.

It made me feel older, and fell in with my spoken and un-spoken emphasis on being old (serves me right), because apart from financial worry and tummy pains I do not feel old at all.   ANGUS WILSON

❧

Very old people age somewhat as bananas do.
                                              EDWARD HOAGLAND

❧

Nasty turn (faint, heart attack, stroke) in Abingdon on our way to lunch. . . . Came to to find myself in the hospital. . . . Next day Prof. Sleight and his boys came round. Home after lunch. On Tuesday . . . had an ambulatory electro-cardiogram attached to me for 24 hours.

. . . Dr. S. . . . told me about a pacemaker that could be fit-ted to the heart but which must be removed at death as it is liable to explode in the crematorium. (He said I could use it in a book.)   BARBARA PYM

❧

Body giving out, will not serve soul . . . leaving no choice but dreams unrealized.   BERNARD BERENSON

❧

Old age has its compensations. . . .

. . . you need hardly ever do anything you don't want to. You can enjoy music, art and literature, differently from when you were young, but in a different way as keenly. You can get a good deal of fun out of observing the course of events in which you are no longer intimately concerned. If your plea-

sures are not so vivid your pains also have lost their sting.
. . . the greatest compensation of old age is its freedom of
spirit. . . . it liberates you from envy, hatred, malice.

W. SOMERSET MAUGHAM

❦

The seat of my office chair, in use for twenty-five years, is
wearing out, my office rug is wearing out, and I am wearing
out. As the Chinese say, "It is later than you think."

H. L. MENCKEN

❦

There are no tasks. I don't have to do anything. I don't need
the money, and I don't need the exercise/aggravation. I am of
an age—I've learned, read, made money, made a career, met
many, many people. I may not even need to write a next book.
I've raised a kid. I don't need any more dresses, houses, cars,
things. (Except for the big deed/dream—to make a peaceful
world?) Places—I've been to all the places I need to go to. The
appointments and projects are just to make life interesting.
What happens when you don't panic to fill in the time?
That tremble on the wire—no use and free.

MAXINE HONG KINGSTON

❦

If I had to die in an hour, should I be ready?

ANDRÉ GIDE

❦

Ray, a Nantucketer, about 25 years old, a good honest fellow . . . fell this morning about day-break from the main top-
sail yard to the deck, & striking head-foremost upon one of
the spars was instantly killed. . . .

. . . all goes on as usual—I, too, read & think, & walk & eat & talk, as if nothing had happened—as if I did not know that death is indeed the King of Terrors.   HERMAN MELVILLE

❦

I am waiting to get my hair cut, reading a crumpled copy of *Life* magazine. There is a picture of an old Greek woman standing behind a church. She is wearing the traditional old woman's garments: black kerchief, black shoes, long black dress. She is toothless, grinning. She is holding in her hand a grinning skull. In the back of the church there is a graveyard. Against the walls of the church there are piles of bones, sorted by type: skulls in one pile, leg bones in another. The old woman asked the photographer to take her picture holding this skull. She could tell, she said, that it was the skull of one of her old rivals. She did not say how she could tell. But she wanted her picture taken, she said to the photographer. "Because she is dead and I am not dead. You can see me here, alive. I want everyone to see me here, alive."   MARY GORDON

❦

We do not count a man's years until he has nothing else to count.   RALPH WALDO EMERSON

❦

If I know anything, it is to expect impermanence . . . and yet . . .   GRETEL EHRLICH

❦

The death of others
Near to us & dear to us
Is death's terror
Is what terrifies us

DELMORE SCHWARTZ

On no subject are our ideas more warped and pitiable than on death. Instead of sympathy, the friendly union, of life and death, so apparent in Nature, we are taught that death is an accident, a deplorable punishment for the oldest sin, the arch-enemy of life, etc. Town children, especially, are steeped in this death orthodoxy, for the natural beauties of death are sel-dom seen or taught in towns.

. . . Thus death becomes fearful, and the most notable and incredible thing heard around a death-bed is, "I fear not to die."

JOHN MUIR

❧

Everywhere I have been I have thought at least once a day of my dead father. He has been dead for over thirty years. In a book he inscribed for me are these words, in his handwrit-ing, a translation of a line of Virgil: "Among the dead there are so many of thousands of the beautiful."

MARY GORDON

❧

In the perspective of the heart,
Those dearly loved, when they depart,
Take so much of us when they go
That, like no thing on earth, they grow
Larger when fleeing from the eye
Till they invest the vacant sky
With their dear presence, an existence
Lost in love's exponential distance . . .

W. D. SNODGRASS

❧

Suddenly getting old, feeling old, looking old, all my friends and contemporaries, and myself. . . . Truly the lyric flight is over and the wedding into life has become firm and lasting.

CLIFFORD ODETS

You never know till you get there, and by then it doesn't matter what you knew.   FRANK CONROY

❦

Death is terrible, but still more terrible is the feeling that you might live forever.   ANTON CHEKHOV

❦

HOW TO DIE—but first, how not to:
Not in a smelly old bloody-gutted bed in a rest-home . . .
Not in snowy whiteness under arc lights and klieg lights and direct television hookup . . .
Not in the muddy mire of battleblood . . .
But how *to*:
Alone, elegantly, a wolf on a rock, old pale and dry, dry bones rattling in the leather bag, eyes alight, high, dry, cool, far off, dim distance alone, free as a dying wolf on a pale day rock.
                    EDWARD ABBEY

❦

Death—backwards, off the high board, at night.
                    JAMES SALTER

❦

The dying Thoreau, asked by some damned cleric if he was ready for the next world: "One world at a time, please."
                    EDWARD ABBEY

❦

Is there any thing beyond?—*who* knows? *He* that can't tell. Who tells that there *is*? He who don't know. And when shall we know? Perhaps, when he don't expect, and, generally when he don't wish it. In this last respect, however, all are not alike: it depends a good deal upon education,—and something upon nerves and habits—but most upon digestion.

LORD BYRON

❧

Whatever this was all about, this was not a vain attempt—journey.

RAYMOND CARVER

❧

The world is always ending; the exact date depends on when you came into it.

ARTHUR MILLER

❧

Yesterday entirely clear and calm from sunrise to set, today perfectly cloudless also. And I—amazedly, sadder and heavier than for many a day, the beauty of all things making my own age and decay more manifest to me.

A stomach sadness and dimness of eyes, or rather swimming and faltering of them plaguing me also,—and this after long walks and rest.

And discontent and failure of hope in heart.

And heard owls cry last night though faint and low.

JOHN RUSKIN

❧

I wonder if it could be true that, as someone once wrote (I cannot remember the author), death itself is a horizon, and a horizon is only the limit of our sight.

DORIS GRUMBACH

I am like a passenger waiting for his ship at a war-time port.
I do not know on which day it will sail, but I am ready to em-
bark at a moment's notice. . . . I am on the wing.

W. SOMERSET MAUGHAM

❧

A man's life is his image. At the hour of death we shall be
reflected in the past, and, leaning over the mirror of our acts,
our souls will recognize *what we are*.   ANDRÉ GIDE

Posterity and Immortality

I hope that in the next world I shall be able to look back at this life and say: "Those were beautiful dreams . . ."

ANTON CHEKHOV

❧

We sometimes congratulate ourselves at the moment of waking from a troubled dream: it may be so the moment after death.

NATHANIEL HAWTHORNE

❧

I am sure I have left at the right time—as early as possible and with success.

EVELYN WAUGH

❧

. . . there are two routes to immortality. . . . In the time that you face death directly, you are immortal. That's the straight-ahead route. The slow-down detour vampire route . . . is a manipulate, degrade, humiliate, enslave route.

So how does one face death head-on? . . . without flinching and without posturing.

WILLIAM S. BURROUGHS

Today I read a . . . biography of Anna Pavlova, whose greatest role was the dying swan. The pictures of her in action make it hard for me to believe she was as perfect as she is described. But I learn that as she was dying, she called her attendant and said, "Prepare my swan costume." The author does not say, but I assume it was brought to her and Pavlova was buried in it.

DORIS GRUMBACH

❧

I am an old man. . . . I have done what I wanted to do and now silence becomes me. I am told that in these days you are quickly forgotten if you do not by some new work keep your name before the public, and I have little doubt that it is true. Well, I am prepared for that. When my obituary notice at last appears in *The Times*, and they say: "What, I thought he died years ago," my ghost will gently chuckle.

W. SOMERSET MAUGHAM

❧

The reward of great men is that, long after they have died, one is not quite sure that they are dead.   JULES RENARD

❧

Real honest work will find its level in time, when the rubbish falls away and is forgotten.   BEATRIX POTTER

"I hope it is said when I am dead His sins were scarlet but his books were read." (Hilaire Belloc)   EDWARD HOAGLAND

❧

Immortality. I notice that as soon as writers broach this question they begin to quote. I hate quotations. Tell me what you know.   RALPH WALDO EMERSON

Contributors

EDWARD ABBEY (1927–1989), noted environmentalist, novelist, and essayist, has been praised as a descendant of Ralph Waldo Emerson and Henry David Thoreau in the American vein of transcendental writing. Abbey's books include *Desert Solitaire, The Brave Cowboy,* and *One Life at a Time, Please.*

DIANE ACKERMAN (1948–) often combines science and art in her writing. Her books include *On Extended Wings,* a memoir of learning to fly an airplane; *The Planets: A Cosmic Pastoral,* a meditation on the nature of the universe; and *Wife of Light,* poems. She has been a staff writer at *The New Yorker,* the director of the creative writing program at Washington University in St. Louis, a member of the literature panel of the New York State Council on the Arts, and the host of a PBS television show. Her work has appeared in many periodicals, including *Life, The Paris Review,* and *The New York Times Book Review.* She resides in Ithaca, New York, with her life partner, author Paul West.

LOUISA MAY ALCOTT (1832–1888), American novelist and poet, became famous in 1869 with the publication of *Little Women.* The novel's protagonist, Jo, has been called the first liberated girl in literature. Alcott wrote a series of novels, including *Little Men* and *Jo's Boys,* based on the characters in *Little Women.* Her sharp evocations of Victorian domestic life and values are perennially popular with children and adults.

HANS CHRISTIAN ANDERSEN (1805–1875) owes his world-wide fame to his fairy stories, among which are "The Red Shoes," "The Ugly Duckling," and "The Emperor's New Clothes." In all, there are 168 tales, which appeared between 1835 and 1872 and have been collected in several English editions. In his lifetime, the Danish author was also known as a poet, novelist, and dramatist.

SHERWOOD ANDERSON (1876–1941) was a central figure in American literature in the early twentieth century. His short story masterpieces, including "Death in the Woods" and "I Want to Know Why," and his novel *Winesburg, Ohio* have touched readers and influenced writers through successive generations up to the present. His work is noted for its poetic expression of lone-liness and its attentiveness to the lives of ordinary people.

MATTHEW ARNOLD (1822–1888), English poet and critic, was Professor of Poetry at Oxford. Among his most famous poems are "The Scholar Gypsy," "Stanzas from the Grande Chartreuse," and "Thrysis," which, with Milton's "Lycidas" and Shelley's *Adonais*, has been called one of the finest elegies in the English language. Arnold's critical works, collected in *On Translating Homer*, *Essays in Criticism*, *Culture and Anarchy*, and *Literature and Dogma*, shaped English and American criticism up to the time of T. S. Eliot.

PAUL AUSTER (1947–   ) is the author of the novels *Mr. Vertigo*, *Leviathan*, *The Music of Chance*, *Moon Palace*, *In the Country of Last Things*, and the "New York Trilogy" (*City of Glass*, *Ghosts*, and *The Locked Room*). His other books include *The Invention of Solitude*, *The Art of Hunger*, and *Disappearance: Selected Poems*. He lives in Brooklyn, New York.

ISAAC BABEL (1894–1940) was first encouraged in his writing by Maxim Gorky, who published two of Babel's early stories in the St. Petersburg magazine *Letopis*. During the Russian revolution and civil war, Babel joined the Red cavalry, an experience on which he drew for his story collection *Red Cavalry*, which depicted the cruelty of war. He became immensely popular and enjoyed rare privileges in Soviet Russia but resisted membership in the Communist Party and, though he served as a military journalist, ultimately avoided turning his art to propaganda for the state. Guy de Maupassant was a primary influence on his work, and in writing about Maupassant, Babel gave his famous dictum: "No iron can pierce the human heart as chillingly as a full stop placed at the right time." Babel was arrested in the Stalinist purges of the late 1930s, and no one knows exactly what happened to him. His writings—fifteen folders of manuscripts, eleven notebooks, seven notepads—were confiscated at the time of his arrest and have never been seen again. His recently published *1920 Diary* covers some of the events that he fictionalized in *Red Cavalry*.

BILL BARICH (1943–) is the author of *Laughing in the Hills*, a lively and perceptive look at thoroughbred horse racing and its lessons for life. His other works include two books of nonfiction, *Hard to Be Good* and *Big Dreams*, as well as a novel, *Carson Valley*. He lives in Northern California.

RICK BASS (1958–) is a noted essayist, short story writer, and novelist for whom love and respect for the environment are integral parts of writing. His book *Wolves* is a nonfiction account of the survival of the species in the Northwest. Bass lives in rural Montana, which forms the setting for his story collection, *The Watch*, and his memoir of a challenging season, *Winter*. His other titles include *The Deer Pasture*, *Oil Notes*, *In the Loyal Mountains*, and *Lost Grizzlies*. He is married to the painter Elizabeth Hughes.

CHARLES BAUDELAIRE (1821–1867), renowned French symbolist poet, translated the works of Edgar Allan Poe and introduced them to Europe, where they became more popular than in Poe's native America. Baudelaire's own poetry consists of a single volume, *Les Fleurs du Mal*. Its subtle nuances, striking images, and attention to shifting, often painful emotional states foreshadowed the development of modern poetry. Baudelaire's decadent lifestyle brought him to an early death at the age of forty-six.

CHARLES BAXTER (1947–) is the author of two novels, *First Light* and *Shadow Play*, and three collections of stories, including *Through the Safety Net* and *A Relative Stranger*. He lives in Michigan, where he teaches creative writing at the University of Michigan.

MARVIN BELL (1937–) is the author of thirteen books, including *A Probable Volume of Dreams*, winner of the Lamont Award of the Academy of American Poets, and *Stars Which See, Stars Which Do Not See*, a finalist for the National Book Award in poetry. He divides his time between Iowa City, Iowa, where he has been a longtime faculty member at the Iowa Writers' Workshop, and Port Townsend, Washington.

ARNOLD BENNETT (1867–1931) was born in the English Midlands. As a young man, he moved to London, where he became a successful journalist, editing a women's magazine and writing "pocket philosophies," such as *How to Live on 24 Hours a Day*, and book reviews. Influenced by French novelist Émile Zola, Bennett turned to naturalistic fiction and wrote numerous novels that achieved literary and commercial success. However, his work came under criticism from Virginia Woolf and is now neglected.

BERNARD BERENSON (1865–1959), Lithuanian-born American art connoisseur, was the foremost authority on Italian art of the thirteenth to the seventeenth centuries. His *Italian Painters of the Renaissance* is a classic work of art history. Excerpts from the diaries Berenson kept from 1947 to 1956 were published as *The Passionate Sightseer*.

MARY BERENSON (1864–1945), at the age of twenty-seven, left her London barrister husband and two small daughters for the love of Bernard Berenson and Italian Renaissance art. They lived together for more than fifty years. Mary attained expertise in art history and assisted Berenson, editing his writing and undertaking business negotiations. The Berensons' home, the Villa I Tatti, near Florence, attracted a fashionable circle of notables, including Gertrude Stein, Edith Wharton, Kenneth Clark, Gabriele D'Annunzio, and John Maynard Keynes, as well as artists, collectors, royalty, and statesmen from around the world.

THOMAS BERGER (1924–   ) is the author of nineteen novels, including *Arthur Rex, Neighbors,* and *The Feud.* His *Little Big Man* has been published throughout the world. He lives near the Hudson River in Rockland County, New York.

ANNE BERNAYS (1930–   ) has written numerous novels, including *The Address Book, The New York Ride, The First to Know,* and *Growing Up Rich.* She was raised and educated in New York and worked for a time in the publishing business. She is a co-founder of the New England chapter of P.E.N. (the international society of poets, editors, and novelists) and has taught writing at Harvard University. She lives in Cambridge, Massachusetts, with her husband, noted biographer Justin Kaplan.

WILLIAM BLAKE (1757–1827), English poet, engraver, painter, and visionary, illustrated his own poems with copperplate engraving and watercolors that evoked his experience of God and the paradoxical nature of the universe. His books of poems, such as *Songs of Innocence, Songs of Experience, The Marriage of Heaven and Hell,* and *The Book of Thel,* reflect his mysticism. His devoted wife once remarked, "I have very little of Mr. Blake's company; he is always in Paradise." Unlike many poets of his day, he was of the working class—a printer by trade—and self-educated.

ROY BLOUNT, JR. (1941–   ) started out as a newspaperman, working on a number of metropolitan papers, including *The New Orleans Times Picayune* and *The Atlanta Journal.* He became known as an editorial writer, columnist, and humorist, and went on to write for national periodicals such as *Sports Illustrated, The*

New Yorker, Esquire, and *Rolling Stone.* His books include *About Three Bricks Shy of a Load, Crackers,* and *One Fell Soup.* He lives in New York City and is a member of the usage panel of the *American Heritage Dictionary* and a contributing editor of *The Atlantic Monthly.*

CAROL BLY (1930–   ) is the author of a short story collection, *Backbone,* and of essays, *Letters from the Country* and *Bad Government and Silly Literature.* Her work has also appeared in *The New Yorker, American Review,* and *Ploughshares* and has sometimes appeared under the pen names Joanna Campbell and Ann Reynolds. For many years she was married to the poet Robert Bly. She lives in Minnesota.

JAMES BOSWELL (1740–1795), Scottish lawyer and man of letters, is renowned as the biographer of English lexicographer Dr. Samuel Johnson.

PAUL BOWLES (1910–   ) is one of America's best-known expatriate writers. During his early years he lived by writing theater music, as well as music criticism for *The New York Herald Tribune.* His story collections and novels, which include *The Delicate Prey, Up Above the World,* and *The Sheltering Sky,* often involve fatal errors made by well-to-do travelers in precarious places. Originally from New York, he has for many decades made his home in Tangiers, keeping an open door for wandering writers and artists.

BERTOLT BRECHT (1898–1956), German dramatist initially known for the expressionism of such plays as *Man Is Man,* turned toward Marxism in *The Threepenny Opera.* In 1933, he was driven from Germany by the rise of Nazism and began a fourteen-year exile in Denmark, Sweden, Finland, and the United States, writing plays, such as *The Private Life of the Master Race,* that attack Nazism.

CHARLOTTE BRONTË (1816–1855), English novelist, is revered for *Jane Eyre*, which many consider the first subjective novel and a precursor of works by Proust and Joyce. Brontë's two younger sisters were also novelists—the middle one, Emily, renowned as the author of *Wuthering Heights*, and the youngest, Anne, all but forgotten as the author of *Agnes Grey*. All three sisters lived with a sharp sense of the limitations and oppression placed on women of their day and expressed dissatisfaction through the struggles of their characters.

ROSELLEN BROWN (1939–   ) has published four novels, three collections of poetry, a book of short stories, and a miscellany of essays, stories, and poetry. Her stories have been anthologized in the O. Henry, Best American, and Pushcart Prize collections. She has received an award in literature from the American Academy and Institute of Arts and Letters and numerous other honors. She teaches creative writing at the University of Houston. Among her works of fiction are *Civil Wars*, *Tender Mercies*, and *Street Games*.

ELIZABETH BARRETT BROWNING (1806–1861) was widely acclaimed as a poet in her lifetime. An invalid from the age of fifteen as the result of a spinal injury, she was forty years old when she eloped from her father's house with the poet Robert Browning. Her diary covers her life prior to the elopement.

FANNY BURNEY (1752–1840) started writing at the age of ten but burned her juvenilia when she was fifteen and began a diary, which she kept for the rest of her life. Her first novel, *Evelina*, was published anonymously in 1778, though the author was promptly identified and highly praised. She was one of the first recognized women novelists writing in English and one of the first fiction writers to deal with the experiences of a young girl coming into contact with the social world; as such, she is noted as a predecessor of Jane Austen.

WILLIAM S. BURROUGHS (1914–) was associated with the beat movement, a bohemian literary and social phenomenon originating in the North Beach district of San Francisco, Greenwich Village in New York, and the Venice neighborhood of Los Angeles in the 1950s. Visionary and quintessentially hip, Burroughs's infamous novels, including *Naked Lunch*, *Junky*, *Queer*, and *The Place of Dead Roads*, flow from dream or nightmare aspects of the American psyche, involving heroin addiction, sex, and death. A cult figure, he is also a member of the American Academy and Institute of Arts and Letters and a Commandeur de l'Ordre des Arts et des Lettres of France.

JANET BURROWAY (1936–) has taught at the prestigious Iowa Writers' Workshop and is McKenzie Professor of Literature and Writing at Florida State University in Tallahasee. Her books include the novels *Raw Silk*, *Opening Nights*, and most recently *Cutting Stone;* the children's books *The Truck on the Track* and *The Giant Jam Sandwich;* a book of poems, *Material Goods;* and *Writing Fiction: A Guide to Narrative Craft*, which is widely used in colleges and universities in the United States.

ROBERT OLEN BUTLER (1945–) is the author of seven critically acclaimed novels, including *The Alleys of Eden*, *Wabash*, *The Deuce*, and *They Whisper*. His book of short stories, *A Good Scent from a Strange Mountain*, was awarded the 1993 Pulitzer Prize for fiction. He has also won the Richard and Hinda Rosenthal Award for first fiction from the American Academy and Institute of Arts and Letters. He lives in Lake Charles, Louisiana, with his wife, the novelist and playwright Elizabeth Dewberry.

GEORGE GORDON, LORD BYRON (1788–1824) inherited his title of baron at the age of ten. At nineteen, he published his first collection of poems, *Hours of Idleness;* five years later, the publication of the first two cantos of *Childe Harold's Pilgrimage*, a fictionalized account of his own travels, brought him fame. Promiscuous, peripatetic, prolific, he created the "Byronic hero"—the defiant, melancholy, swashbuckling image that occupied his life and work. In 1823, he took up the cause of Greek independence and died of fever at Missolonghi before seeing any military action. His masterpiece, *Don Juan*, begun in 1819 and running to 16,000 lines, was unfinished.

ALBERT CAMUS (1913–1960) was a close associate of writer-philosopher Jean-Paul Sartre and, with him, one of the intellectual leaders of the French Resistance during World War II. However, Camus did not accept Sartre's existentialist philosophy of the absolute meaninglessness of life, taking instead a more humanistic view. His novels *The Stranger* and *The Plague* show men doing their best with the tragedies of an absurd, inscrutable universe. Camus received the Nobel Prize for literature in 1957.

LEWIS CARROLL was the pen name of Charles Lutwidge Dodgson (1832–1898), the English mathematician, remembered as the author of the much-beloved *Alice's Adventures in Wonderland* and *Through the Looking Glass*. A lecturer at Oxford who was thought boring, an ordained deacon who never preached, Carroll was shy and stammering and found friendship with a little girl, Alice Liddell, for whom he wrote his famous books.

RAYMOND CARVER (1939–1988) inspired an American short story renaissance in the 1980s. His stories, appearing initially in small literary quarterlies such as *Western Humanities Review* and later in *The New Yorker, Esquire*, and other national periodicals, have been anthologized and translated around the world. His much-loved story collections include *Will You Please Be Quiet, Please?, What We Talk About When We Talk About Love, Cathedral*, and *Where I'm Calling From*. A poet before he was a fiction writer, Carver published several poetry volumes: *Where Water Comes Together with Other Water, Ultramarine, A New Path to the Waterfall*, and *Fires: Essays, Poems, Stories*. He was an editor of *Best American Short Stories* and, with Tom Jenks, co-edited *Amer-*

ican Short Story Masterpieces. In 1988, he was given special recognition by the American Academy and Institute of Arts and Letters. He lived in Washington State with his wife, the poet Tess Gallagher.

RAYMOND CHANDLER (1888–1959), renowned American detective story writer, was a master of the hard-boiled, literate, crime story. He created private detective Philip Marlowe, a rugged realist with an unexpected range of sensitivity. Chandler's novels include *The Big Sleep, Farewell, My Lovely,* and *The Long Good-bye.* Chandler also had a successful career as a Hollywood screenwriter.

BRUCE CHATWIN (1940–1989), originally an art expert at Sotheby's, went temporarily blind and began to travel in Africa and the Sudan in order to recuperate and was converted to a nomadic life of writing. His work combines fiction, anthropology, asceticism, and travel. His books include *In Patagonia,* which won the Hawthornden Prize and the E. M. Forster Award of the American Academy and Institute of Arts and Letters, and *On the Black Hill,* which won the Whitbread Award for a first novel. Chatwin was born in Sheffield, England.

JOHN CHEEVER (1912–1982) sold his first story, "Expelled," to *The New Republic* after he was thrown out of Thayer Academy in Massachusetts at the age of seventeen. By the time he was twenty-two, *The New Yorker* was accepting his work, and for years he was a frequent and celebrated contributor to that publication and other major magazines. His novels include *The Wapshot Chronicle, The Wapshot Scandal, Bullet Park, Falconer,* and *The World of Apples.* His collected stories won both the Pulitzer Prize and National Book Critics Circle Award in 1979. His posthumously published journals revealed his daily attention and habits of mastery in his art, as well as his difficulties with alcoholism and bisexuality.

ANTON CHEKHOV (1860–1904) continues to be the short story writer with whom all others are compared. A Russian medical doctor from a modest family, whom he helped to support, Chekhov initially turned to writing humorous sketches for newspapers as a way of adding to his income. He was taken up by the literary establishment of the day and was increasingly able to devote his time to writing. His collected stories run to a dozen volumes. Among his best-known stories are "The Lady with the Dog," "The Horse-Stealers," "The Duel," "In the Ravine," and "Ward Six." His plays *The Cherry Orchard* and *The Sea Gull* continue to be popular on stage, and the play *Uncle Vanya* has been adapted in film. Chekhov suffered from tuberculosis and died at a health resort in Badenweiler, Germany, in the presence of his wife, the stage actress Olga Knipper.

LYDIA CHUKOVSKAYA (1907–), writer, editor, and biographer of important Soviet figures, is the author of the novels *The Deserted House* and *Going Under*. For many years, her work was not published in the Soviet Union but was circulated underground because she aroused controversy by openly criticizing the Soviet government. In 1974, she was expelled from the country for defending writers Alexander Solzhenitsyn and Boris Pasternak, who had likewise been expelled. Her writing has been favorably compared with that of Solzhenitsyn, Pasternak, and the persecuted Russian poet Anna Akhmatova, who was Chukovskaya's lifelong friend and the central subject of her journals.

JEAN COCTEAU (1889–1963) experimented in numerous artistic media—poetry, fiction, criticism, drama, film, ballet, painting, illustration, opera—and defined the avant-garde in the twentieth century. He promoted and collaborated with artist Pablo Picasso, composers Igor Stravinsky and Erik Satie, and chanteuse Edith Piaf, among others. A dazzling talker and conspicuous opium addict, he liked publicity and was frequently mentioned in the press. His diaries, begun thirteen years before his death, have been published in six volumes, titled *Past Tense.*

SAMUEL TAYLOR COLERIDGE (1772–1834) was the intellectual center of the English romantic movement. His *Biographia Literaria* is among the finest works of literary criticism of the time and contains recollections about Coleridge's close friend William Wordsworth, with whom he published *Lyrical Ballads.* Coleridge's poems "The Rime of the Ancient Mariner," "Kubla Khan," "Christabel," and "Dejection: An Ode," have long secured him a place in the collective imagination of students and readers.

JOSEPH CONRAD (1857–1924), the self-educated son of a Polish nobleman, spent an adventurous youth working on British merchant ships, rising to the rank of captain. A naturalized British citizen, he left the sea to settle in London and write fiction in his adopted language. *Nostromo, The Heart of Darkness, An Outcast of the Islands, Lord Jim*, and *The Secret Agent*, which was the world's first novel of espionage, are among Conrad's masterpieces. With Ford Maddox Ford, Conrad collaborated on the novels *The Inheritors* and *Romance,* using new literary techniques to create effects corresponding to those of impressionist painting.

FRANK CONROY (1936–) is director of the Iowa Writers' Workshop, America's oldest and most prestigious creative-writing program. Formerly, he directed the literature panel of the National Endowment of the Arts and taught writing at the Massachusetts Institute of Technology. His short stories, collected in *Midair,* have appeared in *The New Yorker* and *Esquire* and are anthologized in *American Short Story Masterpieces* and *Best American Short Stories.* His first book, *Stop-time,* a memoir, became an immediate contemporary classic on its publication in the mid-1960s and was followed in the mid-1990s by a novel, *Body and Soul.*

JAMES FENIMORE COOPER (1789–1851), son of the man who named Cooperstown, New York, is one of the founders of American literature. His novel *The Pilot* was the first American sea novel, and *The Pioneers* introduced the character Natty Bumpo, who through many generations of readers became a byword for the natural man uncorrupted by civilization. Cooper renewed Natty in his famous novels *The Last of the Mohicans* and *The Deerslayer,* which depict New England frontier America.

NOËL COWARD (1899–1973), British playwright, actor, singer, composer, screenwriter, and cabaret performer, found audiences on both sides of the Atlantic, for his droll, sophisticated wit. Among his stage productions were *The Vortex, Calvacade,* and *Blithe Spirit.*

GUY DAVENPORT (1927–   ), American short story writer and essayist, is the author of *The Jules Verne Steam Balloon* and *Every Force Evolves a Form.*

ANNIE DILLARD (1945–   ) wrote the narrative *Pilgrim at Tinker Creek,* which won the Pulitzer Prize for general nonfiction in 1975. She is the author of nine other books, including the memoir *An American Childhood* and the novel *The Living.* She lives in Connecticut.

JOHN DOS PASSOS (1896–1970) is remembered for the social realism and documentary techniques of his novelistic trilogy, *U.S.A.,* a vast panorama of American life in the first half of the twentieth century. With a young Ernest Hemingway and e.e. cummings, Dos Passos served in an ambulance corps during World War I. Later, he was a newspaperman, freelance writer, and dramatist whose work focused on individual freedom and social conscience. His diaries were published posthumously, under the title *The Fourteenth Chronicle,* and include his correspondence with Hemingway, Sherwood Anderson, F. Scott Fitzgerald, and other prominent figures of the 1920s and 1930s.

ANNA DOSTOYEVSKY (1846–1918) first met her husband-to-be, Russian novelist Fyodor Dostoyevsky, when he gave her a job taking dictation for his short novel *The Gambler*. Her diaries, begun shortly after their wedding, recount her devotion to him in the face of many difficulties, including the death of their three-month-old daughter, Sonya, and her husband's bouts of despair. From her diaries she wrote *Reminiscences*, published after her death.

FYODOR DOSTOYEVSKY (1821–1881) ranks as one of the world's great masters of the psychologically realistic novel. His classic works include *Crime and Punishment, The Brothers Karamazov, The Idiot,* and *Notes from Underground*. As a young man, he was charged with subversive activities against the czarist regime and was sentenced to death. Facing the firing squad, he was at the last instant given a commuted sentence of four years' imprisonment in Siberia, followed by four years in the army. After these experiences, he traveled extensively in Europe and went through ruinous periods of compulsive gambling in Wiesbaden, Germany. Ultimately, his marriage to Anna had a soothing effect and he was able to work more steadily and prosper, though throughout his life he was plagued by epilepsy. In addition to his novels and stories, he wrote articles on social and political topics for the journals of the day and was a publisher and editor of the periodicals *Time* and *Epoch*.

RITA DOVE (1952–   ) is the author of numerous collections of poetry, a novel, a story collection, and a verse drama. In 1987, she was awarded the Pulitzer Prize in poetry for *Thomas and Beulah*. In 1993, she was appointed by the Library of Congress to a two-year tenure as America's Poet Laureate. She also has received the American Academy of Poets' Lavan Award and the Literary Lion Citation from the New York Public Library. She is Commonwealth Professor of English at the University of Virginia and lives near Charlottesville, Virginia, with her husband and daughter.

THEODORE DREISER (1871–1945) was a prominent American literary figure in the early decades of the twentieth century. While writing his novels, he also worked as the editor of the Butterick's catalogs of women's clothing patterns and later worked in Hollywood as a scriptwriter. Often criticized for the clumsiness of his prose style, he is usually praised for the power and significance of his two great novels, *An American Tragedy* and *Sister Carrie*.

ANDRE DUBUS (1936–) is the author of numerous story collections and novels, including *Separate Flights, Adultery & Other Choices, Finding a Girl in America, Voices from the Moon,* and *The Last Worthless Evening*. His work appears regularly in noted periodicals, and he is much admired for the human complexity and tenderness he weaves into short story masterpieces such as "A Father's Story" and "The Fat Girl." Dubus lives in Haverhill, Massachusetts.

JOHN GREGORY DUNNE (1932–) is the author of ten books and, with his wife, Joan Didion, six screenplays. His novels include *Vegas, True Confessions, Dutch Shea, Jr., The Red White and Blue,* and *Playland*. He lives in New York.

LAWRENCE DURRELL (1912–1990), English novelist and travel writer, was born in India and lived there until he was ten, when his family moved back to England. As a young man, he tried jobs in nightclubs, in real estate, and with the Jamaica police; he once said he had been driven to writing by "sheer ineptitude." American writer Henry Miller helped Durrell publish his first prose work, *The Black Book,* and the two remained lifelong friends. Durrell made his name with *The Alexandria Quartet,* interlocking novels, each narrated through the point of view of a different character party to a single story of relationships, intrigue, and love.

GERALD EARLY (1952–) is a professor of English and Afro-American Studies at Washington University in St. Louis. His essays and articles on modern American culture have appeared in

The New York Times Book Review, American Poetry Review, Antaeus, and *Best American Essays*. His collections include *Tuxedo Junction* and *The Culture of Bruising*.

GRETEL ERHLICH (1946–   ) was born in Santa Barbara, California, and educated at Bennington College and UCLA Film School. In 1976 she moved to Wyoming, where she worked on sheep and cattle ranches. Her books include: *The Solace of Open Spaces,* essays; *Drinking Dry Clouds,* short stories; *Heart Mountain,* a novel; *Arctic Heart,* poems; and *A Match to the Heart,* a memoir. She received the Harold B. Vurcell Award for distinguished prose from the American Academy and Institute of Arts and Letters. She now divides her time between Wyoming and the central coast of California.

GEORGE ELIOT was the pseudonym of Mary Anne Evans (1819–1880), a British novelist whose work defines much of the Victorian era. Forced by the times to publish under a man's name and to live under social opprobrium because her life partner, George Lewes, could not obtain a divorce from his wife, Eliot possessed a keen sense of moral imperatives, as is evident in her writing. Lewes, whom she met while working as an assistant editor at a literary periodical, encouraged her to write fiction, and her first major success came with her second book, *Adam Bede,* which was published when she was forty. Her novels include *The Mill on the Floss, Silas Marner,* and *Middlemarch* and are an established part of the canon of world literature.

RALPH WALDO EMERSON (1803–1882), American poet, essayist, and philosopher, was the chief spokesman of transcendentalism, which is characterized by its reliance on intuition to perceive the spiritual aspects of life. Emerson's well-known works include *Essays, The Conduct of Life,* and *The American Scholar.* His writing and thought influenced the work of his friend and neighbor Henry David Thoreau, who was part of the same literary circle in Concord, Massachusetts. Emerson's gift for epigram and aphorism have made his diaries widely quoted.

LAWRENCE FERLINGHETTI (1919–   ) has long been one of the chief spokesmen of the beat movement. As founder of City Lights Bookstore and Press, Ferlinghetti has sponsored and published such writers as Allen Ginsberg, Gary Snyder, Jack Kerouac, Gregory Corso, and William S. Burroughs. Ferlinghetti's own books of poetry include *Pictures of the Gone World* and *A Coney Island of the Mind*.

M. F. K. FISHER (1908–1992) combined her favorite pastimes, writing and cooking. In books such as *Serve It Forth*, *The Art of Eating*, and *How to Cook a Wolf*, she established a worldview as seen from her dining-room table, a view that extended to all of life. She was a Member of the American Academy and Institute of Arts and Letters. She lived in Glen Ellen, California.

F. SCOTT FITZGERALD (1896–1940), both as writer and personality, defined the American Jazz Age, the Roaring Twenties. His first novel, *This Side of Paradise*, was followed by other hugely successful books, including *Tender Is the Night* and *The Great Gatsby*. With his wife, Zelda, he lived a much-publicized international life, associating with Hemingway and other artistic giants and socialites of the period. Zelda's periodic nervous breakdowns and her death in a fire at a sanitorium to which she was committed marked Fitzgerald's life with tragedy. At the time of his death, hastened by alcoholism, he left behind an unfinished novel, *The Last Tycoon*, considered by some critics to be his greatest.

GUSTAVE FLAUBERT (1821–1880) kept an intimate notebook during his eighteenth and nineteenth years, when he was an unknown adolescent dreaming of literary fame. Many of the themes, events, and elements of style that would develop in his masterpiece, *Madame Bovary*, appear, quite remarkably for a young writer, as conscious concerns in his journal. His painstaking effort to find *le mot juste* created a new level of stylistic accomplishment in prose, and his vision, at once romantic and anti-romantic, opened a new era in novel-writing. Born in Rouen, France, which is part of the setting of *Madame Bovary*, Flaubert is recognized worldwide.

E. M. FORSTER (1879–1970), English novelist, short story writer, and essayist, is best known for his novels *A Passage to India*, *A Room with a View*, and *Howards End*. Forster's famous epigraph for *Howards End*—"Only connect"—is the great theme of his novels and has become a byword for empathy. A series of Forster's lectures drawn together in a book, *Aspects of the Novel*, has long been a recognized source of authority on the art of fiction.

ANNE FRANK (1929–1944) was thirteen years old when she and her parents closed themselves, with another German Jewish family, into the attic of an Amsterdam warehouse to live in hiding from the Nazis. Her diary reveals not only the strain of group survival in intolerably cramped quarters but also the tender, thoughtful development of the author. After two years in hiding, the group was discovered, and Anne Frank died in the extermination camp at Belsen-Belsen. A natural writer, gifted with humor and insight, she is perhaps the world's most widely read and beloved diarist.

LYNN FREED (1945–   ), born in Durban, South Africa, discovered very early her desire to travel and live the life of a middle-class gypsy. She leapt at her first chance to go overseas, as an American Field Service Exchange Scholar. Since then she has lived in New York, Boston, Montreal, and San Francisco and has traveled extensively, often writing about her journeys and contributing personal pieces and essays to major periodicals such as *The New York Times*, *Mirabella*, *Travel & Leisure*, and *Harper's*. Her novels include *Home Ground* and *The Bungalow*, both placed in South Africa. She has taught literature and writing at the University of Texas and at the University of Oregon and now lives in Sonoma, California.

ROBERT FROST (1874–1963) was born in San Francisco but moved east in 1885 and became known for his poetry about New England. He was awarded four Pulitzer Prizes, in 1921, 1931, 1937, and 1943. His poetry is widely anthologized and has been learned by heart by generations of American students. Among his best-known poems are "Birches," "Stopping by Woods on a Snowy Day," "The Road Not Taken," and "Mending Wall." Near the end of his life, he brought a rare moment of public stature to poetry when he was nationally televised reading "The Gift Outright" at John F. Kennedy's presidential inauguration.

ATHOL FUGARD (1932–   ), South African dramatist and theater director, worked as a seaman before settling into a career as an actor. He cofounded the Space Experimental Theatre in Capetown. Under apartheid, Fugard's work met with official opposition and censorship because of his belief in human equality. His plays include *Blood Knot*, *Master Harold and the Boys*, and *Statements After an Arrest under the Immorality Act*.

TESS GALLAGHER (1943–   ), American poet, short story writer, and essayist, was married to writer Raymond Carver, with whom she collaborated on a screenplay based on Anna and Fyodor Dostoyevsky's marriage. Gallagher is the author of a story collection, *The Lover of Horses*, a collection of essays, *A Concert of Tenses*, and numerous collections of poetry, including *Portable Kisses*, *Under Stars*, *Instructions to the Double*, *Willingly*, *Amplitude*, and *Moon Crossing Bridge*, which is a keeningly elegiac volume on the loss of Carver, who died of lung cancer in 1988. Gallagher lives in Washington State.

ANDRÉ GIDE (1869–1951), French writer and editor, was awarded the 1947 Nobel Prize for literature. His varied and passionate writings include poetry, fiction, philosophical and political essays, satire, plays, and autobiography, more than fifty books in all. Concerned with the conflict between the spiritual and the physical, Gide wrote of his early and unhappy marriage to his beloved cousin Madeleine, his troubling discovery and ultimate celebration of his homosexuality, his concerns with religion, morality, integrity, and social justice. Among his better-known works are *The Counterfeiters, The Vatican Swindle,* and *The Immoralist.* He was the founder of the magazine *La Nouvelle Revue Française* and kept up a voluminous correspondence. In his *Journals,* which are comprehensive and cover the years 1889–1949, Gide pursues his ideal of perfect frankness, not failing to include trenchant and witty observations on his famous contemporaries as well as himself.

ELLEN GILCHRIST (1935–) is the author of a novel, *The Annunciation,* and three collections of short stories: *In the Land of Dreams, Drunk with Love,* and *Victory over Japan,* for which she won the National Book Award. She lives in Fayetteville, Arkansas.

ALLEN GINSBERG (1926–1997), emerging from the beat movement, became a leading counterculture figure. The title poem of his first book, *Howl,* was named by his friend the writer Jack Kerouac, who said the poem seemed to release "the pent-up rage and frustrations of the inner being." Among Ginsberg's other works are *Kaddish, The Fall of America,* and *Reality Sandwiches.* He was a recipient of the National Book Award.

GEORGE GISSING (1857–1903) was expelled from Owen's College in Manchester, England, after he was caught stealing money, which he intended to use to help reform a prostitute, whom he later married. His novels, most notably *New Grub Street,* deal with the degrading effects of poverty. Ever hard-pressed, he was driven to produce some thirty books in less than thirty years.

GAIL GODWIN (1937–) has kept journals since the age of thirteen. Her short story "Dream Children" is considered one of the masterpieces of the form. Her novels include *The Odd*

Woman, A Mother and Two Daughters, A Southern Family, and *The Good Husband*. She lives in upstate New York.

WITOLD GOMBROWICZ (1904–1969), Polish novelist, one of the major writers in his language in this century, spent most of his life working as a bank employee in Argentina, where he had gone on a visit shortly before the outbreak of World War II. His works include *A Recollection of Adolescence, Pornography*, and *Possessed*. His diaries, published in three volumes from 1957 to 1966, revealed the personal sources of the sexual and psychological themes of his fiction.

EDMOND (1822–1896) **AND JULES** (1830–1870) **DE GONCOURT,** known as the Brothers Goncourt, collaborated on novels, histories, dramas, memoirs, and a voluminous *Journal*, which records the *Belle Époque* in Paris and offers glimpses of the Goncourts' prestigious contemporaries—Gustave Flaubert, George Sand, Victor Hugo, Charles Baudelaire, Edgar Degas, Ivan Turgenev, and others.

MARY GORDON (1949–   ), noted novelist, essayist, short story writer, and poet, is the author of the novels *Final Payments, Men and Angels*, and *The Company of Women*. Her work appears frequently in leading magazines. She lives in New York City.

MAXIM GORKY (1868–1936) is considered the first great Russian writer to emerge from the ranks of the proletariat. In addition to writing novels and stories, he founded a publishing house that brought out the work of Andreyev, Bunin, and others. Gorky committed much of his literary earnings and his energy to the Bolshevik revolution, endeavoring at the same time to preserve the cultural past. Gorky's diaries and autobiography are particularly interesting as records of his personal and literary friendships with Tolstoy, Chekhov, and others.

JULIAN GREEN (1900–   ) was born in Paris of American parents. He traveled widely, attended the University of Virginia, and later, during World War II, lived in the United States, broadcasting over the radio to the French under German occupation. He has always regarded Paris as his home and wrote his novels, autobiographies (*Personal Record* and *Memory of Happy Days*), and diaries in French. His work is noted for its awareness of sin and human violence. His most recent book, published when he was ninety-five, is *Dixie*.

GRAHAM GREENE (1904–1991), prolific English novelist, essayist, playwright, and short story writer, is known for combining psychological studies, theological dilemmas, and adventure in international settings. Some of his popular books are *The Heart of the Matter, The Quiet American, Orient Express, Loser Takes All,* and *The Honorary Consul.*

SUSAN GRIFFIN (1943–   ) is a well-known feminist poet, essayist, lecturer, teacher, playwright, and filmmaker. She is the author of more than twenty books, including *Woman and Nature: The Roaring Inside Her, Pornography and Silence: Culture's Revenge Against Nature,* and *A Chorus of Stones.* She lives in Berkeley, California.

ROBERT GRUDIN (1938–   ) is the author of *Book*, a novel, which has been reprinted on CD-ROM, with his *A Writer's Journal, 1990–92,* by Voyager. His other books include *Time and the Art of Living, The Grace of Great Things,* and a work in progress, *On Dialogue: An Essay in Free Thought.* He teaches at the University of Oregon.

DORIS GRUMBACH (1918–   ), distinguished American novelist and critic, has been literary editor of *The New Republic* and a regular book reviewer for National Public Radio. Her novels include *Chamber Music, The Missing Person, The Ladies, The Magician's Girl,* and *The Book of Knowledge.* Her popular memoirs, begun as she turned seventy, include *Coming Into the End Zone, Extra Innings,* and *Life in a Day.* She lives in Sargentville, Maine.

DONALD HALL (1928–   ) is the author of numerous prize-winning books of poetry, including *The One Day*, winner of the National Book Critics Circle Award; he has also written essays, children's books, and criticism. Among his works are *Their Ancient Glittering Eyes, The Museum of Clear Ideas*, and *Life Work*, a deeply personal and inspiring meditation on art and life. Hall was married to the poet Jane Kenyon, who died in 1995. He lives on the family farm in New Hampshire.

EMMA HARDY (1840–1912) was the first wife of the English poet and novelist Thomas Hardy. Their marriage was difficult, and Hardy retreated from her into his writing and fame. Her diaries indicate her forceful nature and determined loyalty, as well as the small domestic details of their life. Her death inspired in Hardy one of the finest sequences of love poetry ever written.

THOMAS HARDY (1840–1928) began his adult life as an architect specializing in churches. He wrote a good deal of poetry and fiction and published one novel anonymously without finding a readership. He was thirty-three when a novel published under his own name was successful, enabling him to undertake a literary career. His major novels include *Jude the Obscure, Far from the Madding Crowd*, and *Tess of the D'Urbervilles*. Powerful and naturalistic, Hardy's vision is governed by a sense of the randomness of fate. As a poet, he is considered with William Butler Yeats, to be one of the primary voices spanning the nineteenth and twentieth centuries in the English language.

JIM HARRISON (1937–   ), fiction writer and poet, lives in rural Michigan. He is the author of two collections of novellas, *A Woman Lit by Fireflies* and *Legends of the Fall*, and several novels, including *Farmer, Warlock, Wolf*, and *A Good Day to Die*. A popular literary writer, whose books have never been out of print, Harrison is also a writer's writer, whose intelligence, heart and careful attention to craft have inspired the work of others.

Among his volumes of poetry are *Plain Song, Returning to the Earth,* and *Outlyer.*

STRATIS HAVIARAS (1935–) is the author of four books of poetry in Greek and one book of poetry and two novels, *When the Tree Sings* and *The Heroic Age,* in English. His works have been translated and published in many languages. He is the curator of the George Edward Woodbury Poetry Room in the Harvard College Library, and the editor of *Harvard Review.* He lives in Cambridge, Massachusetts, with his wife, Heather Cole, and his daughter, Elektra.

NATHANIEL HAWTHORNE (1804–1864) was descended from New Englanders who participated in the Salem witch trials in the seventeenth century and, later, in persecuting the Quakers. A sense of inherited guilt informs famous Hawthorne stories such as "Ethan Brand" and *The Scarlet Letter.* He was a close friend of Melville and Longfellow and, with Emerson and Thoreau, was part of the transcendentalist movement and the American renaissance in literature.

EDWARD HOAGLAND (1932–), American essayist and naturalist, teaches at Bennington College in Vermont. His books include *Heart's Desire, The Courage of Turtles,* and *Seven Rivers West.*

GARRETT HONGO (1951–) is the author of two volumes of poetry, *Yellow Light* and *The River of Heaven,* which won the 1987 Lamont Poetry Prize. His most recent book is *Volcano: A Memoir of Hawai'i,* published in 1995. He lives in Eugene, Oregon, with his wife, Cynthia Thiessen, and their two children.

JAMES D. HOUSTON (1933–) has written six novels, among them *Gig, Love Life,* and *Continental Drift.* His nonfiction includes *Californians: Searching for the Golden State,* and *Farewell to Manzanar,* which he wrote with his wife, Jeanne Wakatsuki Houston. He lives in Santa Cruz, California, and teaches at the University of California.

JEANNE WAKATSUKI HOUSTON (1934–) is coauthor of *Farewell to Manzanar*, the classic account of the World War II internment of Japanese-Americans, and *Don't Cry, It's Only Thunder*, about Amerasian orphans during the war in Vietnam. Her essays and stories, first collected in *Beyond Manzanar: Views of Asian-American Womanhood*, are widely anthologized. She is a recipient of a Humanitas Prize, the Wonder Woman Award, and a United States–Japan Cultural Exchange Fellowship.

MAUREEN HOWARD (1930–), novelist and critic, is the author of *Facts of Life*, a memoir, winner of the Book Critics Circle Award. Her novels include *Bridgeport Bus*, *Expensive Habits*, and *Natural History*.

EUGENE IONESCO (1912–1994), Romanian-born French dramatist, lived in Paris, where he pioneered the absurdist movement that emerged in the 1950s and included prominent playwrights such as Samuel Beckett, Edward Albee, and Harold Pinter. Growing out of existentialism and post–World War II angst, Ionesco's work is characterized by non sequiturs, dream logic, and strange metamorphoses. Among his plays are *The Rhinoceros*, *The Bald Soprano*, and *The Chairs*.

WASHINGTON IRVING (1783–1859) has remained a beloved American figure through the popularity of his folktales "The Legend of Sleepy Hollow" and "Rip Van Winkle," which were originally published pseudonymously in *The Sketch Book of Geoffrey Crayon, Gent*. His humorous and satirical pieces drawn from New York history and lore made him famous, but he is also known for his biographies of George Washington, Mahomet, and the novelist Oliver Goldsmith.

CHRISTOPHER ISHERWOOD (1904–1986) was part of the talented group of left-wing young British writers of the 1930s that included W. H. Auden and Stephen Spender. Isherwood's early fiction, collected in *Berlin Stories*, based on his experience of pre–World War II decadence in Germany, became the source of the Broadway play and Hollywood movie *Cabaret*. With Auden, Isherwood wrote several verse plays and traveled to China and collaborated on *Journey to War*, about the conflict between Japan and China. In 1939, he emigrated to California to write screenplays and, in 1946, became an American citizen. He translated *The Yogi Aphorisms of Patanjali* as well as Baudelaire's *Intimate Journals*.

ALICE JAMES (1848–1892), sister of the philosopher-psychologist William James and the novelist Henry James, lived most of her life as an invalid, following a severe illness at the age of sixteen. However, she maintained a frequent correspondence with her brothers and kept a journal, whose eloquence reflects a significant inner life and literary gift.

HENRY JAMES (1843–1916), American short story writer, novelist, and man of letters, is one of the primary and continuing influences on modern fiction because of his psychological insight and artistic mastery, his formal and technical innovations in every aspect of fiction, and his critical writings. His notebooks reveal his imaginative process and his devotion to art. His works of fiction include *What Maisie Knew, Washington Square, The Portrait of a Lady, The Turn of the Screw, The Aspern Papers* and many, many others. In 1915, he became a British subject after many years of living in England and Europe.

DIANE JOHNSON (1934–) is respected for novels such as *The Shadow Knows* and *Burning*. She wrote the authorized biography of crime writer Dashiell Hammett, and she collaborated with director Stanley Kubrick on the screenplay for horror writer Stephen King's *The Shining*. Her literary criticism appears regularly in *The New York Review of Books* and *The New York Times*. She lives in Northern California.

DONALD JUSTICE (1925–) was born in Miami, Florida, and now teaches at the University of Florida in Gainesville. His volumes of poetry include *The Summer Anniversaries, Night Light,*

Departures, and *The Sunset Maker.* His *Selected Poems* was awarded the 1980 Pulitzer Prize.

FRANZ KAFKA (1883–1924), influential Austrian writer, is perhaps most famous for his short story "The Metamorphosis," in which Gregor Samsa, a character very like Kafka himself, wakes up one morning to discover he's turned into an enormous cockroach. Using a precise, lucid style to recount grotesquely unreal occurrences, Kafka points out the comic absurdity and futility of everyday life. His novels *The Castle, The Trial,* and *Amerika* were unfinished when he died of tuberculosis and were edited and published by his friend Max Brod.

ALFRED KAZIN (1915–) is an eminent American literary critic whose works include *The Inmost Leaf, Bright Book of Life,* and most recently *Writing Was Everything: Life as a Critic 1934–1994.* He grew up poor in New York City; it has been said of him that "reading got Kazin out of the ghetto, but writing gave him a home." He was twenty-seven when he published his landmark analysis of modern American fiction, *On Native Grounds.*

EDMUND KEELEY (1928–) has published a number of volumes of poetry in translation, books of nonfiction, and novels, including *A Wilderness Called Peace* and *School for Pagan Lovers.* He is a recipient of the Rome Prize for fiction and the Harold Morton Landon Award for translation. He lives in Princeton, New Jersey.

THOMAS KENEALLY (1935–) has become known worldwide for his Booker Award–winning novel, *Schindler's List,* depicting the German industrialist Oscar Schindler, who secretly worked to save hundreds of Jews from being sent to Hitler's death camps. Keneally's other books include *The Chant of Jimmy Blacksmith* and *A Family Madness.* Australian-born, of Irish descent, Keneally is a founding leader of the Australian Republican movement, a political concern that runs through his novel *River Town.*

JACK KEROUAC (1922–1969), widely recognized as a central figure in the beat movement, became instantly famous with his first novel, *On the Road*. Written in Kerouac's lyric "spontaneous prose," the novel follows a young man's travels across America and through society's fringes and taboos. The book inspired many young people to break with the conventional mores of the 1950s and adopt the beat lifestyle or take to the road like Kerouac's hero, who was largely based on the author himself. His social influence continued into the counterculture of the late 1960s, and today Kerouac remains a legendary figure of the outsider. His other novels include *The Dharma Bums*, *The Subterraneans*, and *Big Sur*. Alcohol and drug use contributed to his death at the age of forty-seven.

MAXINE HONG KINGSTON (1940–), Chinese-American novelist and autobiographer, was born and educated in California. Her work explores the tensions between Eastern and Western cultures and employs techniques of fiction, memoir, and mythology. Her books include the novel *Tripmaster Monkey—His Fake Book* and *The Woman Warrior*, which won the National Book Critics Circle Award for nonfiction. She teaches at the University of California, Berkeley.

CAROLYN KIZER (1925–) founded the literary journal *Poetry Northwest* in Seattle, Washington. Among her poetry collections are *The Ungrateful Garden*, *Knock Upon My Silence*, and *The Nearness of You: Poems for Men*. In 1985, her poetry collection *Yin* won the Pulitzer Prize. Her translations from several languages, including Urdu and Chinese, are gathered in *Carrying Over*.

ANNE LAMOTT (1954–) is the author of four novels: *Rosie*, *Hard Laughter*, *Joe Jones*, and *All New People*. The journal of her son's first year, *Operating Instructions*, and her book-length essay on writing, *Bird By Bird*, have inspired thousands of readers. Lamott lives and teaches in Northern California.

JAMES LAUGHLIN (1914–   ), having suffered a terrible shock as a youth when Ezra Pound told him he would never be a poet, became the founder and editor of New Directions Publishing, which has had a profound influence on world literature. As both a magazine and book press, New Directions brought out the work of Pound, William Carlos Williams, Thomas Merton, and many other important, often avant-garde, figures. Laughlin, in spite of Pound's prediction, also became a recognized poet. His books of poetry include *The River* and *The Bird of Endless Time*. He has taught at the University of California, San Diego, the University of Iowa, and Brown University and is a member of the American Academy and Institute of Arts and Letters. He lives in Norfolk, Connecticut.

PHILIP LEVINE (1928–   ) was born in Detroit. He has published sixteen books of poetry, two of which, *Ashes* and *What Work Is*, won the National Book Award. His other books include *The Bread of Time: Toward an Autobiography* and *The Simple Truth*. He has kept journals and used them in his writing since 1972.

C. S. LEWIS (1898–1963), English novelist, critic, and Christian philosopher, is widely known for his fantasy works for children, *The Narnia Chronicles*, and for his science fiction series, *Out of the Silent Planet*, *Perelandra*, and *That Hideous Strength*. His finest adult novel, *Till We Have Faces*, is a retelling of the Cupid and Psyche myth. Lewis was a professor at Cambridge University.

ANNE MORROW LINDBERGH (1906–   ) was married to American aviator Charles Lindbergh, who in 1927 made the historic first solo flight across the Atlantic. She has written two memoirs of flying with her husband, *North to the Orient* and *Listen! The Wind*, two books of poetry, and a popular book of essays on women's themes, *Gift from the Sea*. The Lindberghs' life was shadowed by the tragic kidnapping and death of their infant son. Sensitive and introverted, Anne Lindbergh wrote in her diaries about the effort to reconcile the demands of being a wife and mother much in the public eye with her own needs as a writer.

AUDRE LORDE (1934–1992) has been described as "Black feminist lesbian warrior poet mother." She is the author of nine collections of poetry and five books of prose. A professor at Hunter College in Manhattan, she received the Walt Whitman Citation of Merit and was named New York State Poet in 1991.

NORMAN MAILER (1923–   ) attained recognition with his first novel, *The Naked and the Dead*, based on his experiences in the military in World War II. A leading writer of his generation, he helped define the "new journalism" that emerged in the 1960s, combining the techniques of fiction and nonfiction. His 1967 Vietnam protest book, *The Armies of the Night*, won the Pulitzer Prize and the National Book Award. In *The Executioner's Song*, he studied Gary Gilmore, a convicted multiple killer sentenced to death. Mailer's work often involves Hemingwayesque obsessions with violence, courage, and sex. His books include *Tough Guys Don't Dance*, *Harlot's Ghost*, *Advertisements for Myself*, and *Oswald's Tale*, a study of John Kennedy's assassin, Lee Harvey Oswald. Mailer is a longtime resident of Brooklyn.

CLARENCE MAJOR (1936–   ) is the prize-winning author of seven novels, a collection of short stories, nine poetry volumes, and three works of nonfiction. He has contributed to *The New York Times* and *The Washington Post*, and to more than two hundred other periodicals and anthologies. He lives in Davis, California, where he teaches at the University of California.

OSIP MANDELSTAM (1891–1938) grew up in St. Petersburg in prerevolutionary Russia and took a pessimistic view of the Soviet era. Following three collections of poems, *Stone*, *Tristia*, and *Poems*, he fell under increasing state censorship and persecution, and no further work of his appeared in publication in his lifetime. He was arrested during the Stalinist purges of the 1930s and apparently died on the way to a prison camp. He is often noted as one of the greatest Russian poets of the century. His *Moscow Notebooks* were published posthumously.

THOMAS MANN (1875–1955), awarded the Nobel Prize for literature in 1929, drew on world mythology and his German bourgeois family background to develop themes of dualism between material life and the human spirit. His novels and story collections include *Death in Venice, The Magic Mountain, Tonio Kröger,* and *Buddenbrooks*.

KATHERINE MANSFIELD (1888–1923), born in New Zealand and educated in England, published only three collections of short stories in her lifetime but attracted enduring recognition. Her best-known stories include "Bliss," "A Dill Pickle," and "The Garden Party." She died at thirty-five of tuberculosis. She was a friend of D. H. Lawrence, Aldous Huxley, and Virginia Woolf, and is said to be portrayed as the character Gudrun in Lawrence's *Women in Love* and as Beatrice Gilray in Huxley's *Point Counter Point*.

MARIE-ELISE (1950–   ) has had several different last names, parental, guardian-parental, and marital, but no longer uses any of them, preferring to create her own identity. In performance she accompanies her poems with the sign language employed by the deaf and with mime; the poems become a dance, intensifying the effects and expanding the potential of the oral tradition. She has been the subject of a video documentary, and her poems, including "Definition," "Diapering This Poem," and "Touching a Friend," have appeared in small magazines and the anthology *Woman as Writer*.

WILLIAM MATTHEWS (1942–   ) is the author of ten books of poems, a book of essays, and two volumes of poetry in translation. His recent books are *The Mortal City, 100 Epigrams from Martial,* and *Time and Money*. He received the 1995 National Book Critics Circle Award for poetry. He lives in New York City.

PETER MATTHIESSEN (1927–), American novelist, short story writer, travel writer, naturalist, explorer, Zen Buddhist, and a founding editor of *The Paris Review*, was born in New York City. His first novel, *Race Rock*, was written while Matthiessen supported himself as a commercial fisherman living on Long Island. Years later, he wrote *Men's Lives*, detailing the struggle of the Long Island commercial fishery to stay alive, and donated the profits from the book to the Long Island Commercial Fishermen's Association. Similarly, when Matthiessen wrote *In the Spirit of Crazy Horse*, an account of the 1975 shoot-out between Native American activists and the FBI, he gave the book's proceeds to the Native American cause, following an extended litigation in which the U.S. government sought to block publication of the book. In 1978, he received the National Book Award for *The Snow Leopard*, an introspective story of his trek across the Tibetan mountains as he sought to recover from his wife's death from cancer and to glimpse the rarest and most beautiful of the great cats. Matthiessen's other works include *Far Tortuga*, *At Play in the Fields of the Lord*, and *Killing Mister Watson*. Matthiessen lives on Long Island.

WILLIAM SOMERSET MAUGHAM (1874–1965) was one of the most successful playwrights on the London stage just before and after World War I. His fame as a short story writer began with the collection *The Trembling Leaf* (1921), which was followed by more than ten collections. His novels include *Of Human Bondage*, *The Painted Veil*, and *The Moon and Sixpence*.

ANDRÉ MAUROIS is the pen name of Émile Herzog (1885–1967), French novelist and critic, best known for his biographies of Shelley, Disraeli, George Sand, Voltaire, Victor Hugo, and Proust. He also wrote fantasies, tales for children, essays on writing, and a history of the United States. He taught literature at a number of American colleges and universities.

J. D. McCLATCHY (1945–) is the author of three books of poems, *Scenes from Another Life, Stars Principal*, and *The Rest of the Way*, as well as a collection of essays, *White Paper*. He has edited many other books and written four opera libretti. He is editor of *The Yale Review* and lives in Connecticut.

JAMES ALAN McPHERSON (1943–) won the 1978 Pulitzer Prize in fiction for his short story collection *Elbow Room*. He is also the author of an earlier collection, *Hue and Cry*. He teaches at the Iowa Writers' Workshop and is a contributing editor of *The Atlantic Monthly* and of *DoubleTake*.

HERMAN MELVILLE (1819–1891), in his lifetime, had only a small following and supported his family during the second half of life as a farmer and then customs inspector. It was not until some thirty years after his death that he began to be recognized as a great American writer. Born into a once-prominent, impoverished New York family, Melville tried clerking in a bank and teaching before taking to a life at sea. At various times, he deserted a ship, lived among cannibals, was involved in a mutiny, and worked as a harpooner—experiences on which he drew in writing travel memoirs, adventure stories, and, ultimately, his masterpiece, the novel *Moby-Dick*. He was a friend of Nathaniel Hawthorne, with whom he discussed the metaphysics reflected in the allegorical layers of his fiction. The final novel published in his lifetime, *The Confidence Man*, is an ambiguous work of literature, reflecting the trickster bent of an author condemned to live in obscurity. In his last five years, Melville worked on a novella, *Billy Budd*, which was published posthumously and has become widely read and dramatized in film. Melville's short story "Bartleby the Scrivener" ranks with the classics of the form.

H. L. MENCKEN (1880–1956), American newspaperman, editor, and writer, began his career on the Baltimore *Morning Herald* and later joined the Baltimore *Sun*, with which he was associated for the rest of his life. As literary editor of *Smart Set* and founding editor of *The American Mercury*, he exerted a strong influence on American political and cultural opinion. His books include *The American Language*, a pioneering work of philology, as well as numerous collections of essays, a three-volume autobiography, various poetry collections, plays, and a study of Friedrich Nietzsche.

THOMAS MERTON (1915–1969) was born in France of an English father and American mother and, from 1941, was a Trappist monk in Kentucky. He is known for his bestselling spiritual autobiography *The Seven Storey Mountain* and for his influence on religious thought. He was a friend of fiction writer Flannery O'Connor, with whom he shared his interest in literature and metaphysics.

LEONARD MICHAELS (1933–) is the author of two story collections, including *I Would Have Saved Them If I Could*, and of two novels, *The Men's Club* and *Sylvia;* he is the editor, with Christopher Ricks, of *The State of Language*, a collection of essays. He has been a longtime professor of English at the University of California, Berkeley.

ARTHUR MILLER (1915–) established himself as the leading American playwright of his generation with his Pulitzer Prize–winning Broadway play *Death of a Salesman*, which has been produced worldwide and continues to inspire stage and film audiences. He won a second Pulitzer and the New York Drama Critics Circle Award for *A View from the Bridge*. His short story "The Misfits," first published in *Esquire*, became the basis for his screenplay for the John Huston film starring Clark Gable and Marilyn Monroe, who was Miller's second wife. Among his other plays are *The Crucible*, *All My Sons*, and *Danger: Memory!* He lives in Connecticut with his wife, the photographer Inge Morath.

HENRY MILLER (1891–1980), son of a German-American tailor in Brooklyn, rebelled against his conventional upbringing and, after traveling and trying several occupations, moved to France in 1930. In the following nine years he published *Tropic of Cancer, Black Spring, Tropic of Capricorn,* and *Max and the White Phagocytes.* Autobiographical and sexually explicit, his work excited interest, protest, and censorship. The American editions of the two *Tropics* were not published until the 1960s, when he settled in Big Sur, California, and became a cult figure of the sexual revolution, only later to be unfavorably reassessed by feminist critics. Recently, the story of the love triangle involving Miller, his wife, and autoerotic diarist Anaïs Nin was made into a Hollywood movie, *Henry and June.* Miller's other books include *Sexus, Plexus,* and *Nexus.*

CZESLAW MILOSZ (1911–   ) Polish poet, novelist, and essayist, winner of the 1980 Nobel Prize for literature, was born in Lithuania. In 1936, his second book of poems, *Three Winters,* established his reputation. With the outbreak of World War II, Milosz began a life of exile, first in Paris and then California, and for forty-five years no book of his was published in Poland. He is the author of a novel, *The Seizure of Power.* His poems were collected in a single volume in 1988.

MICHEL EYQUEM DE MONTAIGNE (1533–1592) originated the literary form known as the essay. His aristocratic father, as an experiment in humanist upbringing, hired a tutor who spoke only Latin to Montaigne until he was six, and each morning the child was awakened to the sound of music. Montaigne became a counselor in the Bordeaux parliament, where he met Étienne de la Boétie, a young judge, who encouraged his interest in philosophy and whose death caused Montaigne to meditate more deeply on life. He retired to his château in Dordogne and devoted himself to reading and writing, publishing his first two books of essays in 1580. His work, characterized by a fearless, all-questioning honesty, sympathy, and wisdom regarding human nature, influenced Pascal's *Pensées* and the subsequent development of the personal essay. Montaigne's diaries detail his travels to the spas of Switzerland, Germany, and Italy, trying to find relief from his gallstones, an affliction he bore with considerable grace.

LORRIE MOORE (1957–), short story writer and novelist, is the author of *Anagrams, Like Life,* and *Who Will Run the Frog Hospital?* She lives in Madison, Wisconsin, where she teaches at the University of Wisconsin.

THOMAS MOORE (1779–1852), a close friend and biographer of Byron, was also known as a popular Irish romantic poet who often set his lyrics to traditional tunes. Among the best known of these are "The Harp That Once through Tara's Halls" and "Believe Me, If All Those Endearing Young Charms."

MALCOLM MUGGERIDGE (1903–1990), British journalist and television personality, was on the editorial staff of a number of periodicals, including the *Evening Standard* and the *Daily Telegraph*. From 1953 to 1957 he was editor of *Punch*, a magazine famous for its wry wit.

JOHN MUIR (1838–1914), Scottish-born American naturalist and writer, devoted much of his life to saving the natural beauties of the West, including the Yosemite Valley, from commercial exploitation. He recorded his journey on foot from Indiana to the Gulf of Mexico in a journal, published as *A Thousand Mile Walk to the Gulf.* His other books include *The Mountains of California* and *Our National Parks.*

MICHELE MURRAY (1933–1974) lived in Washington, D.C., with her husband and four children. She wrote literary criticism for *The New Republic, The Washington Post,* and other periodicals. The discovery at thirty-five that she had cancer impelled her to write four books, including *Nellie Cameron,* a children's book, and

A House of Good Proportion: Images of Women in Literature, which was one of the first anthologies of its kind. Seven months after her death, her first book of poems, *The Great Mother*, was published.

SIR HAROLD NICOLSON (1886–1968) was a British diplomat and member of Parliament, as well as a journalist and critic. His diary, spanning the years 1930 to 1964, runs to three million words. He was married to novelist Vita Sackville-West. With E. M. Forster, Lytton Strachey, Bertrand Russell, and others, the Nicolsons were part of the Bloomsbury group of artists surrounding Virginia and Leonard Woolf.

ANAÏS NIN (1903–1977), American writer, was born in Paris to parents of Spanish-Cuban descent. She is perhaps best known for her erotic sketches in *Delta of Venus* and *Little Birds*, which she wrote to fulfill the fantasies of a male patron who paid her by the page. Her voluminous diaries are a sexually explicit account of her self-discovery.

NAOMI SHIHAB NYE (1952–) grew up in St. Louis, Jerusalem, and San Antonio. She has been an itinerant visiting writer all her working life. Her recent books of poems are *Red Suitcase* and *Words Under the Words: Selected Poems*. She edited the prize-winning international anthology of poetry *This Same Sky* and the bilingual Mexican anthology *The Tree Is Older Than You Are*. Her recent children's picture books are *Sitti's Secrets* and *Benito's Dream Bottle*. She never puts her suitcase in the attic.

JOYCE CAROL OATES (1938–), one of the most eminent of contemporary literary figures and also one of the most prolific, is the author of works of fiction, poetry, plays, and criticism. Her novels include *Because It Is Bitter, and Because It Is My Heart*, *Black Water*, and *Zombie*. She has been a recipient of the National Book Award and is a Member of the American Academy and Institute of Arts and Letters. She teaches at Princeton University and, with her husband, Raymond Smith, founded and edits *The Ontario Review*.

EDNA O'BRIEN (1932–   ), Irish fiction writer, practiced pharmacy briefly before becoming a writer. Among her novels and story collections are *The Country Girls Trilogy* and *A Fanatic Heart*.

CLIFFORD ODETS (1906–1963) was the dominant voice of the American theater in the 1930s. Many of his plays are concerned with socialist themes of class struggle: *Waiting for Lefty, Arise and Sing,* and *Golden Boy.* He was a founder of the Group Theater and later turned to writing for Hollywood.

AMOS OZ (1939–   ) was born in Jerusalem and has made his life in Israel, where he is a leading figure in the peace movement. He is the author of novels: *To Know a Woman, Don't Pronounce It Night, Black Box;* of story collections: *Where the Jackals Howl, The Hill of Evil Council;* of essay collections: *Under the Blazing Light, The Silence of Heaven;* and of a children's novel, *Soumchi.* His works have been translated and published around the world, and he is an Officer of the Order of Arts and Letters of the French Republic. He was also given the German Publishers' Union International Peace Prize.

LINDA PASTAN (1932–   ) is the author of nine volumes of poetry, including *A Perfect Circle of Sun, Aspects of Eve, The Five Stages of Grief,* and *An Early Afterlife.* She has received the Dylan Thomas Award, a Pushcart Prize, and the Di Castagnola Award of the Poetry Society of America. From 1991 to 1995 she was Poet Laureate of Maryland.

CESARE PAVESE (1908–1950) committed suicide shortly after winning Italy's highest literary award, the Strega Prize. His diaries, published more than ten years after his death, revealed his lifelong inner torment and struggle to come to terms with an alien environment and to achieve a delicate balance between emotional maturity and poetic sensibility. His disappointments in seeking a "perfect love" and his pitiless self-analysis make for painful reading. His novels and stories, including *The Devil in the*

Hills and *Among Women Only,* reflect a mingling of realism, lyric feeling, and social sympathy.

SAMUEL PEPYS (1633–1703), son of a London tailor, rose to become secretary of the admiralty, member of Parliament, and president of the Royal Society. His *Diary,* written in shorthand, was not deciphered and published until 1825. It offers a particularly uninhibited view of mid-seventeenth-century England and stands as perhaps the oldest and best known of all English diaries.

SYLVIA PLATH (1932–1963) committed suicide in London several months after publishing her bestselling autobiographical novel, *The Bell Jar,* under the pseudonym Victoria Lucas. At the time of her death, she was separated from her husband, Ted Hughes, who is now England's Poet Laureate. Plath's works include the poetry volumes *The Colossus* and *Ariel.* Since her death, her published journal has become a source of study and interest to admirers, who recognize her as an important voice in the emergence of women's issues.

BEATRIX POTTER (1866–1943), English writer and illustrator, created some of the most famous children's books of all time, including *The Tale of Peter Rabbit.* Fiercely private, she composed her adolescent diary in an elaborately constructed coded alphabet, which was deciphered by cryptologists in 1958.

EZRA POUND (1885–1972), American poet, editor, and critic, was one of the most influential men of letters of his generation, promoting and publishing the early work of James Joyce, T. S. Eliot, William Carlos Williams, Ernest Hemingway, and many others. He was the guiding spirit and chief proponent of imagist poetry and, as a translator, brought important Chinese poetry and Japanese drama to occidental readers. In 1917, he began his epic work, the *Cantos,* and continued writing and publishing its numerous sections throughout his lifetime. In 1945, he was arrested for broadcasting fascist propaganda to the United States from

Rome. In the background of his impending trial, numerous literary figures came together in his support, and in the end, Pound was judged insane and committed to a kind of gentleman's house arrest at St. Elizabeth's Hospital in Washington, D.C., rather than being convicted of sedition and treason. In the late 1950s, the charges were dropped, and he moved back to Italy.

DAWN POWELL (1897–1965), social satirist, was a frequent contributor to *The New Yorker* during the 1930s. Her collections of short stories and novels include *Sunday, Monday and Always, The Bridge House, Dawn Powell at Her Best, Golden Spur, The Locusts Have No King, A Time to Be Born,* and *Wicked Pavilion.*

PADGETT POWELL (1952–), before becoming a writer, was a college chemistry major turned freight handler, household mover, orthodontic technician, and roofer in the southern United States. A protégé of writer Donald Barthelme at the University of Houston's creative writing program, Powell became known with his first novel, *Edisto,* which was successfully followed by a second novel, *A Woman Named Drown,* and a book of stories, *Mr. Irony.* He twice received the Rome Prize and now teaches at the University of Florida, in Gainesville.

ALEKSANDR PUSHKIN (1799–1837) has long been considered the father of classic Russian literature. His work established many of the lyric and narrative styles and character motifs of the poets and fiction writers who came after him. His great works include a verse novel, *Eugene Onegin,* a historical tragedy, *Boris Godunov,* a novella, *The Queen of Spades,* a long poem, *Ruslan and Ludmilla,* and stories, *The Belkin Tales.* His wife, Natalia Goncharova, was a beauty who attracted the attention of a French baron in the Russian service. Pushkin challenged the baron to a duel and was killed.

BARBARA PYM (1913–1980) published her first novel, *Some Tame Gazelle,* in 1950, and for the next thirteen years enjoyed a steadily growing reputation in London's literary world. However, her success seemed to end in 1963, with publishers' rejections of her seventh novel and subsequent rejections of an eighth novel, as being out of fashion. She continued writing and, in the late 1970s, was rediscovered and heralded in England, Canada, and the United States as a present-day successor to Jane Austen.

JULES RENARD (1864–1910), French novelist and playwright, has come to be known chiefly for his *Journal*, which is often compared with those of André Gide and Stendhal for its frankness concerning family relationships.

THEODORE ROETHKE (1908–1963) was the son of a greenhouse owner in Saginaw, Michigan. As a high school freshman he wrote a speech on behalf of the Red Cross that was translated into twenty-six languages. In college he was considered an eccentric and was slow to be accepted by his peers. The title of his first volume of poetry, *Open House*, announced his intention to use himself as the material for his art. Much of his poetry was drawn from the notes he dutifully kept all his life. "I'm always working," he once said. He won the Pulitzer Prize for *The Waking: Poems 1933–53*, and twice won the Bollingen Prize, in 1958 for *Words for the Wind*, and in 1965 for *The Far Field*. He was a Member of the American Academy and Institute of Arts and Letters.

NED ROREM (1923–   ), American composer, essayist, and memoirist, has lived in Chicago, Paris, and Morocco, and now divides his time between New York City and Nantucket. His diaries, portions of which were first published in 1966, are among the best of the form. His works include *New York Diaries, Paris Diaries*, and a memoir, *Knowing When to Stop*. Rorem won the Pulitzer Prize for music in 1976.

JOHN RUSKIN (1819–1900), English writer, art critic, and historian, is known for his five-volume *Modern Painters*, which comprises a spiritual history of Europe and touches on every phase of morals and taste. He coined the literary term "pathetic fallacy" to designate the attribution of human characteristics and emotions to inanimate objects or nature. Ruskin's descriptions of Europe's great cathedrals strongly influenced Marcel Proust in the development of the literary style he would use in *Remembrance of Things Past*.

JAMES SALTER (1925–) grew up in New York City. His father was an army officer, and Salter—an obedient son—followed his example, attending West Point and serving ten years in the Air Force, where he was among an elite corps of fighter pilots. He wrote when he could, often drawing on his experiences in the air, but resigned in 1957—"disobedient at last"—with the publication of his first novel, *The Hunters*. In 1967, he published one of the great literary works of our day, *A Sport and a Pastime*, a tour de force of erotic realism that displays the sophistication, brilliance, and respect for craftsmanship that are his trademark. His works include the novels, *Light Years* and *Solo Faces*, and a story collection, *Dusk*, which won the P.E.N./Faulkner Award for fiction. His recent memoir is titled *Burning the Days*. He divides his time between New York and Colorado.

GEORGE SAND was the pen name of French writer Amandine Lucie Aurore Dupin, Baronne Dudevant (1804–1876). Famous for her love affairs, Sand wrote novels espousing free love and, as she grew older, moved to themes of humanitarian reforms and rustic life. As a source and target of provocative comments, she appears frequently in the journals of other writers of the period. Her books include *Indiana*, *Valentine*, and *Consuelo*.

SAPPHIRE (1950–) is a poet and performance artist whose writing has appeared in *Naming the Waves: Contemporary Lesbian Poetry*, *Women on Women*, *More Serious Pleasure*, and other journals and anthologies. Her books include *Push*, *Keep Simple Ceremonies*, and *American Dreams*.

MAY SARTON (1912–1995) was born in Belgium and emigrated with her family to the United States at the age of four, becoming a naturalized citizen in 1924. Among her numerous collections of poetry are *Encounter in April* and *The Silence Now*. Her novels include *Mrs. Stevens Hears the Mermaids Sing*, which examines lesbian experience. Sarton was a prolific diarist and published several volumes: *At Seventy, After the Stroke, Endgame*, and *Journal of a Solitude*. She lived in York, Maine.

JEAN-PAUL SARTRE (1905–1980) is known as the founder of the existentialist philosophy in modern culture. Sartre's novel *Nausea* and a collection of stories, *The Wall*, dramatized the meaninglessness of life, which is the basic assumption of existentialism. His articles on contemporary literature familiarized French readers with the works of Hemingway, Faulkner, Steinbeck, and Dos Passos. Sartre was an organizer of the political-literary review *Les Temps Modernes* and the author of many plays, including *No Exit*.

JAMES SCHUYLER (1923–1991) was associated with the New York School of poets, whose work attacks the modern middle-class environment. His works include *The Home Book*, a collection of prose and poetry, and *The Morning of the Poet*, which won the 1981 Pulitzer Prize for poetry, as well as a novel, *A Nest of Ninnies*, which Schuyler wrote with the poet John Ashbery.

DELMORE SCHWARTZ (1913–1966) made a startling debut as a poet while still a student and became associated with *Partisan Review*. He was an editor of that magazine and also of *The New Republic*. His titles include *Summer Knowledge, Shenandoah*, and *In Dreams Begin Responsibilities*. His poetry was awarded the Bollingen Prize. His diaries are a painful record of genius destroyed by alcohol. Saul Bellow's novel *Humboldt's Gift* is a fascinating portrayal of Schwartz's life.

SIR WALTER SCOTT (1771–1832), Scottish novelist and poet, is well known for his romantic historical fictions, including *Ivanhoe, Rob Roy, Waverley* and *The Bride of Lammermoor*. In 1813 he turned down the offer of the laureateship in favor of the poet

Robert Southey, and in 1826 he faced financial ruin with the bankruptcy of a publishing firm in which he was a partner. He spent the rest of his life working to pay off his debts. The narrative vitality and skillful portrayal of common people in his novels strongly influenced Balzac and Tolstoy.

GEORGE BERNARD SHAW (1856–1950), Irish dramatist and critic, perhaps best known for his play *Pygmalion*, kept diaries from his twenty-ninth year, when he was still unknown, to his forty-second, when his fame was becoming worldwide. He received the Nobel Prize for literature in 1925. His other plays include *Man and Superman*, *Major Barbara*, and *Heartbreak House*.

MARY WOLLSTONECRAFT SHELLEY (1797–1851) eloped with the poet Percy Shelley in 1814, traveling with him to Switzerland and later Italy, in the company of fellow poet Lord Byron. She is remembered as the author of *Frankenstein* but wrote other novels, biographies, and short stories, as well as edited her husband's work.

PERCY BYSSHE SHELLEY (1792–1822) was influenced early in life by the doctrines of the Enlightenment, ardently espousing liberty and rebelling against the strictures of English politics and religion. The popularity of his lyric poems, such as "To a Skylark," "Ode to the West Wind," and "Ozymandias," has overshadowed recognition of his long, philosophical poems, such as *Queen Mab*, or the elegiac *Adonais*, written on the death of his fellow poet and friend John Keats. At the age of thirty, Shelley drowned while boating in a storm.

CHARLES SIMIC (1938–   ), Yugoslavian-born American poet, emigrated to the United States in 1954. He worked as a proofreader before taking up an academic career and is now a professor of English at the University of New Hampshire. He is a recipient of the Pulitzer Prize for poetry, a MacArthur Fellowship, and a P.E.N. Translation Prize. His most recent poetry collection is *A Wedding in Hell*.

W. D. SNODGRASS (1926–   ) is the author of numerous books of poetry, including *Heart's Needle, Each in His Season,* and *Selected Poems.* In 1960, he won the Pulitzer Prize for poetry; he is also known as a translator and distinguished professor of creative writing and contemporary poetry. He lives in upstate New York.

SIR STEPHEN SPENDER (1909–1995) was a leading British literary figure during seven decades of the twentieth century. A close friend and colleague of W. H. Auden and Christopher Isherwood, he was part of a circle of Marxist poets in the 1930s and served in the Spanish Civil War. He was an editor of *Horizon* and *Encounter* magazines and taught at universities on both sides of the Atlantic. His books include poetry, fiction, criticism, and an autobiography, *World Within World.*

JOHN STEINBECK (1902–1968) was awarded the Nobel Prize for literature in 1962. He is known for his novel *The Grapes of Wrath,* which won the Pulitzer Prize in 1940, as well as for other classic works, such as *Tortilla Flat, Cannery Row, Of Mice and Men, East of Eden,* and *Travels with Charley.* Steinbeck was born in Salinas, California, and much of his work concerns life among the poor, especially the itinerant farm workers who migrated to California from the Midwest and Mexico. Blending realism and naturalism to portray unfair social conditions, Steinbeck's fiction argued convincingly for common justice and reform.

STENDHAL was the pen name of Marie-Henri Beyle (1783–1842), French novelist and critic, who played a major role in the development of the modern novel. Combining romantic and realist impulses, he added painstaking analysis to his characterizations, pointing the way to the psychological novel. His most noted works are *The Red and the Black* and *The Charterhouse of Parma.*

MARK STRAND (1934–   ), Canadian-born American poet, was the United States Poet Laureate in the year 1990–1991. His *Selected Poems* was published in 1981.

PETER TAYLOR (1917–1994) is much revered for his short story masterpieces, including "A Spinster's Tale," "1939," and "What You Hear from 'Em?" His collection *The Old Forest and Other Stories* received the P.E.N./Faulkner Award for fiction, and his novel *A Summons to Memphis* won the Pulitzer Prize. He taught at Harvard University, the University of North Carolina, Kenyon College, and the University of Virginia, influencing several generations of writers with his gifts of discrimination and care. He is survived by his wife, the poet Eleanor Ross Taylor.

ALFRED, LORD TENNYSON (1809–1892) was named British Poet Laureate in 1850. His most notable poems include "The Charge of the Light Brigade" and "In Memorium." Influenced by the English romantic poets, particularly Keats, Tennyson's work is representative of the Victorian upper class. His notebooks contain beautifully handwritten drafts of his poems; an occasional drawing or sketch accompanies the texts, as is often the case in writers' notebooks, particularly those of poets.

BARONESS EMILY SELLWOOD TENNYSON (1813–1896) was the wife of Alfred, Lord Tennyson. Lady Tennyson's diaries give a detailed account of the poet's moods, working habits, publications, and reactions to reviews and criticisms, as well as his meetings with Queen Victoria and his thoughts on writers such as Dante, Kant, Milton, Shakespeare, Chaucer, and others. Her diaries are also a spontaneous and affectionate chronicle of a fifty-year marriage and the family life surrounding the poet.

DYLAN THOMAS (1914–1953), Welsh poet, was praised by critics and loved by readers for the lyrical beauty of his voice, written and spoken. Through his radio performances and public appearances in England and the United States, Thomas achieved wide popular appeal. His works include *Portrait of the Artist as a Young Dog*, *World I Breathe*, and *Under Milk Wood*. His death, as a result of alcohol abuse, was international news, interpreted by many as a symbol of the plight of the artist suffering in the modern, philistine world. Thomas's unpublished prose came out posthumously in *Adventures in the Skin Trade*. Thomas's short memoir, *A Child's Christmas in Wales*, is perennially popular.

HENRY DAVID THOREAU (1817–1862), American essayist, naturalist, and poet, was part of the transcendentalist circle surrounding Ralph Waldo Emerson and an important part of the American renaissance in literature. Thoreau's best-known work, *Walden*, as well as other works such as *Civil Disobedience*, were drawn from his *Journal*, which he kept diligently from the age of twenty to the end of his life.

COUNT LEO TOLSTOY (1828–1910) was orphaned in childhood and raised by his aunts. He began keeping diaries as a teenager, and through his long life they grew to a highly detailed, exceptionally honest record rivaled in extensiveness and literary quality only by the diaries of Virginia Woolf. As a young man, Tolstoy served in the Russian cavalry and lived a gentleman officer's customarily dissolute life of gaming, drinking, whoring, and debt, from which he frequently repented, only to fall again. His early autobiographical fictions *Childhood*, *Boyhood*, and *Youth* and his *Sevastopol Sketches*, based on his military experiences, earned him almost instantaneous fame. When he was thirty-four he married Sophia Behrs, the eighteen-year-old daughter of the czar's physician. As a condition of the marriage Tolstoy insisted on showing her his bachelor diary with its intimate confessions, including his affair with, and illegitimate child by, one of his serfs, revelations that deeply shocked Sophia. During their long and sometimes tempestuous marriage, the Tolstoys read and commented upon each other's diary, leaving present-day readers an unparalleled account of a remarkable union. Sophia served as an amanuensis, copying and annotating her husband's daily work as he wrote his masterpieces *War and Peace* and *Anna Karenina*. In 1897, on learning that he was in consideration for the first Nobel Prize for literature, Tolstoy wrote to the Swedish press, suggesting that the money should be given to the Dukhobors, a persecuted sect of the Russian Orthodox Church. The Russian Church subsequently excommunicated him. He had become a moral and spiritual leader to followers and pilgrims, Tolstoyans, who adhered to his precepts of nonviolence, physical labor, peasant simplicity, vegetarianism, chastity—a utopianism that often contrasted painfully with his own life. A wealthy, landed aristocrat by birth, he set out at the age of eighty-two, wearing bast shoes and burlap clothing and carrying a staff and knapsack, intending to leave home and torment behind and go into the world as a pilgrim. Early in the journey he took ill and died in a small railway station at a rural junction.

COUNTESS SOPHIA TOLSTOY (1844–1919) was viewed by her husband's spiritual disciples as a tedious, self-centered, hysterical, complaining old woman whose greed and materialism threatened to drag her husband down. Tolstoy's disavowal of private property and his intention to give up the copyrights to his works forced her into the roles of estate manager, literary agent, and publisher. She bore Tolstoy thirteen children, three of whom did not survive infancy, and two of whom died in childhood. Her lifetime diary, running to some half million words, shows her to have been passionately, sentimentally committed to her husband and his art, though, as the years passed, increasingly made miserable by the paradox in his character. It was a great tragedy that when Tolstoy was dying, his disciples would not allow Sophia to see him. The Tolstoys' remarkable forty-eight-year intimacy ended with Sophia standing on tiptoe to peer through a window to where he lay, while reporters, photographers, and a crowd looked on.

WILLIAM TREVOR (1928–   ), esteemed Irish fiction writer, is the author of eleven novels and novellas including *The Children of Dynmouth* and *Fools of Fortune*, both winners of the Whitbread Award. Dubbed "the bard of loss, the poet of failed lives and ruinous impulses," Trevor is the author of eight volumes of short stories, brought together in *The Collected Stories*. He is the editor of *The Oxford Book of Irish Short Stories* (1989) and a member of the Irish Academy of Letters. In 1977 he was named honorary Commander of the British Empire. He lives in Devon, England.

MARK TWAIN was the pen name of Samuel Langhorne Clemens (1835–1910), American humorist, newspaperman, lecturer, and writer. His novels *Huckleberry Finn, Tom Sawyer, The Prince and the Pauper*, and *A Connecticut Yankee in King Arthur's Court* are among America's most beloved books. As a publisher, he commissioned Ulysses S. Grant, in the final years of his life, to write his autobiography, in the bargain saving the former President's family from destitution.

ALICE WALKER (1944–   ) is widely known as the author of *The Color Purple*, which won the Pulitzer Prize and the American Book Award for fiction and was made into a popular feature film. She is also the author of numerous collections of poems and of short stories. She is recognized not only as a writer but also as a teacher of writing and of black literature. She grew up in Jackson, Mississippi, and now lives in California.

EVELYN WAUGH (1903–1966), after some unhappy years as a young British schoolteacher, published a hugely successful first novel, *Decline and Fall*, in 1928. He followed with other bitterly humorous satires and farces, such as *Black Mischief, A Handful of Dust*, and *The Loved One*.

SIMONE WEIL (1909–1943), was born and raised in Paris. After a brilliant career as a student, she worked for an anarchist trade union in a factory, shared her wages with the employees, and lived in poverty. She fought against Franco in the Spanish Civil War, and then moved to England, where she died of self-imposed privation and anorexia. Her works were published posthumously and include *Gravity and Grace, Waiting for God, The Need for Roots*, and her *Notebooks*, where she is at her lucid best and concludes that God withdrew himself from the universe after creating it; consequently, man must withdraw himself from material considerations and thus return to God.

DENTON WELCH (1915–1948) had intended to be a painter, but a bicycle accident in 1935 left him severely crippled and an invalid for the rest of his life. He became an author of short stories and two autobiographical novels, *Maiden Voyage* and *In Youth Is Pleasure*, noted for their sexual and emotional honesty. His *Journal* was published posthumously in 1952.

PAUL WEST (1930–) was born in Derbyshire, England, and now lives in Ithaca, New York, with writer Diane Ackerman. West is the author of numerous books, including the poetry collection *The Spellbound Horses* and the novels *Gala* and *Rat Man of Paris*. He is a winner of *The Paris Review* Aga Khan Prize for fiction and has taught at many colleges and universities.

T. H. WHITE (1904–1964), English novelist, born in Bombay, India, is best known for his interpretation of the Arthurian legend, a tetralogy titled *The Once and Future King*, the first volume of which, *The Sword and the Stone*, was made into the ever-popular musical *Camelot*. A keen sportsman, an avid falconer and fisherman, White threaded his love of nature and animals throughout the more than twenty-five books that he wrote.

WALT WHITMAN (1819–1892), the son of a radical, free-thinking carpenter in Brooklyn, worked first in a lawyer's office, then a doctor's, and finally a printer's. He became an itinerant teacher in country schools, wrote a temperance novel, and, in 1846 became editor of *The Brooklyn Eagle*. But he was restless and, during the next few years, traveled and worked as a journalist. His great poem, *Leaves of Grass*, was published anonymously in 1855 in a small folio of 95 pages and grew in eight succeeding editions to 440 pages. Whitman's democratic inclusiveness, his encompassing sense of humanity, the luminous spirit and musicality of his unmetered verse, broke taboos, social and aesthetic, and paved the way for modern poetry. At the age of fifty-four, he was stricken with paralysis and would have fallen into poverty without the help of European admirers. Later, several wealthy Americans helped provide for his modest wants. Some of the best-known sections in *Leaves of Grass* are "Drum Taps," "When Lilacs Last in the Courtyard Bloomed," and "O Captain! My Captain."

OSCAR WILDE (1854–1900), Irish-born poet, playwright, and novelist, began life as Oscar Fingal O'Flahertie Wills Wilde. Advocating "art for art's sake," he attracted attention by an extravagant aestheticism expressed in eccentric and flamboyant clothing and manners, long hair, and flowers carried in his hand when he lectured. Accused of homosexual practices, he was condemned in 1895 to two years' imprisonment and hard labor. After his release he left England and went to France, using the name Sebastian Melmouth. Ruined and bitter, he lived in Paris until his death. His novel *The Picture of Dorian Gray*, his plays *The Importance of Being Earnest* and *Salome*, and the essay *De Profundis* are among his notable works. As a personality, he is recalled for his quick wit and repartee.

THORNTON WILDER (1897–1975) won the Pulitzer Prize for his popular novel *The Bridge of San Luis Rey* and also won Pulitzers for his Broadway plays about American life, *Our Town* and *The Skin of Our Teeth*.

C. K. WILLIAMS (1936–   ) has published many books of poetry and translations. *Flesh and Blood* won the National Book Critics Circle Award. His most recent books are *A Dream of the Mind* and *Selected Poems*. An American, he lives in Paris and teaches part of the year at Princeton University.

SIR ANGUS WILSON (1931–1991), short story writer and novelist, was born in England and grew up in South Africa. His books include *Hemlock and After*, *The Wrong Set*, and *A Bit Off the Map*. For some years he was deputy superintendent of the British

Museum's famed Reading Room, sanctuary to writers and readers since the early 1800s.

EDMUND WILSON (1895–1972), who was considered the eminent American critic of his day, wrote essays, articles, and reviews for magazines such as *Vanity Fair, The New Republic* and *The New Yorker.* His volumes of criticism include *Axel's Castle* and *The Wound and the Bow.* He was a friend of F. Scott Fitzgerald's from their college days at Princeton, and fifteen years after Fitzgerald's death, he put the author's late, uncollected stories together in *The Crack-Up,* which has an autobiographical basis in Fitzgerald's alcoholism and decline. For a time Wilson was married to novelist and story writer Mary McCarthy, who, with his encouragement, bitingly satirized him in her fiction.

THOMAS WOLFE (1900–1938), American novelist and playwright, was known for the intense individualism, exuberant spirit, extravagant rhetoric, and youthful fascination with sex that characterized his frequently autobiographical works. His famous novel *Look Homeward, Angel,* and its sequel, *Of Time and The River,* were presented to the publisher Charles Scribner's Sons as huge, sprawling manuscripts, which Wolfe then edited to manageable size with the help of Maxwell Perkins, who was also known for editing F. Scott Fitzgerald, Ernest Hemingway, and Marjorie Kenan Rawlings. Wolfe died of tuberculosis at an early age, leaving behind an eight-foot-high pile of unfinished manuscript, parts of which were posthumously published as *You Can't Go Home Again* and *The Web and the Rock.*

VIRGINIA WOOLF (1882–1941), English woman of letters, was one of the key figures in establishing the modern literary age. Subtle, original, a born writer, Woolf was a master of the novel and the essay, creating new techniques in prose and opening new possibilities in the study of character and human nature. She was also one of the finest literary critics of the twentieth century. With her husband, Leonard Woolf, she founded the Hogarth

Press, publishing the first works of Katherine Mansfield, E. M. Forster, T. S. Eliot, and others. She is widely known for her novels *Mrs. Dalloway*, *To the Lighthouse*, and *The Waves*, and for her essay "A Room of One's Own," which has been an important foundation in the intellectual and spiritual liberation of women. Woolf's diaries, covering a twenty-seven-year period, reveal her at her core—anguished, triumphant, lyrical, driven, and profoundly creative. Unable to overcome periods of crushing mental illness, Woolf committed suicide at the age of fifty-nine, loading her pockets with stones and jumping into the River Thames.

DOROTHY WORDSWORTH (1771–1855) lived with her brother, the poet William Wordsworth, through his marriage and until his death. Her journals of travel and life with her brother have made her a noted figure, and it is believed that her brother made some use of her recollections in his work.

WILLIAM WORDSWORTH (1770–1850), English poet, is known for masterpieces such as "Tintern Abbey," "Ode: Intimations of Immortality," "I Wandered Lonely as a Cloud," and "The World Is Too Much with Us," which for many years have been standard pieces for memorization in schools. His preface to *Lyrical Ballads* instituted a reform in poetic diction in favor of the "language really used by men." His work is infused by a love of nature, humanitarianism, and an interest in the daily pursuits of ordinary people. Wordsworth succeeded Robert Southey as Britain's Poet Laureate in 1843.

JAMES WRIGHT (1927–1980), American poet, was born in Ohio and educated at Kenyon College. He became a teacher, lecturing at Hunter College in New York City. His books of poetry include *The Green Wall*, *The Branch Will Not Break*, and *Shall We Gather at the River? His Collected Poems* won the Pulitzer Prize.

WILLIAM BUTLER YEATS (1865–1939), Irish poet, winner of the Nobel Prize for literature, is celebrated as one of the world's great writers. He brought poetry into the twentieth century, mixing lyric and dramatic effects, the mythology of Irish folk-lore and the occult, autobiography, and politics in a sensuous and concise realism. Among his many famous poems are "The Lake Isle of Innisfree," "Sailing to Byzantium," "The Second Coming," "Adam's Curse," "Leda and the Swan," "Easter 1916," and "Under Ben Bulben." In addition to his writing, Yeats led a very active and public literary life. He founded the Abbey Theatre and encouraged Irish dramatist John Millington Synge and others to write plays for it, which resulted in a rich heritage of Irish theater. Yeats was also involved in Irish politics, partly through his love for Maude Gonne, an activist who was a central figure in his poetry. At the end of his life, he was elected a senator of the Irish Free State. His epitaph, which he wrote for himself, is one of the world's best known: "Cast a cold eye / On life, on death. / Horseman, pass by!"

Index of Authors

Acknowledgments

Grateful acknowledgment is made to the following for permission to include journal passages and other material:

Diane Ackerman: Excerpt from *The Moon by Whale Light* (Random House, Inc., 1991). Copyright © 1991 by Diane Ackerman. Used by permission of the author.

Paul Auster: Journal entry, May, 1996. Copyright © 1996 by Paul Auster. Used by permission of the author.

Bill Barich: Journal entries. Copyright © 1996 by Bill Barich. Used by permission of the author.

Rick Bass: Journal entries. Copyright © 1996 by Rick Bass. Used by permission of the author.

Charles Baxter: Journal entries. Copyright © 1995 by Charles Baxter. Used by permission of the author.

Marvin Bell: Journal entries. Originally published in *A Marvin Bell Reader* (Middlebury College Press/University Press of New England). Copyright © 1994 by Marvin Bell. Used by permission of the author.

Thomas Berger: Brief excerpt from *Touring Western Europe*, 1956. Copyright © 1996 by Thomas Berger. Used by permission of the author.

Anne Bernays: Journal entry. Copyright © 1996 by Anne Bernays. Used by permission of the author.

Roy Blount, Jr.: "Don't Anybody Steal These" (*Antaeus*, No. 61, 1988). Copyright © 1988 by Roy Blount, Jr. Used by permission of the author.

Carol Bly: Journal entries. Copyright © 1995 by Carol Bly. Used by permission of the author.

Paul Bowles: Excerpt from *Days* (Ecco Press). Copyright © 1991 by Paul Bowles. Used by permission of the author.

Rosellen Brown: Excerpt from "Fingerprints" from *A Rosellen Brown Reader* (University Press of New England). Copyright © 1996 by Rosellen Brown. Used by permission of the author.

Janet Burroway: Journal entries. Originally published in *The Writer on Her Work* (W. W. Norton & Co., New York, 1991). Copyright © 1991 by Janet Burroway. Used by permission of the author.

Robert Olen Butler: Journal entries. Copyright © 1996 by Robert Olen Butler. Used by permission of the author.

Frank Conroy: Notebook entry. Copyright © 1996 by Frank Conroy. Used by permission of the author.

Guy Davenport: Journal entries. Copyright © 1996 by Guy Davenport. Used by permission of the author.

Annie Dillard: Notebook entry. Copyright © 1996 by Annie Dillard. Used by permission of the author.

Rita Dove: Brief excerpt from "The House That Jill Built." Originally published in *The Writer on Her Work* (W. W. Norton & Co., New York, 1991). Copyright © 1991 by Rita Dove. Used by permission of the author.

Andre Dubus: Excerpts from "Love in the Morning." Copyright © 1996 by Andre Dubus. Used by permission of the author.